The Warmth of Fires

The Collected Stories of Ramsbolt #6

Jennifer M. Lane

Cover design by Al Hess – cultofsasha.com

Copyright © 2021

Published by Pen and Key Publishing

jennifermlanewrites.com

ISBN: 978-1-7366691-1-2

ACKNOWLEDGEMENTS

Thank you to Shelly Campbell, Essa Hansen, and Cheryl Murphy.

Special thank you to Al Hess.

CHAPTER ONE

Dean Hessel's office smelled of the orange peeled hours ago, half of which sat festering on the sunny windowsill. A piece of it was stuck in the old man's front teeth, a disgusting gob of slime that made Stuart's stomach churn. Or maybe it was the personal criticism veiled as professional disapproval, as if he couldn't issue enough denouncements on his own. He bit his tongue rather than point out that he hadn't ever asked for the professor job. Yes, he had applied for it when it was offered to him, but it was only offered to him because the world expected him to be just as illustrious a writer as his father had been when he occupied that chair. Stuart Dolan Jr., however, wasn't measuring up to his father's reputation, and it was just as much the university's fault as his that he hadn't yet published a book. Yet. It was hard to be inspired when all his time and energy went into teaching.

Stuart crossed one ankle over the other knee and gripped his shin with his cold, clammy hands. It was framed as a chat, just a good chin wag between academics, but Stuart knew better. He ran his hand through his unkempt hair.

"You have to publish something." The dean tapped a pencil against his desk. "Something that isn't in the school's literary journal. What am I supposed to tell the parents?" His voice was gravel. Cigar-soot coated gravel.

"Are the parents really sending emails demanding my publication history? You know I edit anthologies. I ran the literary society for two years. I have short stories in most of the quarterly journals. What do you want me to say?"

The man's eyes rolled back in his head, revealing the whites. If they came full circle and glowed, Stuart would welcome the demon over the man who sat before him.

"Do you remember the first day you sat in my office? You were a teaching assistant."

"You were my advisor. In grad school." Leave it to him to diminish the history just to embellish the present.

"All these students run together, but not you. You were one of the greats."

"Is it over already? My shot at greatness? Gosh, you talk about me like I'm dead." Stuart smoothed the hem of his jeans.

The dean leaned so far forward in his cheap office wheely chair that Stuart was afraid the man would land on the floor. Long gone were the days the literature department got the gold star, leather chair treatment. Those furnishings were allocated to the business school, where appearances mattered. Here, in the creative writing halls, eccentricity was valued. The ability to artfully do more with less, however, did not extend to Stuart.

The dean's eyes shined. "You got this job because Carter got pregnant."

Stuart winced. At least Hessel hadn't mentioned his father. He spent enough time lamenting his role in his family's literary legacy. "She wanted to raise her child. She didn't lose her job because she got pregnant. You really have to be careful how you word these things."

"You kids and your political correctness. She left. I gave you the seat. You were an assistant professor. It would have taken you years to get this far if it weren't for the circumstances. And you have known for quite a long time now that you have to continue with your professional development…" The man's chest heaved with a deep rattling cough. He spat into a tissue and balled it in his fist.

Stuart leaned back, shoving his hands in the pockets of his vest. He wouldn't shake the man's hand even if it ended with a million-dollar check.

"You need water?"

The man pounded his chest and gripped his throat, shaking his head. When his words came, they were choppy. "Damn cigars. I tell you, spend your time wisely. Do not waste the space you take up on this earth by spewing into it. They used to say that it was the hallmark of humanity that we made tools. Screw the tools. All kinds of animals use tools. And thumbs. You ever see a black bear take the lid off a jar of peanut butter? Huh?"

"Um. No?" Stuart shook his head. "I'm afraid I haven't had that distinct pleasure."

"They can. We're not amazing because we have tools or thumbs or because we can talk. It's because we create something from nothing. For the love of God's green apples, Stuart Dolan. Create something already."

He lowered his foot to the floor and wiped his now-sweaty palms on his jeans. He shifted to stand, but Dean Hessel wasn't done. The man waved a bony finger at him.

"We gave that seat to you because you were loyal and a hard worker. You are here because your father was just as revered at this school as he is with his publisher and with readers. His is a legacy we expect you to match."

There it was. "You can't throw my father's career in my face when you're displeased with me."

"I certainly can, because my department is paying for it. I'm not sure you've been using your time wisely, because I still haven't seen a damn novel come out of the office of my creative writing professor. And you will not explain to me why."

Stuart's breath hung within him, a fog on a humid sunrise. There was no easy way to tell the dean, a man whose works spanned four pen names and could ring the room three times, that facing a blank page had become a brand of psychological warfare, that he'd long ago convinced himself that he couldn't fill that page. He'd censured himself. His ideas were too radical and not deep enough, and he'd be disparaged for writing women poorly or condemned for writing confusing tripe. He'd be compared to his father, whose every word was deemed an instant classic. Stuart's writer's block had grown so large that it had taken him years to analyze its every angle, and for all the reasons it had become immovable it was also insurmountable. With the exception of the short stories he penned for the quarterly journal, every concept that came to him hinted at depth but lacked all substance.

"Well?" The dean demanded an answer. "Why not? Why have you not published a thing? It's not like you don't have the time. You have all your summers. And a sabbatical you haven't used yet. What? What is it?"

Gripping the arms of the chair, Stuart stood and checked the time on his phone. "I know. You're right. I haven't published anything. And I have a class to teach. I have a few ideas I can crank out."

He didn't.

The dean wagged his pencil at Stuart, wiry eyebrows raised. "You'd better. If you need a sabbatical take it. That's what it's for. Or I'll assume you're no longer interested, and I'll have no trouble finding someone who is by fall semester."

Stuart nodded, his mouth too dry to form the words. His whole life he'd aspired to his father's stature. As a kid, he'd wanted to be a journalist, to twirl the coiled cord of a desk phone around his finger, spin in his chair to flag down his colleague to listen in on scoops, to take notes in steno pads with a favorite pen. He'd wanted to wreath access and truth into groundbreaking stories. Journalism had been a higher form of his father's fiction, but nothing had worked out as he'd hoped. Instead of evolving, he'd been trapped in his father's land of tweed and elbow patches.

He swallowed the lump that held his voice for ransom as he turned the knob and opened the door. "I understand, Dean Hessel. I'm on it. Thanks for your patience."

The first breath after closing the door behind him was ten degrees cooler than the air under his collar. He tugged at the neck of his button-up shirt, adjusted his vest, lifted his chin, and dodged students in the hall.

He slipped into the bathroom and paused at the mirror. His hair was getting too long, too wavy. He looked a lot older than his thirty-four years.

This day had been looming on the horizon for months. Hessel's opinion wasn't the only one that mattered. Snide little comments from colleagues aside, there were board members and university shareholders and influential alumni who wanted the degree program to function at its best. They wanted best-seller lists packed with alumni and a professor who'd never published a book was only going to survive for so long. He could skirt his father's criticisms easily enough, but he couldn't dodge the dean forever.

What would he do if he lost this job? It might not have been his first love, but he'd worked hard to get it, teaching every class he could and living with enough stress to make insomnia a close companion. His whole identity was wrapped up in it now. And it had certainly elevated him in the eyes of his father and grandfather, and it made him a favorite in Madison's family. God knew her parents beamed when they introduced him as *Madison's-partner-he's-a-professor.* But their favor wouldn't save him. It wouldn't help him settle on a story and put it on paper. It wouldn't help him find an agent or sell any books.

Dean Hessel wasn't wrong about the importance of being published. It wasn't just a bullet point on his curriculum vitae. He had no practical real-world advice to give to his students. He had no agents or publishers on speed dial.

He pushed through the glass doors and onto the brick sidewalk, hopping over a low spot that gathered the night's rain. Head down, he plowed into a headwind.

Part of him resented all the external pressure. He hadn't asked for any of this. He'd expected to climb whatever ladder, scale the course like everyone else. Sometimes he felt like he'd been dragged to the top against his will and was being dangled off the edge.

If he lost this faculty position, he'd never be able to take this resume to another institution. He'd never be able to look his father and grandfather in the eye again. As if his self-esteem needed more of an excuse to hide under the bed.

He had to write a book. There was no other way out of this.

Taking a worn shortcut from one path to another, the toes of his sneakers wetted from the grass. He hopped a short brick wall, up the stairs, and through the giant wood doors.

Mohl was waiting outside his classroom door, leaning against the wall. He raised his sleeve to glance at a pretend watch.

Stuart dodged flirting freshmen and came to a halt at the door. "We were supposed to meet for coffee, weren't we?"

"Not the first time you've stood me up."

"Hessel caught me after class."

"What'd he want? Another run down?" Mohl adjusted his messenger bag on his shoulder and ran a hand over black hair so short it was barely taller than his scalp. His green eyes darted past Stuart, down the hall. "There's no one coming. Just kids talking. They're not paying any attention. What did he say?"

"Publish a book or get fired trying." Stuart shrugged.

"Damn. Harsh." Mohl waved at someone down the hall. "I gotta run. Stupid lunch conference. Did you get a deadline?"

Stuart let out an involuntary laugh. "Fall semester."

"That seems—"

"Impossible." Stuart nodded, mouth twisted in a snarl. "I know. I might take that sabbatical."

Mohl slapped him on the arm as he passed. "You've probably got a million ideas in that brain of yours. It'll be great. Catch you after lunch."

"Great. Yeah."

CHAPTER TWO

"I've just called to check in."

His father was the last person he wanted to hash out his failing career with. The man had never experienced writer's block and seemed to pull stories out of thin air. He could write anything, anywhere, on any surface. But Stuart was at his wit's end, and with any luck, his father would pull out some anecdote he'd never heard that would lead him straight to the eternal well of tales.

"I put in for a sabbatical fall semester."

"Hassel's on your ass, huh?" Paper shuffled in the background of an echoing room. His father must be in his office. Sound always bounced off the mahogany walls.

"Something like that. I need to focus on getting something down that's worth publishing."

"What do you want your writing to *do*, Stuart? Always start with a purpose."

Was that the missing key? Writing was supposed to be a means to the truth. How was he supposed to reconcile that with the world of fiction.

"Look, son." His father's chair made a crunchy leather sound when he sat. "You were always so intent on journalism. I'm not suggesting you pull a Tom Wolfe and join a band of drug-addled cultural icons, but real-world experiences can count for a lot."

"I don't want to deal with creative nonfiction. There's entirely too much social navigating."

"It does require a certain responsibility to its subjects. I must run. Your mother and I are meeting the Leopolds at the club for dinner."

Their lives were so out of touch with his own. Between his mother's career as a law firm partner with her long list of country club clients, and his father's outgoing professorial lifestyle, they'd been the exception rather than the rule among his peers. Stuart would far rather dine in a corner dive bar than be anywhere near a polo shirt, especially on a Saturday.

"Have a good time, Dad. Tell Mom I said hi."

He put down his phone and picked up his laptop, the cursor blinking at the end of a four-word phrase on an otherwise blank page. Ripping the pencil from behind his ear, he stuck it in his mouth, clamping down hard. Shards of yellow paint and soft wood satisfied his molars but did nothing for his concentration or his writer's block. Of course, Madison decided this was the perfect moment to bang all their pots and pans together in the kitchen and scrape them across the stove top, as if she didn't cook for a living and couldn't be bothered to do it peaceably. A thin wall separated them.

He'd strung four words together, just a phrase, the start of a sentence hours in the making, and Madison slammed a pot against the counter and creaked the oven door open to test something that wouldn't be done for another twenty minutes. The rack grated as she threw a second pan in, mumbling under her breath about electricity being inferior to gas and the audacity of the universe to demand she cook under these conditions.

Stuart spit the pencil from his mouth and wiped it on his jeans. "We've lived here for five years, Maddy. The oven shouldn't be a surprise. You could always pack all that up and take it to work and cook it."

She pulled something wrapped in aluminum foil from the fridge and slammed the door. It hit the counter with a clatter, and she leaned around the doorway to wave a spatula at him. "And I'm supposed to walk your hot dinner back home again? Living here for five years doesn't make this oven any less frustrating."

"Last week you *threatened* to cook at work. You got my hopes up." He shuffled the laptop on his knees and shoved the pencil back in his mouth.

Outside a car horn blared, another victim of the city traffic jam screaming about their pain. Someone returned fire with obscenities. Philadelphia seemed to have the world's longest rush hour. It had been going on for years.

Stuart slammed the laptop closed. It wasn't Madison's fault he couldn't write any more than it was his fault her cooking was crippled by the use of an electric stove. They lived where they lived because it was close to their jobs and being in a relationship meant compromise.

"I don't want to be at work when I'm not working." Madison glared at him. "We can afford to move, you know. We could use more space."

"I don't want to move." The neighborhood sucked, and it was loud. Yes, he was the only college professor in Philadelphia living in a tiny apartment. But he'd searched for months for the perfect place, deep in the thick of things, where he could soak up all of the city's life and energy. And the last thing he needed was to lose it all, back in his parents' neck of the woods, deep in the land of polo shirts and country club memberships. Besides, he liked it most of the time, and he was saving money like he had a plan for it.

He didn't.

"You can write anywhere, Stuart. In a park. In your office at your own work. Here." She took the laptop away and replaced it with a bowl. "It's for Ed's blog post. Tell me what you think."

"Oh, if it's for Edward." Stuart dragged out the name of the man who spent more time with Madison that he did. It seemed Edward slid into every conversation lately. Madison's sous chef took up more real estate in that apartment than Stuart did. For all the lilt in her voice when she said his name and the way she jumped when he texted her, Stuart never allowed himself to entertain the jealousy that threatened to erupt the one part of his life that coasted along just fine.

She rolled her eyes at him and held out a spoon. "Try it. Please. It's chicken, salsa, rice, sour cream... Not the most attractive thing. I know. It's for a compilation of five-minute meals from local chefs."

"Usually when you ask me to try something…"

"It looks amazing. I know. Sorry."

He stabbed a cube of grilled chicken and slathered it with rice and corn held together with salsa and sour cream. It might not look like much, but it tasted better than anything he'd have thrown together if Madison weren't home.

"This is really good." He spoke before he swallowed.

"Thanks. I'll text him the recipe." Madison lifted his gnawed pencil from the love seat like it was a wounded butterfly, and she let it fall to the floor. "That is disgusting, though. We sit here. Really?"

Stuart shrugged. "I gotta write. I can't write without a pencil."

"You're typing."

Wide-eyed, he motioned to the kitchen door. "Doesn't matter."

A pencil, a new notepad, silence, instrumental background music. Too hot, too cold. No place was right, no condition was good enough. Years of opening notebooks and scribbling lines, pushing down the simmering frustration at chirping birds and kids playing outside. Other than a few short stories and some literary journal submissions, he hadn't written much of value. He'd become an expert at railing against the outside world for being too much and not enough, though. The words wouldn't come until inspiration struck, and inspiration belonged to other people. Not him.

"What's wrong, anyway? You're acting really weird. And using a laptop. You never write on a laptop."

The screen door slammed at the corner deli across the street. A bunch of boys just out of school tumbled out of the store with smokes and snacks. Stuart envied their freedom, the careless ease of how they went about life.

"I don't know what to write about. Nothing interests me right now."

A woman clutched her daughter's hand and entered the store, flip-flops flapping off their heels. He didn't bother looking to Madison for reaction or sympathy. She wouldn't understand.

"Just write whatever." She shrugged.

"It's not that easy. I'll never get tenure if I don't publish something. I won't even have a job if I don't write something. I'm the only creative writing professor in the world who's never published a damn book."

"That's not true. You were just in that thing…"

"It was a book review. Not the same thing as publishing a novel. No one wants to pay tuition to learn to write novels from someone who's never published a novel."

She wrapped the dish towel around her hand, one eyebrow arched. "You think they'll fire you?"

"It sure sounded that way." Maybe they'd keep him on staff as the guy who cleaned the dry-erase boards. He chewed another bite of chicken and salsa. "They can do whatever they want," he said with his mouth full. "It's their world. I just teach in it. All I know is I can't just pluck a story out of my head. And, no offense, but it's so damn loud here I can't hear myself think."

She shrugged one shoulder. "Fair. It is loud. If you're trying to write, why are you going outside your comfort zone. You never use the laptop."

"Because I was hoping that using a different method would maybe spark some inspiration. It's not working."

"Well, I guess you'd better get inspired then." She leaned back against the doorway, her blue eyes shining. She grabbed her phone from the side table and woke up the screen. "You should go to Maine. You always talk about wanting to go to Maine. You have the whole fall semester off. The point in a sabbatical is to do some professional development, right? We could rent a place up there."

"We?" Nothing was left in his bowl but some rice. He put it on the coffee table and pulled the laptop back onto his knees. "Too much work. I have to figure out where to go and what to pack, then I'd feel bad for not sightseeing."

"Why not go sightseeing? You need inspiration."

"No, I need to concentrate."

"Look." She held up her phone. He dodged a reflection from the light outside and snagged it from her hand to see. She'd found a little log cabin with a big front porch, set in some faraway zip code. His phone buzzed beside him somewhere on the sofa, and he dug it out from beneath a throw pillow.

"Yeah, it looks nice." He passed her phone back and inspected his own. "Text from Mohl."

Madison wrinkled her nose. "Why do you call him that? Like he's some ground-burrowing rodent. You're not teenagers."

"Mohl. *M-o-h-l.* It's his name. Don't be offensive." Stuart stuck out his tongue at her in a playful attempt at levity. He scrolled through the text message.

"There. Done." Madison muttered and held up her phone.

He squinted at the screen. "What's done?"

"We're going to Maine. I booked that house I just showed you."

"Seriously?" His voice shot up an octave. He couldn't just drop his life and go to Maine. And whose money was she spending? There was no way he was paying to rent some log cabin in Maine when he had a perfectly good apartment under a perfectly good roof. They'd probably lose whatever deposit she just made, too. "Does it have a cancellation policy?"

"I don't know, because I'm not canceling."

Stuart shook his head. "You choose *now* to be spontaneous? Do you not understand that I am under pressure to write an actual book? I can't mess around with this."

"Hardly spontaneous. I booked a vacation for two weeks from now."

"For how long?"

"I'm not telling you. Not right now."

A sour rage rose in his throat. *One sec.* He replied to Mohl's text. *Apparently, I'm doing my sabbatical in Maine.*

He dropped his phone on his lap and ran a hand through his sandy blond hair. "I can't believe you booked it. We didn't even talk about this."

She took a deep breath and looked at him like he was an exhausting toddler. "You need a change of pace. Some new scenery. I'm doing you a favor."

"I don't need a favor. I need to write a book. I don't want to go to Maine."

Madison took his empty bowl from the table and carried it to the kitchen sink. "You do. You just don't know it yet. You'll have a great time."

His phone buzzed again. Mohl wanted to know where. When. What the heck for. Someplace cool?

"What town is this place in? Where?"

"Ramsbolt." She said it like it was the only option, and her look dared him to question it.

He typed his answer to Mohl. *No. Not a cool place. Ramsbolt? Maddy booked it.*

Madison turned away and ran water in the sink. Someday, if they both worked hard enough, she'd have a dishwasher, a gas stove, and enough hobbies to keep her nose out of his business. And maybe he'd have books to write.

Why is she doing this to you??

She thinks I need inspiration.

In the wilderness? What's in that town?

Nothing inspiring, Stuart replied.

Lol. Email me your outline & good luck.

CHAPTER THREE

Madison sang off key to the radio and threaded the Subaru up the tangle of I-95 interchanges. Stuart kept a notebook on his knees, jotting down bullet points and half-formed observations about tiny towns that clotted the drive and the coastline that passed by his window.

She glanced between the road and his notes. "How can you read that?"

"Honestly not sure. I guess I pick out a word here and there." He held up the book. Who was he kidding? It didn't matter if he could read it or not, he wouldn't go back to look at it anyway. He never did. A plastic bin under their bed was full of musings that he gave no value. They sat on shelves and made bookends for his vinyl collection. Nothing he wrote on these pages would be of any more value than the thoughts he'd already spit out and hoarded, unless he planned to crank out a whole novel about a bridge somewhere in Portland.

The dashboard dinged.

"Gas," she said.

If she'd gotten gas when then stopped half an hour ago, they wouldn't have to stop again, but saying that wouldn't make the trip more bearable. He grabbed his phone and found a station. "Two exits. Couple of miles. Stay in the right lane."

She took the off-ramp fast enough for the luggage to shift in the back. He held onto the notebook with one hand and the armrest with the other.

"Why don't I drive the next leg? I'll gas up, and you grab snacks?" He shoved his pen in the notebook's coil and tossed it on the back seat.

She pulled up to a vacant pump, flung open the door and brushed animal cracker crumbs from her lap. Cool air pooled into the car through her open door. He got out, planted his feet and stretched, ran his debit card through the pump and tested the handle.

Bouncing on his heels, hands in his pockets while the fuel ran into the car, he glanced around for a car vacuum, but this place wasn't fancy enough for all that. It was just a few pumps and a convenience store ringed by a sidewalk. Madison had reached the door, head down and eyes on her phone, narrowly dodged by a group of giggling high school girls.

A car full of bags and boxes with a dashboard full of fast-food rubbish pulled up to the pump behind him blaring an Aerosmith song Stuart hadn't heard in a decade. The man waved a hand at him, signaling his impatience.

The pump clicked off, and Stuart grabbed the handle. Gas dripped onto his hand and shoes.

"Figures." He wiped his hand dry on a blue paper towel from a dispenser, but the smell would stay with him for the rest of the trip. The mustached guy in the car behind him flung a thick arm out his open window.

"You 'bout done?" he asked. "Got shit to do today."

Stuart fished his keys from his pocket and dangled them. "I'll move it. Give me a second."

He steered the car to an empty spot by the door, mumbling to himself about fuel mileage the guy would gain if he ever threw anything away.

Inside, the store was bright, and hits from the '70s crackled from overhead speakers. Aisles of bagged snacks and bars of candy were mostly empty of people, except for a few preteen kids who loaded up their arms like an apocalypse was nigh. He made his way to the bank of doors that framed a narrow hallway to the bathrooms, flinging open a door for a Diet Dr. Pepper.

"It's not too bad. A quiet drive." Madison's voice came down the hallway. Stuart peeked around the corner. Her back was to him, and she held up her phone. He couldn't make out who she was having a video chat with, but he didn't want to be seen, so he slipped back around the corner and leaned his back against a cooler of milk.

Madison laughed. It was a carefree outburst, the kind he hadn't heard from her a very long time.

"I'll call you when I can. Not sure when I'll get the chance."

The light from her phone reflected off the glass of a pastry cabinet. It bobbed, a buoy in the dark hallway.

"He'll be writing all the time. I'm sure I'll end up shopping or finding some park somewhere to go for a walk and call. I miss you, too."

The light went out on her phone. He could hear the gentle swish of her shirt as she tucked her phone away. He clenched his teeth and made an apologetic smile for a woman pushing a stroller and stepped out of her way, into the hall, running right into Madison.

"Who was that?" His voice was lighter than the mood that had settled on him, a gentle question bearing an air of curiosity. It did little to portray his interest, but at least he wasn't launching a fight in a convenience store far from home.

Madison put a hand to her throat. "You scared me. You smell like gasoline. Did you bathe in it?" She darted around him and aimed for a tall bag of popcorn. "Do you think this place has crackers?"

"I don't know, Madison. Why don't you look while I wash my hands? Make sure you grab anything that looks good. I wouldn't want you to miss anything."

The bathroom was one of those unisex rooms with greyed tile with black scuffs, a mirror with a broken corner, and pearly hand soap that definitely wasn't the cucumber-melon scent the container claimed to be. Washing the gasoline smell from his hands, he steeled himself in the mirror, straightening his back.

He'd wasted a lot of emotional energy on things that didn't matter over the years, worrying about events that never came to pass, preparing himself for arguments he never had to make. His imagination had a way of running wild. If only he could harness it to write a book.

He gripped the edge of the sink and levelled with himself. Madison wouldn't drag him all the way to Maine if her heart wasn't in it. She would have stayed behind.

She was already in the car when he reached it, a bag of snacks at her feet. She held out a Red Vine.

"Want one?"

He shook his head.

The light at the corner was green. He turned left and took the ramp onto the highway.

"You're gonna have to give me directions." His turn signal clicked as he changed lanes.

"I will. Combos?" She shook the small green and white bag and taunted him with a sing-song voice. "I know they're your favorite…"

"I'll take some." He held out his hand. "I'm looking forward to some alone time with you."

"Yeah?" She dumped three little pretzel tubes into his palm.

"We don't get that much time together anymore."

Silent, she turned her head, letting out a huff at the motorcycle that passed them on the right.

"Look at that guy," she said. "Let's play I spy. I spy with my little eye, something that begins with the letter foolish."

CHAPTER FOUR

Stuart's suitcase scraped across the bumper of their Subaru. Madison was already ahead of him, the wheels of her luggage gnawing up the gravel drive, chewing up dried leaves. He slammed the rear hatch and trudged behind her, scowling in her wake. The porch creaked as he climbed the stairs and avoided a sagging floorboard.

"Are you kidding me with this place? You couldn't find a single place in Maine that wasn't in the middle of a damn cemetery?"

Madison peered into a cracked blue plastic planter, dead plants pouring over the side.

"Which one of these do you think it's under?" Madison scanned the row of pots that lined the porch. Chipped and cracked, no one looked any better than another.

"Your guess is as good as mine. Why not pick the most disgusting one?"

Her lip curled in a sarcastic snarl. He turned away.

Maine had a loamy smell he wasn't used to, like dead leaves and dirt. All the fresh air was making him tired. Maybe it was the drive. He hadn't stretched since that convenience store. Rubbing his eyes with the heels of his hands, he waited for the fireworks to fade and squinted to see across the driveway. Fog was rolling in, sucking up all the tombstones.

Tall trees loomed over the cabin, dropping leaves the size of dinner plates, the kind you get at family style restaurants. The ground was covered in the platters and shards. Tombstones jutted up between them, dull steel blades in a muddy dishwasher. The sun was setting, and the stones cast long shadows that reached for him across the earth that swelled in little rolling mounds. It would be pretty if it weren't so darn creepy.

Stuart grabbed the rail and leaned back, stretching, hoping it would hold him. "Did you know this cabin was in the middle of a graveyard? You didn't mention this at all."

"You're really hung up on this. It wasn't on the website." Madison lifted the edge of a pot using just the tips of her fingers. Obviously, she wasn't any keener on finding spiders than he was.

"It's creepy. Isn't this creepy?"

"I guess." Madison slid a key across the porch rail and pinched it between her fingers. "Got it."

Stuart clutched his stomach. Hunger pangs were setting in. He lifted his shoulders to close the gap in his collar in case a spider dropped on him. Rubbing at the back of his neck, he wondered how far the people of this town had to travel to find a grocery store.

Madison held the knob with one hand and wiggled the key with the other. The lock wouldn't budge. He nudged her hip.

"Here, let me try."

She waved him off. "I got it."

A breeze swept leaves into a tiny tornado. A few landed on the porch roof, and others scraped across the floorboards and piled beneath two rocking chairs and the small table between them.

With the exception of the leaves, the flowerpots, and one sagging plank, everything was clean. Even the ceiling. As deserted as the place felt, at least someone had come by to tidy up.

He placed his hands on the dustless windowsill and peered in. White gauzy curtains with light green stripes framed the window inside. A stream of light streaked across a rug, the back of a sofa, the corner of a bed. There was a fireplace. It was quaint and quiet. Cemetery and potential spiders aside, it was the kind of place he could write in, at least in theory. So much great literature came about in the wilderness. *Walden. Call of The Wild.*

His pulse raced, and when a slow smile threatened to spread across his face, he let it.

"This could work." He turned and brushed his hands on his jeans, though they were clean. "I might be able to get some writing done here."

"Yeah? You might have to do it on the porch if I can't—"

Something clicked in the lock, and the door swung open. He grabbed the handle of Madison's bag and dragged both their cases over the threshold. It smelled of warm wood and the comforting musk of old fires. It was the kind of place that dripped with stories. It wasn't anything fancy, just bare wood walls of round beams that bore the scars of their felling. Axe marks and old nails dented and pocked their skin. Paintings hung here and there at odd heights and angles.

Madison flipped a switch, and all the lights came on. To his right, two lamps on tables bookended the sofa, burning orange through ancient shades. The sofa faced a narrow coffee table and a fireplace too big for the wall. It was large enough to crouch into, and Stuart felt compelled, but didn't want to dirty his shoes.

A bed was tucked against the far wall, big enough to hold two people but too small to qualify as a queen. Madison would complain about it later.

A small table rested beneath a chandelier made of fake antlers that dangled from the ceiling like a trophy from a hunt through a shopping mall. Along the left wall was a tiny kitchen. An almond-colored fridge hummed and shuddered. A single stainless-steel sink was plopped into an old, yellowed counter, some relic from the forties, and to its right, an old electric stove rested on shims above the crooked floor. A tiny window above the sink looked out over the graveyard, as if anyone doing dishes there needed to be reminded of their fate.

The world's tiniest bathroom was tucked in the corner, behind the open door. If the sink were any closer to the toilet, it would be on top of it.

"What do you think?" Madison pressed down on the back of the sofa and sat on the arm. "I hope there are some good restaurants around here because that kitchen looks like trouble."

He spun and closed the front door, and the sunlight disappeared.

"It's not much, but it's not a distraction either."

Whether he'd find inspiration in the cabin's old bones, only time would tell.

Hands on her knees, she studied the room. "Not very uplifting."

He shrugged. "I don't need much. Just some inspiration."

Madison snorted. "It'll probably be delivered by a foot-wide spider while we're sitting on that porch."

"At least there's a three-prong outlet for my laptop."

"Seriously?" Madison grabbed her suitcase and dragged it toward the bed. "How are you going to write here? It's filthy."

"It's not that bad."

Her shoulders fell. "Look at that kitchen. What are we supposed to eat?"

"Madison." Stuart pinched the bridge of his nose. "This whole thing was your idea. We're going to have to make the best of it."

The warm twist of hunger radiated from his stomach and made him sweat. Any hope for peace and quiet, relaxing into a writing trance blew away with the gust of wind that rattled the windows.

"If you wanted gourmet food, maybe you shouldn't have booked a cabin in a cemetery."

She stood and held up her hands. "I wasn't the one who needed a relaxing vacation."

"I never said I needed a relaxing vacation. You did." Stuart turned away from her, clenching his hands so his fingernails bit into his palms. There was no keeping the strain from his voice. "You have this wonderful way of deciding what I need, then complaining when you give it to me. If you'd have asked, I never would have said yes to this."

And she wouldn't be missing Edward so much.

"Let's just focus. This thing is barely cold." The refrigerator door suctioned open, and she moved two beers to fiddle with the thermostat. "I can't relax if I can't eat. Did you see any restaurants out there? I sure didn't."

He rubbed at his wrist, his chest tightening. It would be a long month if this tension didn't break. "We'll find a store, and we'll come up with some meals that will make you happy."

Madison pulled the sheet off the bed and inspected the mattress. "I'm not excited about a vacation from food, but I'll make it work. And there are no bedbugs, so that's a bonus."

Stuart inched open the cabinet doors, one by one. There were five glasses, three plates, two bowls. The drawer beside the sink had so much silverware that everyone in town must have donated their bent forks to the cause. Beneath the sink were some cleaning supplies, bug spray, a candle, a flashlight. There were a few old baking sheets, pans, some dented pots. The usual stuff. He almost missed the note on the counter, hiding in the shadow.

"What's this?" It was folded in half, just a scrap of paper.

Dear Madison + guest. Welcome. If you need me, I'm at the newsstand across from the market on Main Street. My number is at the bottom here if you got an emergency. I put two beers in the fridge for you. I'll come by to clean. When you leave, put the key under a pot.

"What is it?" Madison edged closer and peered at it, upside down. "No Wi-Fi password?"

Her discontent was palpable enough without her words to go with them. He folded the note and stuck it in his pocket.

"No, Madison. No Wi-Fi."

"Good thing you don't write online. I gotta pee. Then we can go find food."

Madison slid into the bathroom. Stuart searched a map on his phone. There was a small main street not far away with little shops. It looked pretty vacant, if street view was current, but there was a market and a place to get tea.

Madison's elbow banged something, and she cursed the walls. The sound of paper unspooling from the roll filled the cabin, and the toilet flushed.

She washed her hands and spilled out of the room. "It flushes slow. And the towels are really thin."

If he replied she'd only dig in further and find more reasons to hate the place. He checked his pocket for his wallet. "We'll make do. I found a place to stock the fridge. There's a market on Main Street. Wherever in hell that is."

She closed the bathroom door, and a painting fell to the floor, glittering dust motes into the stream of light. She rolled her eyes and picked it up, brushing her hand across it. Holding the painting up for him to see, she pointed at the image, darkened with grime.

"Do people really like these old paintings of boats? Is there a market for this stuff?"

"Yeah. Hotels and rental properties." He took it from her and hung it back on the wall, nudging it until it was straight. He tilted his head. It wasn't a bad painting of a ship being tossed on a storm sea, as the genre went. A little cliché maybe, but it was pretty good. He squinted at the shaky scrawl of tan paint in the lower right corner. It blended into the sea, and he couldn't make out the letters.

"When you're done making out with the bad art, can we go?"

Madison left the door open as she stepped into the sunlight. A leaf blew in. He kicked it out and stepped on it as he fit the cabin key on the ring, next to the car keys. Madison was already at the car, clutching her purse strap, the very image of impatience.

"Don't you even want to look to see what kind of tools are in the kitchen before you buy food you have to cook?" he asked. "What if you don't have some pot you need or something?"

The door closed behind him.

"Oh, it doesn't matter what's in that kitchen. It doesn't matter what's in that market. This place is going to be the death of me."

* * *

As impressions go, Ramsbolt didn't make much of one. The cemetery came to an abrupt end and storefronts began. Empty stores with dark windows lined both sides of the street. Leaves scraped up the sidewalks. It was as if the whole town got up and left.

"There's a florist." Madison jabbed her thumb at the window. "Doesn't seem like there's enough people in this town to support a florist."

"Or toys." A light was on in a narrow toy store, the window packed with teddy bears and toy trains. It was out of place among its neglected neighbors, nostalgia in a derelict desert. "I bet that place was cute back in the day. It looks like one of those classic Christmas cards."

Madison hummed a reply. "Halloween, more like it."

The road opened to a roundabout, as if there'd been so much traffic at one time that it needed management. In the center was a park on a gentle hill, a statue of a sailor pointing toward the east. He cast a long shadow that broke the circle of road and blotted out the sun as they passed.

Main Street was no bustling mecca, but the palpable proximity to humanity made it seem like a different planet. Cars were parked along the street. A lanky mailman rushed from an outdoor store and crossed the road without looking. A guy threw paint cans in a blue pickup truck outside a hardware store.

"Cinnamon buns." Madison wound her window down and leaned into the gust of air. "Do you smell that?"

Stuart pointed. "Bakery." A pink and white awning above a brick front shop declared it to be Marissa's.

"Thank God. At least there's some kind of civilization. Maybe they have coffee." Stuart craned his neck to read the sign of a broad building. It cornered a narrow alley. "There's the market."

He parked at the curb, and she led them inside. Groceries had always been her domain. Happy to claim no side in debates about avocados or apples, he put his hands in his pockets until the time came to make a few condiment suggestions and pick out some morsels to tide him over between meals.

"Do you want me to come up with some ideas?" It had been years since he last offered to cook. Not only was he bad at it, but Madison had staked early claim on the chore, despising it bitterly, complaining about more time on her feet, but unwilling to relinquish the task to an amateur.

She glared at him. "No. Why would you want to do that?"

"I figured it's your vacation, too. Maybe you didn't want to cook."

"I'm picky. I don't mind doing it." She put down a small pulp basket of blueberries and moved on to grapes.

He couldn't blame her for hating his cooking. When most of her life revolved around making consistent award-winning dishes for restaurants with wait lists, making hamburgers in her spare time couldn't possibly be exciting. After hours on her feet, smelling like food and oil, of course all she wanted to do was sit. Their meals were easy, from a box or a can. Madison had no intention of giving up her kitchen crown, and he had no desire to wear it. But he still had to offer.

He pushed the cart behind her, one of its wheels pointing sideways.

She lunged at apples piled in baskets and grasped one. "These are gorgeous. I could bake a pie maybe. I could try anyway. I'm not much of a baker, and who knows what that oven has for temperature control. Or pie plates. Apples and pork chops maybe."

Stuart nodded his agreement with pork chops.

Two men stomped into the store like something out of a lumberjack catalog, beards and flannel, plaid and denim. They passed the bag boy with a choppy greeting and made for an aisle across the store. One of them, the shorter one, locked eyes with Stuart and scowled. The two men muttered at each other in voices too low to hear over the music. The taller one stroked his beard.

Stuart was well acquainted with his own imagination, and while ordinarily he might embrace the fanciful spin of an imaginative tangent presented by two leering strangers in a store, there was no denying their curious gape held a sinister edge. Their stares almost demanded to know who he was and why he was there. Their eyes burned with opinions, and Stuart didn't want to hear them.

"Can we take a look back there?" Stuart pointed to the dairy case, pushing the cart with its one wheel facing sideways. "Real quick."

"Ice cream. Great idea." Madison placed apples in the cart as she skipped to keep up. She mumbled about a la mode and cream sauces, changing her mind because she wouldn't have the right pots. Stuart kept up his pace, the wheel jerking and clicking.

Madison overtook him, aiming for the ice cream. The two men were bearing down on him from the rear. He made a sharp right, deflecting, cutting over an aisle. Madison must have heard the cart turn because she looped around from the other side, facing him. Her face lit up.

"Kitchen wares. And this stuff is cheap." She grabbed a plastic ladle, eyed it up and put it back. She was blocking the aisle, and his heart pounded in his ears, drowning out Boston singing "More Than a Feeling."

The cart jittering, wheel scraping the old tile floor, Stuart made for the next aisle. Cereal and coffee. The men followed his every move. There was no way their paths were a coincidence. Confrontation wasn't his strong suit, and intimidating lumberjacks in creepy little isolated towns who leered and followed his every move couldn't possibly be there to present him with a welcome basket. He grabbed a blue can of something he hoped wasn't decaf, not taking the time to look. The cart wouldn't budge. The wheel was stuck.

"Come on," he said under his breath. "Move."

He gave the cart a hefty shove, and it lurched, slamming into a thick hand, twice the size of his, with dirt-caked nails and grease-filled lines.

Lifting his eyes, he came face to face with the largest bearded man he'd ever seen. Blue eyes shining so bright they could be full moons over a deliverance corn field.

"Watch what you're doing there, boy."

Stuart tried to swallow the lump in his throat, but he only had the voice to say, "Sorry."

Head down, he wrangled the cart into a U-turn and aimed for Madison, still gushing over cooking tools.

"I am not buying a whisk just for this trip," she said. "I'm tempted, though."

"Whatever. Get one. Or don't. Hurry up."

"What's the rush?"

His heart hammered in his throat. Taking slow breaths to steady himself, hands on the cart, he steered past her.

The dairy case was packed with the labels and logos of local farms he didn't recognize. He tugged at his collar and wiped his forehead with the sleeve of his shirt. He was cornered back there between dairy and frozen vegetables. The two large men were on his heels. Heavy boots clunked the linoleum and pitters of dried mud flaked onto the floor as they approached. A large arm thick as a log, veins bulging on the back of a calloused hand reached past him, and Stuart jumped aside, a breath hitching in his throat as he fought against the urge to cower.

"Whoa, little pantywaist." The smaller lumberjack held up his hands. "Just tryin' to get us some cottage cheese."

Stuart cleared his throat, flung open a door, and grasped a dozen eggs. "No problem. Have a great day." The carton shook in his hand. He placed it in the cart and spun, wheel wobbling, toward an aisle where boxes rested at chaotic angles. Madison prattled on.

"I can't wait to sit on that porch tomorrow with some tea." She brushed dust off a box of tea bags. "Does that sound good to you?"

Good? As far as Stuart was concerned, he wasn't stepping foot off that porch again until it was time to go home.

CHAPTER FIVE

The sun came up over the cemetery. It was so quiet Stuart could hear a squirrel digging up a nut ten headstones away. If he didn't sway the rocking chair, he could probably hear the dew evaporate as the sun warmed up the earth.

He stuck his pencil in his mouth and ran his hand over the blank page of his notebook. It was cool, soaking up the morning chill, and as empty as his mind. His father used to sit in his study and stare at the wood walls. Stuart would ask him what he was doing, and he would say he was writing. Even when the mind was at rest, he'd say, the wheels were still turning.

"Bullshit."

Leaves rustled a few headstone rows away. A black lab nuzzled the ground, lifted his head, and cocked an ear at Stuart, a harsh critique for the intrusion.

"Hi, doggy."

The dog bolted toward the woods, and the squirrel skittered up a tombstone, stood on his hind legs, and did a double-paw tuck. After a flick of his tail, he scampered off to another nut.

Stuart dug an old writing prompt from the file cabinet of his brain. *Pick an object in the room*, he'd say. *Make it the cause or the source of a conflict.*

In his most boring all caps handwriting, he jotted the first word that came to mind at the top of his page.

PORCHES.

There had to be millions of famous porches. Warren Harding famously ran his presidential campaign from the front porch of his Ohio home. Philadelphia had a long history of porch sitting, of people spending summer days out of doors, chatting with neighbors. There were woodsy porches, and coastal cottages, lake houses, porticos on giant stone mansions, and the giant wraparound porches of Southern gothic romances. What were they good for?

Waiting. Waiting for someone to show up. Someone to leave. Someone to drop something off or pick something up. For kids to come home late. Waiting for sunrises and sunsets and storms to roll in. For Madison to get out of the shower so he could find out what mood she'd be in today.

He tucked his elbows in to fend off the chill as the morning sky went from pink to yellow.

"Not the perfect place to wait for a story to show up. Apparently."

If only the cemetery could talk. It was built on hundreds of stories.

Mist followed the sun. It closed in, hugged the tombstones, caressed the ground. Stuart saw without really seeing, skimming, picking up feelings from the scene instead of the details. He didn't need the pebbles or the sharp edges. He needed the aspect, the element to take form with him, but all it gave him were broken senses. Damp earth and birds on the rise. Pastel fog and cold morning coffee. There was no flesh in it. No meat and bone. There were no stories out in that graveyard.

He grasped the arms of the rocking chair and pushed to his feet, grabbing the back to silence the wobble. He had no right to make all that noise. Sticking the pencil in the notebook's coil, he rested them on the seat, silent, and scanned the intersection of the cabin, the worn and gritty porch railing coarse against his palms. There was no one but bugs and furry transgressors infringing on the morning.

The screen door slammed behind him, and he jumped. Birds took off from a tree by the drive, showering the leaves with water droplets. Madison blinked at him, her hair wrapped in a thin green towel.

"Water pressure sucks. And the shower has that kind of mold in the caulk that grows from the inside out." She moved his notebook and fell into his chair. It creaked and rocked. Stuart clenched his jaw at the intrusion on his silence as she rubbed the towel from her hair and scrubbed at her scalp. "I'm never awake at this hour. Is this what the world looks like?"

"Not Philly." Stuart's nostrils flared with his strained smile. "It's loud. And bright. We should… Never mind."

There was no good way to ask her to respect the stillness.

A flock of birds came in from the west and landed on the vacated tree. More water showered to the ground.

Madison inspected his notebook as if he'd been writing in hieroglyphics. "Did you come up with anything? Porches?"

He turned his back on her, facing the rising tide of light.

"Just a place to start."

"Gosh, every romance needs a great porch scene." She rubbed at her hair.

Stuart spun to face her, leaning against the railing. "I don't think this is a romance. No idea what it is, to be honest, but it's probably not a romance."

She folded the towel and placed it on her knees. "This place has a ton of porches. Did you see them all yesterday? Every house has one. I guess it's all the snow. They need some shelter while they get in the door."

"I bet winter here is brutal." He could imagine the sound of it, boots stomping ice on old wood steps and snow shovels grinding away at brick walks.

"You could write about that. Maybe a really cool murder mystery scene with blood covered snow on a porch. That'd be cool."

"Hmm." The porch rail squeaked when he shifted his weight. "I'm not sure I'm a murder mystery guy either. Maybe. But I don't think so."

She smoothed the towel. "That's what all my friends are reading. Mysteries. You should give it a shot. What's the worst that could happen? You won't have a book? You don't have one now."

"Hey, Madison. Why don't I write the books?" He shook his head and jabbed at a loose nail with his toe. His feet were cold, and now they were dirty too.

"I'm just trying to help you because it seems to me you don't have any ideas here. Porches? That's your big idea?"

He held back a frustrated snip. Fighting with her was only wasted energy. He'd snap back, and she'd say he was being mean. She went through the trouble of booking the trip, after all. And it was clear he didn't have a solid idea of his own. He gave her the benefit of the doubt.

"I'm not going to write for the market," he said. "It moves too fast anyway. I'll write what I want to write and see where it gets me."

She shrugged and rocked in the chair. "Suit yourself. I'm just saying the bookstore by the restaurant has nothing but thrillers and mysteries in the window. If that's what sells, it might be worth writing. Edward said the same thing."

Stuart's throat closed up. The tightness in his chest squeezed the air from his lungs. He couldn't catch his breath. Swallowing hard, he dove in headfirst.

"What the hell are you doing talking about my career with Edward?"

"We're around each other all the time." She went to the porch rail and peered over it. "What am I not allowed to talk about my life now?"

"Oh, not at all, Madison. You can talk about my life all you want. But Edward can't talk about my life. He's not a part of my life. In fact, I'd like him to be a little further away from my life. Do you know what I mean?"

He turned away and faced the lifting mist. It would be easier if she would just agree with him. If she'd just say nothing and go inside and stare at her phone or bang pans together in the kitchen.

From the corner of his eye, he could see her face turn three shades of red.

"If you deny it, you'll be lying to me. You're a lot of things, but you're not a liar."

"Edward is not involved in your life."

"That's bullshit, and you know it. Why don't you go back inside and cook something out of bananas and pasta sauce and write a blog post for him all about it. Then he can call you and tell you..."

He picked up the notebook and propped it on the railing. This page, this blank page, was a new start. A new story.

"Forget I said anything." Madison threw the towel over her shoulder and went back inside. The screen door slammed behind her.

"You should go for a drive this morning. Find a bookstore. I bet there's one around here somewhere." Her voice was artificially chipper, higher and louder than it needed to be, as if nothing had happened between them at all. All the commotion startled a chipmunk, who raced from the base of one tree to the rotted stump of another. "You could do some research by looking at books there. Don't they have bestseller racks? Staff picks? Something like that. All I'm saying is that my friends are reading mysteries."

All her friends could jump in a lake.

Everybody knows you don't write for the market. The market moves. It shifts. It dodges every manuscript you throw at it. Writers think they're going to catch the vampire wave, but by the time their book is ready to submit, the market goes sour on vampires and wants biographies instead. Nobody writes for the market. But Madison wouldn't know that.

The tightness in his chest spread to his heart. It pounded against the intrusion, and his nostrils flared with hot breath, puffing steam into the air. His pulse throbbed in his neck. Was this a panic attack? Eyes wide and fixed on the back of a leaning tombstone, he wanted to let out a primal scream, release all the pressure building inside him before he exploded. He wanted to rush inside, hands clenched into tight fists and scream that he's a creative writing professor, and he knows what people read, and he didn't need her pressure or unsolicited advice about how to write a novel. She couldn't even get the punctuation right in a recipe for a blog. He wanted to scream that the clock was ticking on his career, and she'd done enough damage dragging him to Maine and wasting all those hours in the car. And if he didn't come up with anything while stuck in this cabin in the middle of a cemetery, he was going to have to live here with the birds and the barking chipmunks because his career would be over. But if he opened the door on that, he would also let loose a torrent of emotions and accuse her of messing around with another man. And he couldn't face that. Not right now.

"There aren't any bookstores here," he said. "I already looked. Thank you for the unsolicited advice, but I got it."

His anger at her was misdirected; he knew it. He wasn't mad at her. Not about his writing, anyway.

"I know." She clung to the door frame, peering at him, an expectant eyebrow raised. "Science fiction. You always watch that show from England."

She spun back into the cabin, and he rolled his eyes. *"Doctor Who.*

Fine. That's a great idea. I love sci-fi."

Looking up at the night sky, imagining fantasies playing out among the stars, had been a childhood past time. He'd been obsessed with the question of what lay beyond that giant brick wall at the edge of what he could fathom, begging the universe for hints at what lay beyond. But his grasp of science wasn't strong enough to pull off the genre. He'd give an arm and a leg to hop on a ship to Mars, though.

CHAPTER SIX

Stuart warmed his hands over the toaster oven in the cabin's corner kitchen. A cat clock on the wall taunted him with its precision, cranking out seconds without analysis or hesitation with the mere swish of a tail. How many passing moments had it counted without questioning its own purpose?

Stupid clock has one job. It isn't even self-aware. Don't compare yourself to a clock, you dolt.

The toaster popped. His breakfast, scalding toast just this side of burned, seared his fingertips as he fumbled the molten slabs onto a plate. He smeared them with crunchy peanut butter. There was no jelly, though.

"We have to go back to the store soon. We didn't get much."

Stuart plopped on the sofa, and his pencil rolled to the floor. Madison was on her hands and knees in the giant fireplace, staring up into the flue. She grunted something about bugs.

"Did you hear me? About the store?"

"I did." She tilted her head to peer up the chimney. "We would have gotten more than pasta and peanut butter if you hadn't freaked out about the locals. I wanted milk and coffee creamer, but here we are. Do you think bugs can get in here? We should get more bug spray. Lots more bug spray."

Madison stood and brushed off her yoga pants. She twisted trying to see her rump, and Stuart gave her a thumbs up.

"All clean." He risked being scowled at, but it was worth the effort at levity. "Nice butt."

Without crescendo, a deafening crash rattled the cabin from the direction of the porch. It seemed to come from the wall and the roof at once. Not as loud as he'd imagine a falling airplane engine to be, but loud enough to make him gasp for air brace himself as the cabin shook. The lamp wobbled on the table, and Stuart caught it before it crashed to the floor. In an instant, the ship painting slipped from the wall and plunged, landing with a thud. Eyes wide and a hand to heart, Madison jumped in a graceless pivot that ended with her crouching behind a chair, gasping Stuart's name, as if he were to blame for the disturbance.

Stuart broke out in an adrenaline sweat. He dropped the lamp as the fight instinct sent him hurtling for the doorknob. Chest heaving, his back to the door, he paused, ears straining to gather every sound, every sense heightened. He winced at the metallic slide of the latch bolt as he turned the knob in a fluid but ever so slow opening.

But wait. If he opened the door, he could be facing the unimaginable wilds of Maine. He'd faced down little more than a possum in his scant thirty-four years. And there were worse things to consider. The town had been barely more than hostile so far. The two men from the market came to mind, every fiber of their being fit the trope of axe assassin.

His heart thundered in his chest as he froze, one hand on the cool brass knob, the other clasping his robe shut within a white-knuckle grip.

"What the hell was that?" His voice was barely above a whisper.

Madison peered around the chair on her hands and knees, palms flat on the hardwood floor. Her voice shook. "I don't know! Bears? A moose? A meteor?"

He jabbed at the phone to unlock it. Who would he call? 911? And say what, he's in a cabin in a graveyard, and he's freaked out by a noise?

Madison crept into the kitchen and grabbed the paper towel holder. It was just a wooden dowel screwed into a little plank of wood, but she wielded it like a well-heeled slayer.

"What are you going to do with that?" he asked.

"I don't know." She pushed it into his chest. "You do something with it?"

"Do what?" His voice went up a pitch, and he pushed it back at her. "Shake it at them? Dowse for water?"

He shimmied along the wall and pulled back the edge of the curtain. One of the rocking chairs had tumbled over, and a brown dog of no discernable breed stood scared, tail between its legs, a few feet off the porch.

"It's a dog." His relief unfurled into a sigh. "Just a dog. He must have tried to jump on the chair, and it moved and scared him."

"Does he have a collar?"

"How would I know? I'm in the house. It's out there." He rolled his eyes.

Madison snagged his sweatshirt from the sofa and shimmied into it. "I'll go find out. You should finish your breakfast. You need to write, anyway."

The resigned obligation in her voice lit a fire in him. Who was she to tell him when to eat and when to write?

"I'm so honored you would sacrifice your time to save me, but it's a dog. Why don't you cower behind the sofa while I go outside and see if it has a collar? Two seconds ago, you wanted me to wage war against zombies with a paper towel holder. Now I'm an incompetent fool? I think I can handle a stray dog."

"I didn't say you were incompetent." She waved an arm at the cat clock and its swinging tail. "Ticktock. That sabbatical isn't going to last forever, and you should—"

He folded his arms. "You implied incompetent. I know about the ticking clock, thank you. I can hear the thing all day long. I've been hearing it for years. It's annoying."

"If you're so damn competent, why don't you have a book yet?" She leaned in with her hands on her hips, face red and chin set, voice like liquid fire. "There's always some excuse with you. It's too loud, too hot. The wrong paper. You have to chew on a pencil. I brought you all the way up here for a month to help you get rid of distractions, and if all you're going to do is chew on pencils, you can't complain when you still haven't written anything when we get home."

His pulse throbbed, and a vein in his neck ached. He grinded his teeth. "It won't ruin my career if I look at a dog outside."

Madison turned away but gave him a healthy dose of side-eye. "I'm only trying to give you room to write the book that could change your future."

"I don't want my future to change. I just want—"

He wanted a million things. Some job security, stability with Madison, less criticism, less pressure from everyone. His mouth watered, and his skin frizzled with the static charge. Any closer to her electrical current, and he would go off.

"What, Stuart? What do you want?" She slapped her hand against the door, and the curtains fluttered. "Don't get mad at me because you can't write."

If he said one word, if he so much as opened his mouth, he would explode. Why did she have to pluck at his strings? She was right; it wasn't her fault he hadn't written a book. He could edit papers on a train, read a novel at a football game. There was no reason he shouldn't have been able to come up with a concept worth turning into a novel even if she turned every pan in their kitchen into a drum. It wasn't her or the noise, it was the pressure she applied to his wound that hurt like hell.

"Madison, I really don't want to get into this with you. Not right now."

"Really? It's been years. You grunt and moan and blame the weather, you blame kids outside and the phone for ringing. You blame me for making noise or working too much. You want silence and distractions. You can't have both." Her mouth hung open, and she shook her head. "I don't…I can't…"

He was just as lost for words as she was. Jaw set and nostrils flaring, a million angry bees swarming in his head, he tried to calm them with a deep breath.

"Why don't you just apply yourself instead of jumping and running? Sit down, grab some paper, and…" She pursed her lips, eyes darting as if searching for words in the walls. "Just start. Just write something. Don't you want things to get better?"

"Better? Hell, yes, I want things to get better. Especially between us. And I'm pretty sure I can pinpoint exactly when they started falling apart. You haven't paid one bit of attention to me or my career for a very long time. Other than bragging about my job to your friends or name dropping my dad, you live your life, and I live mine. We used to be inseparable. You don't even know me anymore. And all the sudden you're really concerned about how I spend *my* time? So, yes. I really do want things to be better, because this is garbage. What is it that you want for me that you're suddenly so eager to come all the way to Maine? It sure as hell has nothing to do with me."

She pulled the neck of his sweatshirt up over her chin and ran it across her lower lip. "I do want more for you. A little inner peace. You constantly say you want some quiet. Fine, then. Write a book and sell it. We'll move to the suburbs."

Arms folded, he dug his fingers into his bicep. "Selling a book doesn't make that kind of money. And that's not the point. I like where I live. We'd need a second car."

"Sometimes I think that job is all that matters to you." She moved to the kitchen and flung open a cabinet door. She grasped a scratched and pitted glass, filled it with water and stared down into it, an oracle at a well.

She wouldn't find her own fault there. Fact was, she never did. She just projected her role in their rift onto him. He wasn't blameless, but his sins didn't weigh nearly as much as hers did, and if she was blaming him for the demise of their relationship, she truly didn't see the depth of the divide. Pointing them out wouldn't make the cabin any more tolerable. At least she was still saying *we*.

He ran a hand through his hair to discharge the static. "That's not fair. My job isn't the only thing that matters to me."

She clasped the glass and drank deep. "You want to write a book? Write a damn book. All I'm trying to do is help you."

The only word that came to mind was *salvage*. Conflict had always been that way for him. As everything shattered, he picked up the pieces, hoarded them in a secret place deep down inside. It was just another argument, another broken moment to glue back together. Unlike his father, he had no study to run to for retreat.

"I don't want to fight." He grasped the back of the sofa, squeezing the fabric in his hand for the sake of seizing something malleable. "I'm sorry. I can't… Every time I sit down to write, my mind goes blank. It's like I've been keeping this in for so long, feeding it for so long, that it's bigger than me now. I'm afraid I'll never come up with a story, and that fear is all I ever think about."

Madison loosened the grip on the glass, her knuckles no longer white. She set it on the counter without a sound and faced him. "What are you afraid of? Do you even know?"

"I'm only a failure if I fail. And I'll only fail if I try. It's like…I have this dream, and it's always on the edge of being real until I try to do it. Once I try, if I fail, I'll lose everything. My job, my security, myself. My dream."

The floor beneath her feet groaned when she pushed away from the counter. She picked at a hangnail on her thumb, looking like she'd rather be anywhere else. Stuart knew she hated talking about feelings or working through things. She had a standard set of solutions in her toolbox. Lemon, sugar, fat, salt. If she couldn't add tangible things to a pan and stir, she wasn't getting anywhere. He appreciated that about her. Usually, he didn't have to put his feelings into words, and she didn't have to make sense of them.

She shook her head. "I don't get it. I wanted to be a chef, so I cook things."

"Okay. Say I do finish this book, and I'm madly in love with it, and it won't sell, or people hate it, or it does sell, and the second book isn't half as good. What then?"

"You can't just go through life being afraid to pursue your one greatest passion. What kind of life is that?"

"I don't know, Madison. It's a giant unknown, and I hate unknowns. And I know you're not happy. Here or with me. I'm constantly worried that you're bored. You were just on your hands and knees staring into a fireplace thinking about bugs, for God's sake. This is the last place you want to be, and it's obvious."

She rolled her eyes. "I did this for you. This isn't about me."

He sighed, but it didn't budge the air between them. He tried to crack his stiff neck. "What if someone were standing over you while you cooked, screaming at you to cook."

"I kind of do that to other people for a living."

"Negative motivation doesn't work for me. In case you can't tell." He rubbed an eyebrow and shot an instinctive glance at the door, feet itching to flee. He could grab the keys off the counter, hop in the car and drive back home, to Canada, to Florida. Anywhere. But that wasn't the answer. This place was just as good as any. It was better than home, that was for sure.

Dammit.

He pulled the crocheted afghan off the back of the sofa, balled it up in his arms, and threw it on the floor. "I don't know. I don't know what the answer is. I just need some quiet to figure it out."

He didn't hear Madison move or see her shadow cross the floor, but her hand was on his arm, and he fell into her hug. When she pulled back, her smile was a sad one.

"I'm part of the reason you can't write. I know that. I'm making too much noise."

"That's not it. It's not the sounds—"

"Emotional noise. Dissonance. Even if I'm not trying to be, I'm pressure you don't need. I shouldn't have come. I'm some of the noise you need to get away from. Maybe there's a park somewhere I can go to, take a walk and give you some space."

"That sounds familiar." His sarcastic sneer was involuntary. Other than a set jaw, Madison made no motion that it registered with her. He wasn't letting her get away that easily so she could run off and be with Edward. If she wanted to leave him, she'd had plenty of chances. But if she truly wanted to make their relationship work, she would. After all, she'd come this far.

Stuart shook his head. "No. I'm sorry I snapped at you. I know you're trying to help. This isn't your burden, and I'm such an ass lately. You took a month off work to come up here with me. You wouldn't do that if you were being selfish."

She pulled back. "You're right, though. I hate it up here. I'm bored, and I miss the city. I miss work. This isn't the place for me."

She walked to the bed, changed into her jeans, then fell to her knees and dragged the suitcase from beneath. Throwing her pajamas in, she said, "I want to go home. Now."

His breath hitched in his throat. "What? What are you doing?"

"I can drive myself to the train station and leave the car there." She spun, pulling her hair into a ponytail. "There's one in some town called Colby. About a half hour from here."

She'd already looked. She had an escape plan the whole time.

"Don't go. We can figure this out." The world started spinning. Everything moved too fast.

She pushed past him to the bathroom. "I need to do this. I need to clear my head. And I need the car to keep warm until the train comes. The drive will be good for me. You can get an Uber or something to pick up the car."

Bottles rattled together in the shower as she collected her shampoo. She pulled her toothbrush from the glass on the sink. His insides wound together like rope, contorting and binding with every item she collected in her arms. Her toothpaste. Her floss. He folded his arms across the middle, trying to close the gaping void.

"What are you doing?" Stuart tried to block her as she passed, but she skirted him. "Please. Talk to me."

Her eyes were empty. It was like looking into the soul of a stranger. There was a time he could predict her every word.

The shake of her head was almost imperceptible. "Listen to me. Please. For once. You're brilliant. You just don't see what I do. Don't you dare come home until you have a book deal."

She threw bottles and tubs of creams in her little bag and zipped the suitcase. It landed too soft on the floor, like the sound had dropped out of the room when she grabbed the handle.

"No. Eight weeks, Maddy? I can't get a book deal in eight weeks. It's a nice sentiment, but don't be unreasonable. You should stay. We should talk."

The suitcase wheels made a hollow sound as they wobbled along the floor. "Make the most of your time here, Stuart. It's the best gift I can give you."

"Wait. I'll come with you. Let me change into something." He looked down at the hole in the knee of his pajama pants."

"Don't," she said. "I'd rather drive alone. Plus, you'll just waste a bunch of time sitting in the car, waiting for the train. You can go get the Subaru in a few days."

She flung open the door. The dog was gone.

CHAPTER SEVEN

"I wish you weren't going." Stuart kicked a gnawed acorn, and it skittered into grass wet with morning dew. But did he really mean it? The silence would be nice as would the freedom of not wondering if she was happy or bored. Of course, if she weren't there, she'd be with Edward.

"It's for the best." Madison slammed the car's hatch on the last of her bags. Next time she opened her suitcases, she'd be back home in Philly. She'd throw it all on the bed where it would stay. She'd text Edward and say she was coming back to work, and he'd be thrilled. Stuart winced at the mental picture.

He'd still be in this cabin, trying not to think about another man touching her, trapped with his failing career, comparing himself to his father and trying to claw through insecurity long enough to throw a few words on the page.

Half of him wanted to climb into the car with her, but another part, a curious and stubborn part, wondered what would happen if he sat alone in that cabin, if he were forced to be with himself in silence and put himself and his own needs ahead of all that fear. Would his brain finally crank out something worth thinking?

"Come here, you." He pulled Madison into a hug. It might be the last time for a while. "Have a safe trip. Call me when you get home."

She pulled back and smoothed his hair. "Don't...don't forget to shave."

"It's the middle of nowhere. Why would I shave?"

She opened the car door and caught it with her hand as it swung closed again. "I didn't know what else to say."

"What are you going to do on that long train ride?"

"Read, maybe. Think up some new recipes." She swung the door open wider. "I'll miss you. I'm really sorry we argued."

Something in her half smile said she didn't mean it. She looked like that every time they fought, and she sputtered some apology that she didn't want to give him. It was her way of saying an apology was just an obligation. She didn't want peace, she just wanted to have her way. If he pressed it any further, she'd turn it around on him and say he was the one who always caused it. He nodded but didn't budge.

"I don't know what I'll do." She hugged herself and rubbed her arms. "I won't be writing a book, I can tell you that. I'll probably play games on my phone or something."

"That cooking game with the penguins?"

She nodded at the ground, lips pursed.

"You'll enjoy that." He sure wouldn't.

She inched to the car and threw one leg in. "Okay. Take care of yourself."

"Call when you get home."

"Will do. I'll let you know where I parked the car."

She climbed in and fastened her belt. He grasped the edge of the car door as she nudged the rearview mirror. It was cold and damp, slicked with morning mist. A voice in the back of his head begged him to stop her, to keep her there, but another, louder voice told him to let go.

"Have a safe drive."

The door slammed shut, and she gave him a wave that he returned as she pulled down the path. The crunching gravel and engine whine faded into the fog.

He shivered and wrapped his sweatshirt tighter, soundless. Leaves rustled between the tombstones, a squirrel or chipmunk returning to its solitude perhaps. Maybe he was reading the vibe in the graveyard like tea leaves, but the silence and stillness finally gave him comfort. There wasn't any life chapter-ending ache or flush of grief. That emptiness he feared in her wake just failed to settle in. It would all work out. What if she had a guy on the side. His mother had on more than one occasion, but she'd stayed with his father. If Madison wasn't in it for the long haul, she would have left him by now.

Turning to the house, he stuck his hands in his pockets, tilted his head back to take in the tallest branches of a white birch.

"Book's not going to write itself."

A squirrel hopped up on a leaning mossy headstone, did a double-paw tuck, and flicked his tail in agreement.

Stuart climbed the porch steps. Arms wide, he stretched and

cracked the tension from his neck. The morning air was still thick, and dew would cling to the bits of grass for a while yet. The whole town was at his disposal. He could walk down the streets, check out the stores. He could drag the dining room table into the graveyard and write among the stones.

"If absence was designed to make the heart grow fonder, kudos to the architect."

Coffee. He could sit on the porch with a cup of coffee in his shorts and try to put something down on paper. He didn't need Maddy to do it. And he wouldn't stop trying to write just to spite her.

Inside, he closed the door to keep out the bugs and the wayward dogs, scooped her wet towel from the floor, and made another pot of coffee. It sputtered into the glass carafe with its yellowed plastic band made half a lifetime ago while he paced the kitchen, wearing his expectations into the grooves in the linoleum. Thousands of cups of coffee hadn't proved their worth before. There hadn't been a storm in a single ounce. Café tables on crowded sidewalks. Suburban malls and arboretums. Nothing had worked. But this cup of coffee. It had a lot to prove.

He filled the blue ceramic mug and warmed his hands with it. Early autumn was frigid in Maine, colder than he expected. He hadn't noticed while Madison was there. Her warmth was still in the room, but the chill was getting brutal. Especially the corners where Edward lurked. He grabbed the crocheted afghan from the couch, and Madison's sweater fell to the floor.

She was far too gone to reach by foot, and if she hadn't wanted to stay for him, he sure didn't want to know if she'd return for a sweater. He folded it neatly and laid it on her side of the bed.

Out on the porch with the blanket over his knees, coffee in hand, and notebook by his side, he couldn't help but imagine his days this way. It looked like the writer's life. A little log cabin in a charming graveyard. Rocking chair creaking on an old wood porch. The air was frigid, but it wasn't yet bitter.

He flipped to a blank page in the notebook, one without drawings of cats and car wheels, and wrote at the top: Murder Mystery.

Chewing on a pen, eyes fixed on the back of a tombstone pockmarked by the weather and moss-covered by time, he sat still so as not to disturb the crows playing hopscotch in the shadows.

The two men moved through the town like buffalo, large and lumbering beasts. They carried water for no one, and their gruff exterior had become part of the scenery in the derelict town. That was the safest way for those two to live, out loud and in the open. The tall man knew that the shorter would never live up to the lies they might tell. And the shorter man knew his comrade would lose patience in the end. Not friends but never enemies, they made their lives in that small town, answering to no one. And no one questioned the boxes as they arrived. Chain saws and drills. Vices and knives. Nor did they question the visitors. Not when they came and not when they left. The population of that small town would have been double if not for the men, who kept departing souls in their chambers beneath the village. Tortured. Tormented.

Tripe. The scary local in a small-town story had been done to death.

Stuart rolled the tension from his neck, but there was no relief in it. If this was the kind of work he'd crank out under pressure, the trip was going to be a long one, and he'd go home empty handed.

Heroes who refuse the call to adventure often need to be rescued from their boredom. Stuart was no hero, but he sure could use some rescuing.

He ran a hand down his face and slammed the notebook on the porch. Grasshopper sparrows cried out at the anarchy and took jagged flight paths from the shrubs to the ground.

For days his jaw had been aching from clenching his teeth. Terrible habit. Worth breaking before it got worse. He rubbed at it, searching the cobwebbed porch rafters for answers, and came up empty. A tiny spider made a path from one ceiling joist to another, drawing together strings, making his net to catch a feast. It had one job, and it did it well. Weave, catch, eat—all admirable, life-sustaining endeavors. And Stuart was cursed to be among a higher order in the food chain. Not content to merely weave, catch, and eat, he was obsessed with the burden of a meaningless life and haunted by his own pointless endeavors. His entire career was fueled by a desire to write fake stories that felt real enough about fabricated lives, hoping they would change some real person's world, but if the words wouldn't come, what was the point? What would he have to fall back on? His career would be toast, but so would his ambition.

How could he change someone else's life with words if he couldn't pull enough of them together to save his own?

CHAPTER EIGHT

Midday sun streamed through the cabin windows, but its reach was far too short to warm Stuart, sprawled on the sofa, one arm dangling to the floor. The notebook of scribbles rested on his chest, seesawing with his breath. A conscious part of his brain kept him just this side of sleep, urging him to write something, anything at all, but his creative juices were out of shape, thick and slow, pinning him to an impending nap.

An alarm went off on his phone, jolting his heart rate, and his arm flung out, thumping the floor in search of the imposing chirp.

T-minus 26.

Twenty-six days left to come up with something. A story. A struggle.

Holding the phone above his face, squinting into the light, he silenced it and let it fall to the floor, only for the chirping to become incessant.

"What? I turned it off." He pushed himself up on his elbows, the notebook falling to the floor.

It was Madison.

"Hello?"

"I made it home." Water ran in the background. She gulped it down.

He rubbed his free hand over his eyes. "Safe trip?"

"Yeah. I got in late yesterday. Exhausting. The car's at the station under a light. You can't miss it." Outside of their apartment in Philly, a traffic argument erupted. Car horns made their way across the network and into his ear in Maine.

He cleared his throat and sat up. "I'll get a cab or something. What's all that racket?"

"Same old Philly. Hey, did you find my sweater?"

"Yeah." It was draped over the end of the bed with a sliver of light piercing its heart. "I'll keep it safe."

"Thanks. I'm proud of you. It takes a lot of courage to lock yourself in a cabin in the middle of nowhere the way you did."

It wasn't worth pointing out that it was her idea, but it was for his own good.

He flung his feet over the edge of the sofa and planted them on the cold floor. "At least it's quiet."

"I was thinking about it on the train." She rustled through a plastic bag. Pretzels, perhaps, or some salty snack. They were her favorite. "You're really determined. I know you'll write a great story up there. It'll come to you."

"That's what I'm hoping. I already have some ideas."

He grimaced, no idea why he said it. She hadn't asked him to lie; it just fell out of him. Unless she considered the concept of two lumberjack axe murderers a story idea.

"That's good news. I had a great idea for a dish—" She cut herself off, loud car exhaust tiring itself somewhere outside their city window. "You're not into cooking anyway. I should let you get back to writing. I have another call coming in. Probably a robocall."

Probably Edward. "Yeah. Thanks. Have a good time up there."

"Don't be a stranger."

The line clicked, and she was gone. Don't be a stranger? Funny, the person in the relationship who keeps moving further away is telling him not to be a stranger.

He pushed to his feet. The window was cool to the touch. Sun picked up dust that clung to the outside, making little ghostly streaks of cleanings past, and it warmed his skin where it fell on his arm.

A distant hum grew closer and louder, swelling an engine pang. Someone heading out of town or passing through, perhaps. His mind unspooled, kicked out a hook, hoping to snag a story.

A family of four with a pet cat, dressed in their Sunday best, fleeing a vampire zombie invasion that started as a small-town flu and morphed into viral undead while singing "American Pie" to keep the kids calm.

The engine cut the air, growing closer, crunching up the drive. Stuart ran a hand through his tousled hair and tugged his T-shirt down over his jeans. A dark-skinned older man with wiry curls tinged with white climbed out of an '80s Pontiac Grand Prix, silver and red. He slammed the door, and Stuart jumped. The quiet country life had softened him already. What had it been, two days? No, three.

He threw the door open and stepped onto the porch before the man could knock. The words were on the tip of his tongue, that he'd rented the place and was there to write. He wasn't a squatter or a random thief.

The men met at the edge of the cabin, Stuart on the porch and the interloper on the walk. The sun cast shadows on the man's deep wrinkles. His face was lined by age and sun.

"Warren. Nice to meet you." His voice was deep, and his hand was soft when Stuart leaned down the stairs and shook it.

"Warren. You left the note on the counter. Nice to meet you. I'm Stuart."

Warren stuck his hands in his pockets and rocked on his heels. "The house okay? You need anything? No one's rented it for a while. Half expected the water heater to blow."

The twinkle in his eye said he wasn't all that worried.

"Nah, everything's good. Nice little place you have here."

"Thank you. I'm glad to have a renter for a bit. Keeps the kids from breaking in here and hanging out."

Stuart's eyes grew wide. Kids breaking in? "Is that a thing? Something to worry about?"

Warren shook his head. "Nope. Just kids looking for a clubhouse. Like kids do. But they leave food wrappers, and ants follow them around." He craned his neck to peer at the cabin with a critical eye, as if Stuart had painted it pink and orange. "What brings you to town then? Going into Canada?"

There was a hint of paranoia in the man's question, as if he already had his answer, and by the time it settled into Stuart it was a full-blown accusation.

Stuart rubbed at the back of his neck. "I'm not a fugitive or anything. I'm here to write a book."

Warren shrugged. "Most people who rent this place are just stopping through on their way to Canada. Seems like a long way to go to write a book."

His snort became steam in the chilly air. Little did Warren know, the journey would feel ten times as long if he didn't actually write anything.

"Tell me about it. I'm just here for the peace and quiet."

"I always wanted to write a book." Warren glanced up, at the trees that towered over the cabin perhaps. "Never had the time or energy. Never came up with a good idea, either, I guess. I'm impressed."

When his gaze returned to Stuart, it carried the same look of awe Madison's family gave him at holiday dinners. Sure, the ability to make a story out of mere breath and paper had been valued by mankind since the dawn of time, but it rarely felt justified to those on whom it was bestowed. It was hardly an award of valor. He'd built a career out of telling people that anyone could do it, teaching people to chip the hard edges off the stone of their art. He'd never grown comfortable accepting the compliment of the writer label with any grace, and he'd long ago given up the notion that he'd wear it with any ease. Something about the expectant focus of Warren's attention, in light of the war he waged against himself in that cabin, made him reject the commendation all the more.

He loosened his set jaw. "It's not all it's cracked up to be."

"I sell a lot of paperbacks at the newsstand." He jingled his keys in his pocket. "I read them to pass the time. You writers are like magicians. Should get more credit than you do."

Stuart laughed and turned to the door. "I should earn the credit I get."

"All it takes is one idea."

The guy was only trying to be nice, and Stuart had heard the sentiment a thousand times, but something about it set him off this time. The idea that anyone could do it if only they could find the right idea made him want to punch a wall. He ran a hand through his hair and fixed his eyes on the grass that edged the drive. He'd brushed this conversation aside a thousand times before. How many students never wrote? How many should have but quit too soon? How many tried and never finished?

Stuart pulled his phone from his pocket and checked the time. He pinched the bridge of his nose. "I should get back to it. Sorry to rush you."

Hot anger rose in his throat. He was so sick of hearing people say *I keep meaning to write a book* like it was laundry unfolded or dishes in the sink. Writing, putting words down on paper, anything at all, was the only thing he could do to stop feeling this way, and it was the one thing he couldn't do. Madison was right. There was only one way to get a book down on paper and sitting around wasn't going to do it.

Warren waved a hand and twirled his keys around his finger. "No problem. Just wanted to swing by and see if you needed anything. I'll get out of your hair."

Every pebble grinding beneath Warren's feet sounded like a bomb blast. The car door creaked open. Even the squirrel on the tombstone twitching his nose at the air seemed offended.

"Hey, you said you have books at the newsstand?" Stuart blurted out the question before he realized he'd asked it.

Warren paused, one foot in the car, and shook his head. "A couple. Trade stuff. Paperbacks. No new releases, though. Mostly people buy them when they're sick and waiting for their prescription at the pharmacy."

"Is there a library?"

"Sure is. You just go straight across the roundabout and take your first left. It's down the street there. It's got a sign. Can't miss it. Tucked in an old house."

"Thanks. That sounds perfect."

"It's small. Don't get too excited."

CHAPTER NINE

The library was tucked between quaint little homes on a potholed street, just like Warren said it would be. Set back behind a short stone wall with a narrow wedge of lawn, it was three stories high with white siding that dripped like sharp-edged layers of fondant. Where Stuart came from, libraries were cut from two cloths. They were clinical and municipal bunkers designed to protect the books from the people, and imposing university libraries that cost so much to access that the contents seemed unreachable and disappointing once you got there. But this little library was positively charming, promising. It was like warm cookies and a hug at the same time.

From where he stood on the broken sidewalk, Ramsbolt's library begged him to go inside, plop in a chair at a long wood table, place his notebook beneath a green banker's lamp, and write out the horrors that hid beneath the shingles and the terrors Warren would inflict on the small town that were taking shape in his mind.

He warmed with a swell of affinity for the library, his mood lifting for the first since he'd stumbled into the little town, and his fingers ached to write within its walls. Perhaps things were looking up after all.

Pulling his phone from his pocket, he snapped a quick picture, indulging in the dream that he'd sit in an interview someday and wax poetic about the tiny library in Maine where he got the inspiration to start his first great novel.

In a neighboring yard, birds pittered beneath a feeder. A tattered garden flag with last year's snowman on it flapped in the breeze and branches of a shrub rustled. There wasn't a single human-made sound for miles. If some horse sauntered up with a weather-worn rider who declared Stuart the sole survivor of an apocalyptic storm cloud, he wouldn't have been the least bit surprised.

He climbed the few wooden steps, the hollow thud of his feet like thunder in the quiet neighborhood.

The porch was covered in chalk drawings of elephants with large ears and skinny trunks, and pink zebras with blue stripes. The corners of sun-faded flyers lifted in the breeze. Stuart pushed the latch on the handle and nudged the door open, an electric chirp warbling about his entrance. Inside, a woman in her late twenties, her face illuminated by the tablet she read, looked up. Her dark brown hair was tied up in a bun with a pencil shoved in it.

Her dark eyes narrowed, her back straightened, she wore the stern visage of a woman not to cross. Were she a troll tasked with guarding a bridge, he would have turned and run home, but there was nothing troll-like about her, though she guarded precious treasure.

"Library, right?" He closed the door behind him.

She lifted her chin. The familiar nightmarish feeling erupted within him, that he'd forgotten his homework, left his lunch on the bus, and had stumbled into the wrong classroom all in the same day. She was about to demand a toll to cross the bridge, and something about the look in her eyes said it would require a currency he didn't carry.

"You don't have a library card here." She spoke the monotone fact without inquiry.

Stuart tugged on the hem of his shirt. He wasn't dressed for the chill in that place. "That's true. No library card. Do I need one to sit and write for a while? Can I just look at the books?"

She lowered her glasses to the end of her nose, sizing him up without obstruction. "As a librarian I'd much rather you read them than look at them, yeah. I mean, no. You don't need a card. And yes, you can go in." She fidgeted with her tablet reader, turning off the screen, then placed her glasses on the desk and seemed to focus on her hands. They were the telltale movements of an extreme introvert, and the bristled armor of his defensiveness cracked a bit. There was no easy way to declare kinship.

Behind her a narrow doorway led to the library proper. The door had been removed from the hinges, but the hardware remained, like the library was saying you were welcome to come in, but we can still keep you out if we want to.

He considered her deference permission and took a step, but she cleared her throat, bringing him to a halt.

"You're not from here. Just passing through?" Her voice was strong. She wasn't done with the scrutiny just yet. Pushy for an introvert.

"Um. Just passing through town, yeah." He swallowed hard. Did he look like a book thief or a vandal? The kind of guy who walked into libraries across the country to remove the last page of every book?

She sighed and pushed away from the desk, getting to her feet. "Come on. I'll give you a tour."

"Oh, I know how it works, I'm a—" But she was steps ahead of him, through the doorway and into the library. He followed in her current, a spicy trail of orange and cinnamon and something he couldn't place. "Does everyone get the guided tour or just me?"

When she turned to face him, her cheeks were red. She draped her fingers on the back of an orange vinyl chair. Six identical seats, straight out of the seventies, formed a ring around a midcentury modern coffee table. It would be cozy and retro if it didn't have such an air of permanence.

"You're welcome to stay here. I mean, sit here. While you read. If you want." Her eyes were fixed on the coffee table, on the perfectly fanned arrangement of last year's magazines. Some blond celebrity smiled, clutching a big floppy hat, while a headline promised to help diagnose cancerous moles on page thirty-three.

His insides twisted a little. He wasn't making her nervous on purpose. Turning from her, his eyes fell on the closest books. Nonfiction. Structures in landscape architecture. The shelves they sat on were solid wood, built to last. The entire room, though simple and plain, was clearly cared for. It lacked the chalky paint and resilient carpeting of his university's library. Peel away the shelves and the books, and it looked nothing like a library at all. It was *Whistler's Mother* and *American Gothic* and the kind of simple warmth his heart yearned for.

Chewing on her lower lip, she pointed to a box of pencils on the coffee table. "No pens. Pencils only. You don't have to put books back when you're done. Just leave them on the cart there." She pointed to an empty library cart tucked against the wall and gave him a smile that lifted her eyes. "What research are you doing? Let me guess, it's something about wildlife. You're a journalist, aren't you?"

He raised his eyebrows. "No. Wildlife journalist? Is that a thing?"

She grew another shade redder and shrugged. "Just a guess. Climate change. Environmental stuff."

"I hope I don't smell like a wildlife journalist. I am a writer, though. A college professor. Creative writing. Just visiting town. I'm staying in a log cabin in the cemetery."

"Warren's place. I know it. No one ever stays there. How long are you here?" Her grip on the chair puckered the orange faux leather.

"A month. It's just part of my sabbatical. I…" He ran a hand through his hair while he tidied his mind. "I'm here to write a book."

"A whole book?" Her eyes widened. "In a month?"

He shrugged. "Definitely not a whole book." Probably not a chapter either, if he didn't get started. "Maybe an outline."

She pulled a folded piece of paper from beneath the magazines and shoved it in his hands. "You should fill this out and get a card so you can at least check out some books to read at night. I ordinarily wouldn't encourage a short-term visitor to get a library card, but you're a professor. You could always return them on your way out of town. I know there's no television there. Cozy little place. Kind of romantic."

It was his turn for red cheeks. He cleared his throat with a hard swallow. "Thanks. For the offer."

"Yeah. I mean, you teach creative writing, right? Unless you're lying, and you're actually a serial killer renting a cabin in a cemetery as a convenient way to hide the bodies." She leaned on the chair, and it scooted an inch, knocking her off balance. Her ears blazed red as she regained composure.

His stomach fluttered with the charm of her awkward uneasiness. He felt suave by comparison. The butterflies settled as she righted the chair and smoothed the cushion.

"Anyway, you have a great little library here. Thanks for letting me have a card. I promise to bring the books back. It's not like I'm irresponsible with books or anything. I absolutely promise not to bury them with the bodies."

She blinked at him, nose wrinkling with her smile as she plucked at a stray upholstery thread on the chair. "We appreciate that. Or me. I do. I'm the only librarian."

Their eye contact melted a hole through his chest that sent molten lava through his veins. A younger Stuart would have inched closer, but this one cracked his knuckles to discharge the current.

"Want to know a secret?" He leaned in. "I can't write books."

The angel on his shoulder that feigned to be his conscience jumped up and down and held up a neon sign with Madison's name on it while the playful little devil who rarely spoke started counting the miles between Maine and home. It wasn't really flirting if he didn't expect it to go anywhere, right? But his imagination reeled. Someday this glowing librarian with a messy pencil bun might open a box of books to find his on top. She would toss it in the trash can as she said, "He came in here and said he couldn't write books. He's just a player and a liar."

Her easy, sympathetic smile lifted the weight of a thousand unwritten stories from his chest. Saying it out loud to someone, especially someone well-read who worked around books was freeing. She was practically a colleague, after all. And it wasn't like she could do damage to his reputation or call him an idiot. He'd never see her again after this. He could drop the books in the return slot at midnight and never think of her again.

He returned her consoling smile without thinking, without filter.

"I'm Sandy." She beamed and stuck out a hand, clammy and warm, and he shook it.

"Stuart. Nice to meet you."

"Same."

She pointed to the far corner. "Books about writing craft are back there. You probably don't need that, though. Oh, God. Here I am telling a writing professor where to find books about writing. Did I insult you? I didn't mean to."

He waved a hand. She could have described every book in detail, and he would have enjoyed her company, but it seemed cruel to let her nerves get the better of her. "No. Not at all. Don't worry about me."

She walked backwards, hand trailing the back of the chair, eyes fixed on his. She was definitely flirting with him. His heart responded, throbbing in his neck.

"Okay. I'll leave you to it. Enjoy," she said, turning back to her desk. "Let me know if you need help with…anything. At all. Anything."

"Thanks." Stuart tugged on his collar again, though it wasn't tight, letting the heat escape from his neck.

Plopping down on an orange vinyl chair, he propped his notebook on his knee. He pushed her dimples from his mind, gripped a tiny golf pencil, and coaxed himself into the slipstream, where words took form and, with any luck, arranged themselves into a story.

Warren's hands were lined with ink from old newspapers and trade paperbacks. His skin was trenched with papercuts, but the deeper scars had been fatal. Not for Warren, though. For fifty years he'd reigned supreme over the town of Ramsbolt from his place behind the newsstand counter. It seemed nearly everyone in town had met their end in some twisted tangle except for Warren. The others left, telling themselves they wanted opportunities, warmer weather, and a sun-drenched beach, though they knew it was fear that drove them away. Those who remained were smart enough not to ask why. One by one, Warren plucked them off like pages torn from a to-do list, and Warren's list was almost complete. The town was almost empty.

Stuart scrawled a little line beneath the paragraph, cutting it off from the blank page below.

It was an interesting premise, a small town on the verge of collapse being demolished from within. What would drive a man to destroy the thing he needs the most? It would need a hero, though, a tall and stoic mailman who would put the pieces together and save the predator from himself. But something about the core of the story didn't sit right with Stuart. His heart wasn't in the brutality, at least not enough to flesh it out as a book.

He felt eyes burning into him and looked up to see Sandy peeking at him over her shoulder. Turning from the searing impact of the moment their eyes met, he feigned interest in a distant shelf of nonfiction, leapt from the chair, and took a book in his hands, the glossy cellophane cover cool and soothing.

No, Warren seemed too kind to inspire such ferociousness. He needed a downtrodden hero, the embodiment of need. He needed action and wanting that stood in opposition to everything his character believed. There would have to be an outside force strong enough to push the champion further from his goal, into the darkness, until he realized that what he wanted and what he needed were two very different things. Torn between the darkness and light, with his soul on the line, his character would have to risk it all, whatever *all* was, in an epic battle with the Big Bad. But who was that hero and what was that need?

He held the book as if it were a tray of precious gems, perched on his fingertips, the overhead light catching on the glossy cover, reflecting it onto the books as he walked. There weren't a lot of options. This had to be the world's smallest library. If this was the only entertainment in town, Sandy had her hands full.

He tossed the book and gripped its spine as it fell.

Wildlife of Maine.

It was a tall, thin book with a full cover image of an owl in a tree wrapping the spine.

The bottom row of his childhood bookshelf had been full of books like this. Wildlife and trucks, landscapes of Africa. He would sit on the floor with his legs crossed and a book in his lap, imagining scenes unfolding like movies. It smelled like his childhood, too, musky ink and paper, bringing back memories in torrents. Rainy fall days when summer was too far gone to grasp anymore, skimming the shelves in search of adventure. Sick days when he stayed home from school and got lost in a flu-filled haze of pictures, eating grilled cheese sandwiches, tomato soup, and animal crackers. Making pillow forts on snowy days and reading at night with a flashlight. He stuck his nose in the book and filled his lungs with it.

Sandy appeared in the doorway, soundless. He jumped at the intrusion.

"I love that they always smell the same," she said, leaning against the door frame.

"I was just thinking the same thing. Reminds me of being a kid."

Slipping closer, the smell of her washed over him, the leading edge of a tide sure to sweep him away. She took the book from his hand, and he let her.

"Are you checking this one out?" Delicate fingers turned the pages.

"I am. I am checking it out. Taking it with me." His voice was barely above a whisper. It was all he could manage, his mouth dry. He cracked his neck and pinched the spine of another book.

How to Build a Car.

He tucked it under his arm and stepped back. "And this one. I should get these back to the cabin. Get to work."

And stop being distracted by orange and cinnamon and those brown eyes and hands that look soft and not at all like they suffered papercuts.

Sandy held out a hand, and for the briefest moment he was inclined to take it, to hold it, to know her knuckles and nails and the soft pads of her fingers. He handed over the book instead, leaving his own hands empty and vacant.

"I'll check these out for you if you want to come with me and fill out your form." She turned from him, returning to the desk. "I can't believe this is all you're checking out. This is one heck of a book you're writing. A race car driving owl."

He collected his notebook and bag and followed. "Yeah. I'm just looking for inspiration, that's all. A springboard."

She flung open a drawer and handed him a pencil. "And a library card is all it takes to check out the inspiration and take it with you."

He filled out his application, leaving his home address in Philly, his driver's license number, his date of birth. He added his email address to receive courtesy reminders, but his mouth dried at the option to leave his cell phone number. What if he messed up and left the book at the cabin? What if she called while he was in Philly and Madison saw the call?

He glanced at her as she stamped the slip and stuck it into the book's pocket. She seemed to be moving in slow motion.

She wouldn't call. Why would she call? All he had to do was return the book. Even if she did call, Madison was probably too busy with Edward to notice, anyway.

He fought back a snarl, wrote down his cell number, and held out his application.

She took it from his hand and replaced it with the books. "Due back in a month. Or when you leave, whichever comes first." That wrinkle in her nose when she smiled sent goosebumps down his arms. "Hope these bring you some inspiration."

He squirmed under her grin, held his breath, and smoothed his shirt. Her attention made him jittery, his stomach like Jell-O.

"Oh, I put regional authors' books on the mantel in there. The old fireplace is all blocked off. I mean, who would set a fire in a library. It's probably not even up to building codes to have a working fireplace in a library. But you would know, right? Maybe that's not part of the college curriculum. We don't even have a code enforcement guy here." She let out a nervous laugh and ran a hand over her forehead. "Stop talking, Sandy."

She took a deep breath that lifted her shoulders. Stuart squeezed the books so hard he was afraid they would turn to pulp. It was all he could do to keep from touching her shoulder, calming her, completing the electrical circuit.

"Anyway, I'll keep an eye out for books by you. It would be an honor to put your work on the mantel."

He swallowed hard, pushing down the fluttering in his belly. It had been a long time since he'd had that effect on a woman. And it had been just as long since a woman had that effect on him. Clutching the book to his chest, he nodded.

"I'll take you up on that one day. I'll mail you a signed copy."

<h1 style="text-align:center">CHAPTER TEN</h1>

Stuart's walk back to the cabin was the longest haul ever taken by a man. He kept his head down, eyes shielded from the bright midday sun, the books tucked under his arm. There weren't any threatening lumberjacks out and about, no townsfolk to weigh him down with their scrutiny, but he was embarrassed nonetheless about marching to his doom armed only with glossy pictures of wildlife and a book about cars. It would take a miracle to craft them into fiction. And nothing served as a better reminder of his daft mortality than the ringing of his phone and his father's name splashed across the screen.

With a sinking stomach, he walked through the shadowed pool of the sailor statue and answered the call.

"I got your email about Maine." His father was distracted, his voice distant, as if he were holding the phone away, but the lilt of snark came through just fine, and Stuart rolled his eyes at it. "Buckling down to write a book, finally?"

"If I didn't teach four classes a semester, I'd have more time to stare at blank paper." He winced. The door he opened to his father's criticism was so old it barely closed anymore. He didn't need to hear yet again that teaching was a waste of time.

"You don't need a job to write a book," his father said. "You didn't need all those degrees to do it either."

"Not everyone can afford to live a life of leisure. I didn't inherit your father's money."

"The good news for you is that it's all safe and sound. It wasn't luck that I learned how to make a good living, it was hard work. It'll be there for you when I'm gone. In the meantime, you get to learn how to live without it."

"So I've heard. Being a professor is a pretty good way to do it, you know. Plus, I don't have to fly around giving speeches." Stuart looked both ways and crossed the street.

"Don't knock it until you've tried it. I made twenty thousand dollars in speaker fees last month. All the things I know and have seen, all the books I've written, and they still only come to ask the same questions. What was it like to be the son of an assassinated senator? Are any of those political scandals in your books real?"

Stuart laughed. "For twenty thousand dollars, I'd be happy to dish on your life."

His father snorted. "Just wait until I'm gone. Do you need money, though?"

"No, not at all. What I need is inspiration."

His father grew quiet but for the gentle stretch of his leather chair and the creak of wheels on the area rug beneath his desk. "Writers love to say that the imagination is a muscle, and it gets stronger the more you use it. I don't care much for that comparison, Stuart. Because that implies that everyone has it. That if you don't have it, that something is wrong. It isn't a muscle at all. It's a gift. And sometimes… I'm not saying this is you, of course, because I don't really know…but sometimes, we spend so much time or effort focused on the gifts we didn't receive that we don't recognize the ones we did. Do you know what I mean?"

His words were tight and measured. Stuart knew exactly what he meant. Addicted to his own wit, if he was right, he'd claim the validation, and if he was wrong, he'd own his role as a motivating influence.

"When did you publish your first book, Dad?" He braced himself for the math to come, but he wouldn't get a straight answer and didn't expect one. His father was always *quite young* when he published his first book. *Right out of school*, he would say. The man was a mythology of tweed and smoke, a crafted cool and aloof figure who never struggled or tried very hard but deserved everything he'd achieved.

"Immaculate conception, son." The telltale clunk of the chair reclining told Stuart his father leaned back, satisfied. "Don't ever let anyone question your journey."

"I can't believe people pay you for that advice."

His father sighed, and the chair groaned upright. "I queried agents. I figured out what they wanted, and I sent it to them. If it makes you feel better, consider it precise luck. Of course, it was so long ago that it feels like overnight success. It's been ages since I needed an agent.

Definitely not *that* woman."

"I know. I've heard the story." Stuart had been young, but the battles of the ego clash between his father and his agent rocked the house and brought his mother to tears over the unnatural end to the friendship they'd shared. The older Stuart got, the more faith he put in his father's role in the demise of their relationship.

"And before you ask, I do not need an *editor*." His father had fired him, too, negotiating his way out of it with the publishing house. "You, however, do need both. And, no, I can't give you the name of my agent or a leg in the door."

"I wasn't asking to ride your coattails." Far from helpful, they taunted him more than anything.

His father must have run a hand down his face; Stuart picked up the sound of gritty stubble and a huffed sigh. "You wouldn't want to anyway. I doubt we're in the same genre. Besides, there's nothing more humbling than facing down your own ego."

Stuart gripped the books tighter as he reached the edge of the cemetery. Taking a shortcut, he rounded the house by way of the kitchen window. A squirrel skittered down the trunk of one tall tree and darted between drifts of leaves and up another trunk, hanging upside down, his chest heaving, breathless at the intrusion.

He paused at the bottom of the stairs, yet again the small boy who looked up at his father begging for a morsel and being served gruel. Leaves crunched beneath his stomped foot.

"You know what, Dad? I'm good with the negativity. I don't need any more of it. Every time I ask you for fatherly advice you've either had a charmed life that can never be replicated, or you worked hard for it in ways I never can. You've never once congratulated me for a single thing I've achieved. In fact, you counter every one of my achievements by calling it a hindrance. Unless, of course, you can somehow take credit for it. So why, exactly, did you call?"

"I'm taking your mother to Cabo for her birthday in December. If you want to send her a card, send it early."

"Yes. Thank you. I will."

Stuart fumbled the books while he ended the call and climbed the stairs. He left the keys dangling in the lock, dropped the books on a rocker, and gripped the railing with all his anger.

"Don't blame the stars for the darkness, just because they're all that you see. Don't blame the stars."

He'd written the line in his twenties and long forgot why, but it had served him well as a mantra ever since.

"He's not your problem. You just need to write." Moss fluttered from the porch railing when he kicked it with his foot. "I should fail just to spite him."

His phone rang in his pocket, buzzing his hip.

"What?" He answered without looking. "Did you forget to mention another way I've disappointed you today?"

"Damn. Madison's phoning it in, these days?"

It wasn't his father's voice on the line. The sarcastic snicker came from Mohl.

"Sorry. Rough day. I thought you were my father. You couldn't have called at a better time."

"Madison isn't distracting enough?"

"No." He kicked at the railing again. The wind had already pushed dried leaves over the depression the Subaru left in the path. "She left. Took a train back home."

"Maybe she did you favor."

"I could do with fewer favors lately. What's up?"

"I have news. You remember that student you had who wouldn't share his work? The one you used to eat lunch with. You said he was brilliant."

"Markus." Stuart had misjudged the freshman as being in the majority who sought life outside of books. Clad in combat boots and a trim green jacket, he stuck to the back row and kept his head down. A few chance encounters in the dining hall opened Stuart's eyes to the witty satirist who was too timid to share his work.

"Yeah. That guy. He got a multibook deal," Mohl said. "Rumor is it's worth seven figures. I found out from the woman who writes the campus newsletter. She saw the announcement."

"Holy crap." Stuart stepped back into the shadow and leaned against the wall. "I'll have to dig up his email address and send him a note. That's…it's fantastic."

"How's your book coming?" There were rattles and clangs from Mohl's end of the line. A peal of laughter that seemed to come from a bar.

Stuart banked on his friend being too distracted to probe for details. He didn't want to lie, but the truth didn't want to form itself into words either. Running a hand down his face, he mustered the shortest response he could without committing to it.

"You know. Writing."

"I've been waiting to see an outline, man. When are you going to email me something?"

"You were serious?" Stuart knew he'd been serious.

"Of course I was. The stakes are high, my friend. You have to come up with something or the dean's gonna lose his shit."

Stuart let a chuckle loose. "You don't have to tell me that."

"Did you just dive in? No outline."

"It's not that—"

"I find it hard to believe that Mr. Structure isn't working from an outline this time. Can't even watch a movie with you without a full blown second-act critique. Or are you just cranking out the pages so fast you don't want me to interrupt your flow?"

He'd brought five notebooks filled with ideas that weren't worth his time. He'd filled four pages of a new one with doodles about lumberjacks, a vampire, and the start of a grocery list. "You're not interrupting anything. No, I'll...I'll send it over soon. But I do have to run."

"Yeah, I hear you. I gotta hit the road, too. I have an evening class to get ready for, and that coffee place on Broad has long lines this semester."

"New barista?"

"Adorable. Little brunette thing. She could break me."

"Wish I was there to see it." He'd rather be anywhere than stuck in that cabin, surrounded by death and the dismemberment of his life.

"Coffee. Not the breaking."

"All right. I gotta run. Take it easy. And send me the outline already. Stop messing around."

The line clicked and went silent. Stuart let the call swirl around him for a moment, filling in the sensory gaps with the dark scent of coffee and the acid bite of overheard gossip. He missed the sound of Philly traffic slowing at a red light, the sharp tongue of neighborhood parking spats. Life seemed so far away here. Subdued. Even downtrodden. He yearned to cross a street with a dozen other people, to walk where the air would still belong to summer, but a cool breeze would careen between the buildings and dip into the canyons between them. The glass doors of convenience stores and student centers would swish open and shut as laughing students would pour in and tumble out. He couldn't lose those things.

If he lost the respect of his students, he wanted it to be because he was tough, because he cared too much, not because he didn't have a fraction of their talent or skill. If their own professor couldn't publish a book, what would that say to them? If he had to change careers, where would he start?

He wanted to keep that life, and that meant living up to a different measure. Not his father's nor the dean's. He'd have to create on his own terms. He'd have to go in there and write.

But inside wasn't any more comforting. It was dark. Nothing lurked there but the insurmountable feeling that his father was right, that he didn't have *it*, whatever *it* was, and he'd been taking up space that his father had earned.

Could he have been Markus fifteen years ago, if he'd spent more time creating than studying the craft? Would he have an outline started by now if he wasn't flirting with a librarian and checking out books that weren't any use?

Stuart dropped the books on the table and stuck his tongue out at the owl on the book cover. If he were going to make anything of value with his time, he'd need to change his perspective and create a routine around writing. That's what he told his students who were prone to distraction.

His growling stomach demanded attention, and the miles between him and the comfort food of home seemed to double. There had been that bakery downtown, the one that smelled like cinnamon buns.

He clutched his notebook and molar-marked pencil, locked the door, and bolted off the porch. Lungs straining with brisk air, he plunged across the cemetery toward Main Street in search of food.

He wound through the tombstones, cut through the gravel parking lot behind stores, and slid through an alley onto the wide road lined with little shops. No map was needed to find Marissa's Bakery. Located just a few doors down, past empty storefronts, the pastel pastry shop looked like a six-year-old girl's dream come true. It was pink and blue with hints of yellow, and the glass display was packed with so many cookies and cupcakes, the town must have a daily quota to meet. Garish in a way only confectionaries could get away with, he suddenly knew what Dorothy must have felt like as she took her first step on that yellow brick road.

A woman with a brown ponytail stood at attention when he opened the door. Soft pop hits crackled from an overhead speaker.

"What can I get ya?" She shoved a book beneath the counter.

"Um. Do you have cinnamon rolls? I smelled them the other day, and I've been craving them ever since."

"I do have cinnamon rolls." Lifting her chin, she studied him. "The other day? I thought I knew everyone in this town."

"Just visiting." He dug his wallet from his pocket. "You take debit?"

"Yup." She pulled a paper from a box and hovered over a tray of pastries. "One or two?"

"One, please. And a cup of coffee?"

"This for here or to go?" A defiant fire in her eyes seemed to demand something of him he couldn't quite interpret. He shrugged it off. Perhaps he just looked familiar.

He squirmed under her gaze. "To go. Please."

She wiggled a paper cup from a stack, her eyes never leaving him. She passed it across the counter with the pastry. "Four bucks even."

He handed over his card. She slid it through the register and passed it back. "You visiting family? We don't get many tourists."

"No, I, um…" He fumbled the card back into his wallet. "Just looking for some quiet."

The receipt spit from the register. She gave him half and put the other half in the drawer. It chimed and clanged when she slammed it shut. "You hit the jackpot if you were looking for quiet."

"It's been perfect so far." He offered a smile that he hoped closed the door on the small-town chatter and turned to the coffee station to fill his cup.

Going back to the cabin wouldn't achieve his goal. Neither would walking around the town or plopping on a bench for some people watching. Every minute that notebook remained empty he was another moment closer to losing the only thing that defined him. He had to sit and buckle down. Choosing a chair that faced the street, he sank into Mohl's warning.

He'd worked hard to be a professor. Went to college, got an advanced degree, edited anthologies and published short stories. He taught and tutored and networked. He'd been in the right place at the right time more than his fair share, and when he arrived at his dream, he found he'd missed out on the biggest milestone. Silencing his father's voice in his head to achieve it was one thing. Arguing with his inferiority complex was another. And they'd never gotten along all that well.

He would sit there looking out that window until he had twenty, no ten, good story prompts. At least eight. A guy arguing with his inferiority complex seemed as good an idea as any.

A car door slammed down the street, and three young boys pumped their bike pedals, leaning into the urgency of youth on their way toward the park. What they didn't know could hurt them yet. He craned his neck to follow their path up the street, to the steps of the church, where they circled.

He dragged the molar-marked pencil across the page, digging a dark line at the top, separating this new drive from his old droll.

It was hard to be from the good side of the tracks in a town crisscrossed by railroads. Every side was worse than the other. But it wasn't the tracks that defined the town, it was what came in on them. And the woman who came to stay made them famous. Marissa: the cinnamon bun serial killer.

Outside, the boys on bikes swarmed and stopped, dumping their bikes on their handlebars and crowding on a bench outside the newsstand. Their bikes lay in the street, angular machines of frame and tires. He chewed his pencil and squinted to make out what they had in their hands. Surely some marvel of childhood, a dirty picture or a stray pack of smokes, a frog or a lottery ticket.

Drumming the pencil on his notepad, he jumped when he sensed someone nearby. Marissa poured coffee into his nearly full cup.

"Whatcha got there?" She asked, peering at his page.

"Just some ideas." He pushed a napkin over his notebook, obscuring her name, assuming she was Marissa. His voice cracked when he thanked her for the refill.

"You looked like you could use another cup." Her voice was flat and her jaw set.

Funny. He'd only taken two sips.

She locked eyes with him, the carafe so steady in her hand the level of the coffee didn't even quiver. It wasn't her judgment he shriveled under nor was it her study that sent the wave of nausea through him. Hers was the countenance of a woman whose decision was made. Her mouth curled and her lips pursed, eyes glancing at the door.

He wasn't welcome.

Leaning back and clutching his stomach, he smoothed his shirt, brushing away crumbs he hadn't yet made, his cinnamon roll as yet untouched.

"Well?" She raised her eyebrows, imploring an answer to a question unasked.

He glanced at the door. "I'm sorry, I—"

"What are you writing? Exactly."

Running a hand through his hair. "Nothing, really. I'm doing a bad job of it, to be honest."

He had a book to write, an idea to grab, inspiration to snatch out of thin air like catching a snowflake on his tongue on the hottest day of July. He didn't feel like pretending to be a successful writer for five minutes.

"I'm having a hard time concentrating."

"Mmm." Marissa held the carafe close to her chest, knuckles white and her free hand cradling it. Their eye contact was a stalemate in a battle Stuart didn't understand. Why was she staring at him like that?

A piercing ring shattered the coarse quiet between them. Stuart jumped, his knee knocking the table. He caught the pencil before it rolled to the floor, and when he looked up, Marissa was gone, on her way behind the counter. She took the call from the kitchen.

Stuart turned his back on her, returning to the boys and their discovery, but they were gone. Closing his eyes tight, he deprived himself of one of his senses, putting all his attention on the call.

"I'm glad it's you, Adelle. I have some news."

She took steps. Closer. Farther. The rest of the chat was out of earshot, but the tone was light and cheery. Two women chatting about a friend's good fortune perhaps. Just another small-town moment he'd stepped into that would have played out the same whether he was there or not, and it tugged on something in his chest. It pulled at some string that had wicked up so many hopes and fears about writing. Standing in front of bookshelves as a kid, marveling at the words and the tomes he'd someday read, being immersed in classics, clutching to every word and phrase written by people hundreds of years before, each with their own hopes and fears that they spread out on pages with quills. They were legacies. All of those books were their legacies.

He didn't have one. His biggest fear was what he couldn't put down on paper. And the more it tugged on that string around his heart, the more his throat closed.

Taking a giant bite of the pastry, he flipped to a blank page and pushed up his sleeves, pinched the pencil in his fingers, and ignored his pounding heart.

The lady behind the counter was known for the gifts she baked. There had to be two hundred people in that town, every one of their births ushered in with a cake, their deaths marked with pastry trays. In between it was cookies and bagels, but little did they know that her real gift to the town was herself. And as the storm raged outside and the full moon wiped the sky, she kneaded the dough with aching elbows and bulging forearms for the very last time, compounding the poison. No one yet knew that this Founder's Day would be the last, but the world would remember it for eternity. After tomorrow, Ramsbolt would be famous for the slaughter of the lambs. Marissa, the shepherd and baker, would lead them all to the butcher. And then the dragons would come.

No. He peeled back the page and faced down a blank one.

False starts. That's all the boys ever had. Short bike races down the town's only Main Street, zinging between cars and shoppers carrying bags. They started their school year with so much promise. Promise to do homework, to keep the book covers clean. They started their summers intent on building tree houses and finding a way to break into that cabin by the cemetery to smoke cigarettes and ogle girly magazines they stole from their dads. But nothing ended quite the way they planned as the summer of 1987 faded to fall. And fall they did. Straight into their graves at the edge of town. When the full moon rose, they would start again. This time, more confident than ever. That's how the werewolf pack of Ramsbolt, Maine came to be.

Maybe. Probably not, but maybe.

CHAPTER ELEVEN

He was faster than everyone thought. Not because of his natural skill. He'd spent most of his life in the shadows of others, pushing the paper in a sweat stained shirt, huddled in concrete rooms without windows while men with half his talent starched their collars and played monopoly. But he was in it for the long game, for the tournament, biding his time and saving his pennies until he could afford the bite. And last night he'd parked his car at the top of the garage and plodded down those dank stairs, his lungs rattling in their cage, straining against the bars of his ribs. He'd paused at the landing and coughed up the last bloody clot he could stomach. Then he slinked through the alleys, dodging the streetlights, careful not to be followed, just like the Joan Jett look-alike he met at that bar demanded. Waif of a thing, but he wouldn't want to cross her. Not yet anyway.

He'd paid his ten thousand and sank onto that old crusty sofa. When it was his turn, he became preternatural.

For now, he'd keep the job, toil away, push the paper. He'd say yes sir and no ma'am. He'd do his job and collect his check, the sharp edge worn off their words by his newfound lineage. Eventually someone would notice that the years had stopped passing for him. And then he would dine like a king and sew his own cape from their coffin upholstery.

A light, warm breeze swept over the porch, rustling his notebook pages while Stuart read over what he'd written in bed the night before, choking down each paragraph and wincing as his teeth dug into the stolen golf pencil. His stomach could only hold down so much cringe.

Sipping hot coffee before it went tepid, he held down the pages of his notebook, protecting them from the gale and keeping it from sliding off his knee. Beyond the porch, squirrels played tag, zigzagging across the tombstone-littered lawn. He could get used to all this quiet, if not for the nagging thought that there was something he'd forgotten to do. The spat with his father had claimed more space in mind than its due. He hadn't even paused to speak to his mother before he...

Grabbing his phone from the small table, he pulled up a florist website. Flowers cost more than they ought for something so disposable, but he opted for roses to spare their cat the harm of lilies and selected a delivery date that would ensure she could enjoy them before they ran off for Cabo.

While he was there, he opened his work email and started a blank note to Markus. It would be easy to give into the jealousy of the moment, to fall victim to his own darkness, but he truly was happy for his student, who'd overcome heavy blanketing fears to put the fullness of ideas onto paper, unspooling the tendrils of the art within him. The commonality between them was what had drawn him to Markus at the start. The gripping fear of rejection, recoiling from the sting of eternal judgement over words laid bare for the here and now.

Markus, I heard of your achievement from a colleague. I am sincerely proud of you and inspired by your accomplishment. While I would like to say I've seen you progress in the craft, and I have, it is the overcoming of obstacles that has inspired me the most. Sharing one's work with the world takes bravery, and you deserve all the accolades that come your way. I regret that at your age, I lacked the nerve to bring bold works to life.

His heart sank at the lie. At least it felt like a lie. It wasn't just bold works he lacked the nerve to create. He hadn't created anything of length at all. It had been short stories and little quips, social commentary, and reams of outlines. There were passive ideas and active exclusions, stories that didn't deserve the light of day. Maybe his father was right after all, and he wasn't a life-giver. Maybe he was a life-tender, an editor, a mentor, or a counselor. But he'd never be a sage without walking the path his students took. And they were treading it without him.

He deleted the last line, signed off, and hit send.

New emails loaded as his note flew off, his neglected inboxes screaming for attention. He took one sip of now-cooled coffee and set it with the notebook on the tiny wobbly table. Spam and inconsequential banter deleted, an email from his father stood out.

Long gone were the days of rapid apology. They had always been from Stuart's side, anyway. What he could see from the terse preview, however, told him the cordiality had ratcheted to a lower peg.

I have always been direct with you.

His father offered no salutation.

If I felt you needed or wanted me to hold your hand as an adult, you gave me no indication when you were a child. You took off on your bike as you pleased and learned the hard lessons on your own. From the youngest age, you let me know that I was not to hold your hand, so here we are. You come to me in search of something you refuse to name, and I only know how to respond with the directness and truth you have always expected from me. Sometimes, my son, swords stab at old wounds. There is often truth in the harshness. Indeed, I mean you no ill will when I say that your quietude would be well spent considering whether you want the thing you have not yet been able to grasp. Man is no worse off for seeking his true path, but he is lesser for building a fortress on land that will never be his.

Yours, Sam

The blast of cool air that pushed against the cabin tingled Stuart's nose. He let the phone lie in his lap and rubbed the sting away. The push and pull with his father had always been there, wearing the guise of negative reinforcement cloaked in a translucent veil of emotional manipulation. Some days it seemed his father wanted him to earn his own name in battles that left him wearing scars. Other days it seemed like the war was the point. Long gone were the days he sought his father's approval, but the man still insisted on withholding it anyway. What was the point?

Stuart let the rage simmer and boil over until it was white hot. Then he hit reply, pounding furiously on his phone.

Thanks so much for feeling free to share your opinion. Your level of support for me has never wavered. For years I have absorbed the blows of it, let them land, and nursed my own wounds. Perhaps my failing is not having told you how they land. It may come as a surprise to you, but I never wanted to be raised by a writer. I wanted a father. I needed someone to teach me about the world and how to live in it, not a running dialog about how little of life I deserved. I am no longer the boy who came to you in search of approval or validation. Rather, I am now a man living on my own terms. Your suggestion is under advisement.

Yours, Stuart

It should have felt good to hit send, and perhaps it would have if he were years younger. Instead, the anger ebbed on the shore, leaving behind a frothy scum of grief for the tact that had died between them. The late-coming resolve sat hard in his stomach. He wouldn't wait for a reply and hit refresh, waiting for his father's barbs. If he truly believed that truth lay in harshness, maybe this time he would finally see it.

He tossed his phone on the little table. It knocked into the coffee cup and toppled over, coffee splashing onto his notebook, soaking the page and bleeding through. Jumping to his feet, he snagged the notebook by the spine, shaking brown drops to the porch, waving the pages in the air.

"Cheap paper." Ten pages soaked through. "Why can't anything go right?"

Spreading the papers out on the railing to dry in the sun, holding them down with rocks from the lawn, he took a mental inventory of what might be lost.

"Who cares? It was garbage anyway. I should just go get a new one and start over."

He inspected the mug. At least it didn't break. And his phone had stayed dry.

"On the bright side, you could get a little exercise."

The bright side was getting harder to see for all the shadows it cast, but it would be good to walk away for a bit, get some juices flowing. The newsstand was bound to have some kind of paper, and with any luck, it might be less absorbent than a paper towel. He threw on his sneakers and a jacket, checked his pocket for the keys, and locked the cabin. He shot a parting glance at the notebook, and his stomach roiled. Why did it always feel like he was being pushed two steps back without the fun of taking one step forward?

Lungs full of wet autumn sky and leaf mold, he coughed as he lunged down the steps. Crows picked at twigs at the edge of the cemetery, and he imagined them a murder of bone collectors, scavenging the digits for their little punch bowls of poison. He crossed the street and hopped onto the sidewalk, tracing the curb as crisp leaves swirled in the doorways of vacant shops and scraped the pavement. His own footsteps and the swish of his jeans cut through the wind and the clatter.

Light spilled out of a window, and he slowed to stop where it puddled on the sidewalk. A cluttered antique shop of sorts filled the building. Chairs dripped from the ceiling like stalactites in the caves he'd visited as a kid, like they were minerals seeping from the very room that birthed them. A little orange cat was curled up in the window, next to a box of gold-rimmed teacups. The furniture in that place could probably fill every house in town.

Funny, he thought. *Imagine buying a haunted teacup, drinking in someone else's anxieties and fears with every sip.*

Across the street was the florist shop. A woman in a green apron stomped out of the store and tightened her ponytail, giving him side-eye as she watered some plants on a bench by her window.

Ingredients for her potions, no doubt.

He felt his face redden with the shame of staring, lost in his vivid imagination. At least he knew who brewed the tea for all those cups.

Turning up his collar, he shuffled down the sidewalk, passing the toy store full of gremlins that came to life at night and wreaked havoc throughout the town. He didn't pause to take it all in. He'd been nosy enough for one day. But he couldn't resist the statue in the park, not for its countenance or the skill of its maker. It was miles from the ocean, hours of driving from any semblance of ships. Why did a sailor stand in the turning circle, looking out at some horizon no one else could see?

Degory Howland, the plaque said. *For Those Who Never Saw The Sea.*

He shrugged his shoulders against the cold, shielding his neck from the bite. What kind of town has only one monument and puts all its eggs in a basket of irony?

Whoever the bearded bronze man was, he had stories to tell, and Stuart was more than a little jealous. But the temperature was dropping fast, and he needed another notebook. Resisting the urge to give Degory Howland a wave, he tugged his jacket over his chin and trudged across the street, heading down Main.

A mother tugged a boy from a car seat and plopped him on the sidewalk, slamming the car door. A guy half his age ran up the sidewalk, dodged a stationary trash can, and half tripped in the market door. An older woman with a cane in her hand tapped at the edge of a cast iron bench.

This humanity wasn't the comforting buffer of home. There was no salve from being among people, no shared identity, no common ground beneath their rush and hurry. He wasn't a guest in their cradle, he was an intruder. He didn't even want to be there. None of this had been his idea, and he had his way, he'd be teaching a class and wondering what to have for dinner.

He quickened his pace as he neared the newsstand. The woman tugged on her child's hand, dragging him out of the way. She leered at him, if he read her look right, and the woman with the cane, who had taken a seat on the bench a few doors down, clutched her purse on her lap like a child whose candy was threatened. His shoelace slapped at his heel as passed.

"Damn it," he said. Pausing at the empty bench outside the newsstand, he raised a foot and tied the lace tight. Three girls left the store clutching chocolate bars and sodas, and they squealed as he lowered his foot to the ground. Wide-eyed and frantic, they scrambled down the street. The woman on the next bench down shook her head at him, lips pursed, lipstick bleeding into the lines around her mouth.

He put up his hands. "I didn't do anything to them. I swear."

She turned away, staring across the street as if he never existed at all.

His eyes followed hers and fell on the tea house across the street. Two women stumbled out, laughing. His ears strained to hear what they were saying, just to feel a part of something after so much isolation in the cabin, but it was just mumbles and laughter, warming all the same.

The woman on the bench cleared her throat, one hand perched on her cane. Her eyes burned through him, and he swore she could see every little sin he'd committed since he was born. Tugging his sleeves down over his wrists, he pushed open the door to Warren's Newsstand.

A bell chimed when he entered. Warren stood behind the counter in a yellow sweatshirt, counting down change for a man buying a magazine. Neither looked his way, so he counted it a blessing and moved through the ether of paper and ink and pencil lead. Warren hadn't been lying when he said the paperbacks were old. Stephen King and Nora Roberts were prominently represented, pages yellowing where they stood. Beneath them were perfect rows of magazines grouped by subject, in alphabetical order. Pencils and erasers, pens and markers hung from hooks above shelves of paper. It tugged on his nostalgia for back-to-school shopping, brand new boxes of number two pencils and filling three-ring binders with loose-leaf notebook paper. There was nothing in adulthood that stood up to the clean slate of a new semester, before the wheels came off the bus, the pencils were chewed, and the paper wrinkled.

He found notebooks on a shelf in the back corner. Spiral bound and composition. He grabbed a green-covered book of college line paper. At the end of the aisle, he grabbed the day's paper to keep him company, some national collection of yesterday's news. He still needed a pen, so he stood on tiptoe and scanned what he could see of the shelves. His best bet was two aisles down, where boxes of chalk and scented kids' markers hung on a pegboard.

Rolling up the newspaper and tucking it under his arm, he turned the corner and walked right into Sandy. The newspaper fell to the floor, sections fanning across the aisle.

"I'm so sorry." He bent to collect the pages.

"No, it's my fault. I didn't even see you." Her face was three shades of red. The tips of her ears were crimson.

He smiled down at the markers in her hands.

"They're for the kids. Evening programs. Not my kids. I don't have kids."

"I didn't think you did. I mean, you didn't say so. Most moms say so." He bit the inside of his cheek to stop himself from chattering. "You have a very nice library."

"Thanks." She held up the packet. "It's easy to keep up with. As long as I keep the markers away from the books."

She smiled at her own quip, and the store peeled away in layers. Magazine pages and shelves, walls, Warren, and the town all flitted away, and it was just him and Sandy fumbling in a little bubble.

"Hey," he said. "I have to get to a train station. Somewhere called Colby. To get my car."

It seemed to take forever, but her shoulders fell, and the lines at the corners of her eyes smoothed as something like disappointment overtook her.

"I'm so sorry. I sold my car." She waved the marker packet toward the window. "A few years ago, I bought one. I thought I needed one, you know. To get to Colby for things. But I had everything I needed here in town and never used it."

"Oh, I didn't mean you had to take me. But I would—"

"I would have, though. It would have been nice. We could talk about books or…you probably read a million of them a year." The tips of her ears flushed pink again. "I can't read books. I mean, I can read, of course. Obviously. But books. I prefer my tablet."

Stuart tested the strength of the shelf beside him and leaned, his elbow wedging between a box of Snickers bars and a display of mints. "Why is that?"

"No idea."

"A lot of people prefer reading on tablets." He ran a hand through his hair, and she blinked at him, little gold flecks in her eyes getting bright and dimmer as her irises expanded and contracted in the light.

"Are you leaving already?"

"What? No. Do you need the books back? I can return them if you need them." He shifted his weight, and the box of Snickers bars teetered to the edge of the shelf.

"Yes. I need the books back. There's a sudden deep interest in race car driving owls." Sandy reached out and pushed the box of candy bars further back on the shelf. "No, I mean your car."

He plucked a roll of mints from the display, the kind you put in a bottle of soda to make an explosion. That's what his stomach felt like. "I just need to go get it at some point. Is there a taxi around?"

Sandy's eyebrows lifted. "Here? No. You could try Jaleesa, but she's a mechanic. Sometimes she takes her truck out to get parts. Same with Grey. He's probably a better bet, actually. He's a plumber and goes out of town a lot for things. Hangs out at the tavern in the evenings."

"That's the place on the corner, right?"

"Yeah. By the red light."

"Thanks." He tightened his grip on his newspaper.

"You're welcome. Good luck." Sandy turned to the register. He paused for a beat to put some space between them, so as not to crowd her or follow her around the store. Maybe one more browse of the magazine covers.

Pen. He almost forgot that he needed a pen.

He took a step to the side, down the aisle of colorful boxes. It got him out of her wake. But she had turned back, disturbing the flow, and he walked right into her. Face to face.

"We could go to the tavern sometime. If you want." She shrugged and picked at the corner of her marker packet. "If you're bored maybe. We could talk about books."

His heart pounded in his ears, and his brain stammered before his mouth. His throat dried, and his hands went cold. There was no mistaking the subtext. In a town this small, a girl like Sandy must get very thirsty for excitement. And she was right; he was bored. Getting his mind off the writing would probably help him untangle the knot he was in. And it wasn't like he was under any obligation to turn it into a date.

"Sure. Let's do it." A voice that sounded like his own floated, weightless, from him.

"Great. Is there a night that's better for you? I usually close up the library around six, but I set my own hours, so I'm flexible." She hugged the markers in her folded arms. "There's no food there, so after dinner is probably best. Dinnertime. After dinnertime."

"Tonight, works fine. Six is good." He reached down and grabbed a pen. It was one of those slider pens, with a transparent barrel and a scene inside. He tilted it, and a bobcat slid before a row of pine trees. It said Maine on the side in a scripted, white font. "See you there."

He mirrored her grin and admired the skip in her step as she sauntered the few paces to the register. Pretending to shop for sidewalk chalk, he waited until she had left before paying for his items and thanking Warren.

Outside, the door had barely closed behind him when a blast of cold air took his breath away.

He should have been honest about Madison, found a way to slip her name into conversation. There shouldn't be a gap, however narrow, for Sandy to think he accepted anything more than an invitation for a drink. There was no mistaking the way she looked at him, the way her fingers plucked at things and her ears went red. Of course, she may not have wanted to seem too forward, and she was clearly an introvert. But weren't drink invitations a hint at intimate inclinations?

He stepped off the curb. He'd walked this far, he might as well pick up some snacks at the market, even if he'd destroyed his appetite.

Another blast of cold air made his eyes water.

Sandy had definitely been flirting with him.

CHAPTER TWELVE

Helen's Tavern was quiet, as bars went. It was more like walking into a hospital waiting room than a neighborhood pub. No one cheered for a sports team, and no announcer's voice set the tone. There were no arms reaching over shoulders to grab glasses from the bar. Just two women, generations apart, tending a handful of patrons who nursed their beers and an older man in the corner, hunching over a newspaper. He lowered it and sneered. Stuart offered him a twisted grin, the kind that said he was sorry for the intrusion, sorry for dragging his newcomer gaze across the settled scene and making a spectacle of them and a critic of himself.

Stuart shuffled onto a bar stool as quietly as he could, not daring to ripple the waters. Sandy wasn't there yet, but Stuart meant to be early. Taverns made for great writing spaces as long the air wasn't too disturbed, and they rarely failed to deliver good people watching. What this one lacked in people it more than made up for in cozy quiet. It was a gamble, wanting to test the tavern's writing waters against seeming too eager and risking the escalation of Sandy's affections. He didn't want to lead her on.

Maybe she wouldn't come. That might be a good thing. Or not.

He set his notebook on the bar and dug his new pen from his pocket, letting it sit on top. It was too thick to fit in the metal coil. He glanced over his shoulder at the door, his jaw tight, his throat constricted. The yeasty traces of beer swirled around him as the older woman scuttled up to the taps and lowered her chin, her eyes fixed on him.

"What can I get ya?" She clung to one tap, clearly for balance, and it occurred to him that beer might not be good for the tide of nausea that had started to rise. Madison would kill him if she could see him sitting at a bar, waiting on a girl. He had no business being there. Skimming the taps, he spotted a familiar salve.

"Lager. Yuengling, please. Thanks." He threw the notebook cover open and twisted the pen, making a tiny circle at the top of the paper to work out the ink. Leaning back in his chair, he picked apart the tavern. The younger woman shuffled paper in the back room. He imagined her the last descendant of a long line of town natives, a defiant yet humble woman who only ever wanted out, but all she found as she pulled at the exits were locks that held her in. He pictured the old woman as an overbearing grandmother, intent on bequeathing the legacy of her tavern to the only descendant who never wanted it at all.

Two women behind the counter, he wrote.

She placed the beer in front of him, foam clinging to the glass. It made a wet ring on the bar, no napkin.

"You need a tab started?" Hands on her hips, she waited, eyes teasing at his page.

"Yeah." He dug his wallet from his pocket.

"Don't need a card. Just a name." One of her eyebrows arched.

Across the bar, the old man peeked around the newspaper. He rolled his eyes and hid his nose in the paper again.

"Stuart. Thanks."

After a pause of considered assessment, she turned away. Holding in a sip of his beer, head down over the blank page, Stuart studied the man's hands. Lined and spotted, his fingers curled in arthritic knots, he had the look of a man who worked for a living. A carpenter, perhaps, or a mechanic. Someone who spent his days in the sun, his arms tense with work, and now that he's retired can barely lift a paper, preferring to stay indoors where the lights were dim and the noise out of reach.

He could smell it, the faint metal twinge of a car garage, the soothing thickness of air damp with oil. Healing happened in garages, or so the poets said, for cars and their makers and fixers. His grandfather had always been out there, tinkering with things, making them better, making them work. He'd been the kind of man who'd grab a wrench and approach any problem, even if the solution were a hammer. His mother's father had been an unafraid and intimidating man but warm when he was in his zone, humming and tinkering. Stuart had always wanted to go out there, to play along, but the fear of being in the way and under foot kept him in the driveway, perched on his bike.

Stuart's pen led the way, and the tavern dissolved around him.

Arthur had raced more than cars in his youth. He'd raced his family's reputation. He'd raced his fears of growing up like his father, giving into the rush of a drug or the blitz of a drink, plowing through jobs and women as if unrefined solace were all that could feed him. Instead, he stuck his head in engine bays, tinkering and fiddling, scraping his knuckles for the affirmation of life. And when he lifted his head, it was to peer out the windshield, plowing past fields, eyes flitting to every threat, dismissing anything harmless in favor of anything he could chase.

That's what racing used to be. He'd raced himself until he could race someone else. Until he could rent a ride, then buy his own. Until he could make a few bucks at the checkered flag, making bank on the corners. Then he chased the finish line, counting down races until his hands were too tired, his neck too thin to handle the strain of the track.

These days, he chased curbs. His body spent, there was nothing left to gamble. Unable to hang his head beneath the bonnet, he hung it over drinks instead. He might have been eighty years too late, but he would catch his father's tail eventually. If he tried hard enough.

Now that his family was gone, scattered by the torrential divorce and the diaspora of his kids, it was Arthur against the grains, tracing the fields in the rural Maine town he chose as his last course. No one knew him here. Not the bartending woman who tried to catch his eye or the mailman or the lady in the bakery who talked at him too loudly. And definitely not that boy who moved in next door with his restless mother. If that boy knew him better, he wouldn't look up to him so. He wouldn't sneak into that garage while Arthur struggled, and beg to help. And Arthur wouldn't be pacing his driveway, marking time till Noah got home from school so he could teach the lad, if he were willing, how to change a timing belt.

If there were one thing any man should know, it was how to get the timing right.

Stuart dropped the pen. His hands were sticky with sweat, his heart pounding.

He'd made enough false starts in his life to know what one felt like, that imposing wall of writer's blocks mortared at the end of the road. He knew what it was like to keep going for pages, reams, just to hit the inevitable wall that was thicker and darker than night, with nothing on the other side. No ending. No cliffhanger. No fancy twist that would leave anyone breathless. Dead-end stories were his specialty, but this was a feeling he didn't recognize. This was the feeling of a clear path, a character with purpose, a story of universal truths.

This was a story he could write. Sandy would love it, wouldn't she?

He craned his neck, peered over his shoulder in search of a clock, but the tavern had none. He checked his phone. Sandy was late. He shouldn't be bummed out about it. He shouldn't want to see her at all.

Cheeks burning, he hunched over the screen. No one was there to see his face, so no one could see the shame he felt. He should be missing Madison. She should be the first one on his mind, the first one he wanted to tell about the rush of sudden promise.

"Refill?" The younger brunette tossed her hand on a cocked hip. He hadn't noticed his glass was empty.

"Yes, please. Thanks."

He pushed the empty glass across the bar and flipped the page of his notebook. He scribbled a bullet point and added *sticky bottles* next to it. *Clutter. Like walking on the sticky side of tape.* Things he could use later.

He thanked the bartender for his refill, and as she turned away, Stuart felt Sandy before he could see her, before the orange and cinnamon wave washed over him. He turned to her as she slid into the empty seat at his side, pushing his notebook away to make room for her.

He tried to keep the elation from his face, but the cool contrast was too cold and impersonal, so he gave into the broadest grin that suited his mood. His stomach did a little twist that he brushed off as a reprieve from the loneliness of the cabin, but he knew better. It was her, that smell, the way she looked at him. He liked it. He just couldn't allow himself to accept it or admit it.

He couldn't wait to tell her about his story idea.

She shimmied into the seat, her hip in those tight jeans touching his, but she rocked the stool and shuffled away.

"Sorry about that," she said.

"No problem." Warmth seared up his side. "Can I buy you a drink?"

"Sure. Thanks. I'll have what he's having." She nodded at the younger woman who waited with a lifted chin and a suspicious smile behind the bar. "Is this a real-life author's real-life notebook?"

Stuart winced and shrugged. At once, the urgency to tell her about his story idea faded, and he nudged the notebook aside. "I guess. It's new. There's not much in there."

"Blank slate, huh?"

A laugh escaped him. "They rarely progress past that point, if I'm honest. I usually jot down observations. Little inspirations. I'm not so great at writing something worth finishing."

"It can't be that bad." Sandy nodded at the bartender and thanked her for the drink.

Stuart took a sip of his beer, drawing in his bottom lip to catch a drip. "To be completely honest with you, I've never even taken a book past a second draft. I am a complete fraud as a professor."

"Is that a prerequisite? Like, you can't be a creative writing professor unless you've published sixteen novels?"

"Technically?" He shrugged. "They usually like you to have at least one success to your name before hiring you to teach. I just happened to be in the right place at the right time. A lot." He left his last name out of the conversation. Just once, he'd like to be judged on his own merit. "Unfortunately, the dean will have my head if I don't publish something. Ticking clock."

She tilted her head, her eyes sympathetic. "It'll come to you. When the time is right."

"I do have an idea. It's a little early to know where it's headed yet, but it has potential."

Sandy adjusted her drink on the bar. "Out of curiosity, how does one end up in the right place at the right time and just fall into being a college professor?"

"I was in grad school. A teaching assistant. One thing led to another. I don't even know if it's the right place for me, to be honest. I'm starting to wonder if it's the right career for me. Like, maybe I'm digging my heels in on this thing just to spite my critics."

She shook her head. "No, I'm sure you're a great teacher."

He skimmed the wall of bottles behind the bar, looking for the truth. "Maybe. My students like me. They form critique circles and make friends in class. Several of them have done well for themselves and found careers in publishing. They send me emails and stay in touch. That's nice, but it won't pay the bills. And it will only be fulfilling for so long. Eventually, helping others achieve their dreams won't be a suitable consolation prize for never achieving my own."

Sandy put her hand on the notebook cover, as if swearing an oath. "Clearly you know how to do it. Sometimes the pressure to reach some big milestone just takes over, you know? It becomes a lot to chew."

"Tell me about it." He rubbed his thumb along a sticky drip on the outside of his glass. "I guess that's why I'm here. I had to get away from the distractions and be inspired by something new. All the ideas I was coming up with felt trite."

"Does a book have to be unique?" She ran a hand through her hair, stirring up the scent of her shampoo. It fell against her back in a soft wave. "Jane Austen's work still resonates, and it was written two hundred years ago. People come back to the library and check out the same books, over and over. They don't want unique stories. They want the comfort of not being alone. It doesn't have to be something bold and new, not at its core. It just has to tell the truth. That's what people identify with."

"I suppose when it comes to universal truths…" She was right. He gulped in a bit of sultry tavern air, threw his elbow on the bar and rubbed a spot above his ear. "I guess sometimes I wonder if my truths aren't wise enough. If the characters I make out of thin air are too thin. Do I have enough of this life thing pegged yet?"

His eyes met hers. He saw understanding there in her barely perceptible nod.

"You won't know until you take a risk." Her voice was a whisper.

"Until I jump in. Yeah." He broke their chain, took a sip. It was a blind faith leap at someone else's urging that brought him here, but it was his own conviction that drew him to Sandy. He could tell her the truth without any consequences. He could admit how he felt because it wouldn't damage his reality. No one who knew him understood how out of place his heart was, how disconnected he felt from his own day to day. He couldn't tell Mohl or Madison that when he sat down to write, it felt like trespassing, on the brink of being caught, of being seen and not forgiven for treading where he didn't belong. And it wasn't just the writing. He was in Madison's way at home, an alien in her culinary landscape. He was an outsider at work among men and women twice his age with more accomplishments than he could count. Every place he went was someone else's. Was that why he fixated on making space? Porches and cafes, patios, parks. Sitting in the car at the airport long-term parking lot. He'd tried them all. He'd adopted random benches on bustling streets and set up writing space on rooftop bars at noon, when the sun was high enough to cast no shadows on his text. None of them had felt like home.

"Sometimes." She cleared her throat. "Sometimes you need to immerse yourself in a new space. You know, like those people who take off into the woods to discover who they really are."

"On the brink of the unknown." Woozy, he was too lightheaded to blame his beer-and-a-half.

He ran his thumb along the corner of the notebook, flicking the pages like a flip book without the moving pictures. He opened the cover back to the lines he'd just written and pushed it in front of her, breath glitching in his throat, a respiratory misfire.

Her back straightened, eyes widened. Glancing between the paper and his eyes, she said, "You have impeccable handwriting."

"Lots of practice."

She laid a hand on the page. "I can read this?"

"Yeah. I just wrote it. Just now. It's not even first draft, but I—"

She slid the notebook closer, nudged her drink away. "You don't have to apologize for it."

"I'll just let you be."

He gripped his glass with a sweaty hand, his eyes fixed on the bar, the way the dim light overhead made a little pool around him, he felt like an actor who forgot his cue. In the corner, the man shook the paper. Stuart's heart pounded in his ears.

"This is good." Sandy's head snapped up, and she fixed her wide eyes on him. "I would read this."

"It's just a framework. A blurb. Figuring out a character."

"It's a great starting point." She threw an elbow on the bar and rested her chin in her hands, looking down at his writing. "You have a lot of opportunities in here. Does it feel right?"

He rubbed an eye with the heel of his hand. "I think so, yeah. I'd need to flesh out the characters a bit more, but I'm excited to see where it might go."

She smiled and slid the notebook back to him. "Looks to me like you just found the entrance to your wilderness trail."

His stomach tensed, and his nerve endings tingled. It had been a long time since he'd been this energized by an idea, but this time, he had to follow through. He closed the cover, reluctant to put the story away, but it was too precious to put at the mercy of spilled drinks.

"I've taken so many wrong turns. It's the best I've felt about a story in a long time."

"What made you want to be a writer?" She wiggled on her stool, decreasing the angle between them.

Birthright? Saturation? He gulped his sip of beer. It was growing warm too fast. "It's not something you choose to be, I guess. It's something you just are. My head has always been full of the lyrics, you know? I've always been making up little stories. Since I was a kid. They helped me overcome fears, not feel so alone, then you grow up, and they fill your time. But they just keep coming, no matter what." Until he needed them, and then they stopped. "What made you want to be a librarian?"

She swallowed a sip of her beer. "Anthropology. Parents come in and check out the books they read when they were little to share with their kids. The book club gushes over these shared experiences. Since mankind was young and slept under the stars, stories have been our shared morality. They're how we learn about other experiences and find empathy for each other. All those books are the glue that hold us together."

"The hero's journey."

Chin in her hand, her eyes shined. "What kind of books do you write, Stuart? What stirs your soul?"

His insides turned to ice, and his fingertips went so cold they could chill his beer. He wanted to fall at the feet of this warm, soft woman who wouldn't judge him and tell her how heavy the want and loss had been, how he'd lost his purpose and couldn't find his way back. How he used to dream up vivid worlds in brilliant color, and he would wake up yearning for them to be real, but it had been years since he could remember his dreams in the morning light. He wanted to tell her about cozy dystopias that once ran feral through his daydreams, but all fell flat on paper, and how hard it was to flesh them out and make them worth the words. But it all sat in his brain, a wet lump of mush, and his mouth was too dry to form the words.

He should want to say those things to Madison.

He gave his beer a weak smile. "What's my genre? All I know is that murder mysteries aren't my thing."

She nodded. "They're big sellers, though. They fly off the shelves at the library."

The older woman behind the bar put a hand by Sandy's near-empty glass. Stuart resented the intrusion.

"Another round for you two?" She wore the suspicion that had become familiar over the past few days, people eyeing up his outsider attributes, staining him with their cynicism. Her eyes fell on the notebook. "Whatcha been writing about?"

She looked like a mother standing over a pile of broken toys demanding to know who did it. Stuart burned under the demand.

"Just notes and things in my head, for now."

Across the bar, the man cleared his throat and shook his newspaper so hard Stuart was surprised the news didn't fall out.

"Some kind of creeper. Everybody says. Perv."

The older woman waved a hand at the man, shushing him like a traffic cop.

"Don't listen to him," she said. "Shut up, Arvil. Grumpy old man."

Sandy shifted her weight on the stool. "Helen, this is Stuart. He's nice. He's from out of town. Have you seen Grey?"

"Nice to meet you." Helen's look softened. Either Sandy's introduction counted for something or she was good at playing hostess.

He nodded. "Nice to meet you, too."

Helen turned back to Sandy, throwing a bar rag over her shoulder. "Grey had a mess at the market to fix. Won't see him around here tonight, but he'll be in tomorrow. Probably around four. Young man, did I hear you say you're trying to sell a book?"

He ran a hand down his face. "Trying to write one."

"Not many people around here have that kind of leisure, sitting down and writing a book. Takes a good artist to make stories out of thin air."

"Takes a good liar." The man in the corner shook his paper again.

"Ignore him. You want to write a book, don't let anyone tell you no." She took the rag from her shoulder and wiped the bar where his beer spilled. "I got another round for you. Coming right up."

"I lied to my friends." The words lurched out of him.

Sandy snapped to attention. "About what?"

"I told them it was going well. That I had a ton of ideas up here." He ran a hand down his face, pausing to scratch at two days of stubble on his chin. "It sucks that I lied to them. I don't know what it says about me, that I couldn't just tell them the truth, that I'm so damn scared that my ideas aren't good enough." He bit the inside of his cheek to rein in his unspooling deficiencies.

"It's easier to tell the truth to strangers sometimes," Sandy said.

"That's the truth." He nodded his thanks to Helen, who placed two beers before them. She wiped her hands on the rag and left the way she came.

Sandy touched his arm, and an electric shock went right to his heart. He took in a shallow breath and let his eyes find hers.

"Hey. If telling the truth to strangers is easy, then it should be even easier to tell it to imaginary characters." She patted his arm and took her hand away.

His jaw unclenched of its own free will. "Yeah. As soon as I figure out what I have to say."

CHAPTER THIRTEEN

Stuart was small for his age, smaller than all the kids in class. His hair was still fine and his features still soft. He hadn't noticed it until the doctor said so to his mom, and now it was all he could think about. It made him different, not good enough. And maybe that was why he was scared, like a baby, when everyone else seemed so happy.

A loud bang reverberated, and the sky crackled. Fireworks fizzed, and his room lit up in red then blue, white then red. Outside, the street erupted in cheers. Stuart pulled the covers over his head, flinching with each boom, wiping cold sweat on his sheet. His hot breath filled the little cave he'd made, and he wiped his upper lip with the back of his hand.

The baseball team had won again. Dad said if they won, they would go to the playoffs.

Footsteps pounded on the street below, women in clicking shoes and men in boots. They shouted at each other and laughed, all the words blending together in a chunky stew of adult things he didn't understand. Glass shattered, and Mrs. Metz from next door yelled at some rotten kids to pick it up.

Stuart felt around for his little red flashlight, the one he got at school for Halloween to keep kids from getting hit by cars. He flipped the white plastic switch, and the pale-yellow light fluttered to life. The batteries were dying. He shook it, but it didn't help. Covering the light with his shaking hand, he ducked under the cover again just as another blast went off, dragging his Pound Puppy by the ears under the blankets with him.

"It'll be okay," he said, breathless. "Let me tell you a story."

He snuggled under the blanket, face to face with the brown and white stuffed dog.

"Once upon a time, there was a doggie who lived in a football stadium. He had to hide when people were around, but at night, he had the whole place to himself. He ate hot dogs and pretzels with lots of mustard whenever he wanted, but it was loud sometimes, and the doggie was so scared and lonely. One day, a little orange cat came along. His name was Dorito. And Dorito said that only scaredy cats were allowed to be scared."

His bedroom door creaked open, and light poured in from the hall. "Stewie?"

"Mom?" He peeled back the sheet.

"Who are you talking to?"

Stuart dangled the puppy off the edge of the bed. "Norbert."

The mattress wobbled when his mom sat, and he wiggled out of the covers. Her hair was pretty, and she smelled like she did when she went out with her friends, like perfume from the little pink bottle on her dresser.

"You're such a good storyteller." She petted the dog as if it were real.

He snatched the dog back. "Norbert isn't real. He hates being petted like he's real."

Mom put her hands up. "I forgot. You're right. And you're getting to be such a big boy. Not even scared of fireworks anymore. And I bet Norbert won't be scared anymore either. Not since you told him a story like that."

"You think so?"

"I know so." She shifted her weight and untangled the flashlight from the blankets. The light was still on, dim. She switched it off. "I also know it's time for bed. Your dad has a big day tomorrow, and he can hear you through the wall."

She rubbed his hair and took the flashlight with her when she left.

Arms wrapped around Norbert, he settled back beneath the sheets. The fireworks were over. Next time, he wouldn't be so small or so afraid.

CHAPTER FOURTEEN

Stuart's phone let out a bloodcurdling alert that could have woken the dead. He rushed from the sofa, dropping his notebook and tripping over his shoes, to grab his phone from the small dining room table. No one needed that much upheaval about a heavy frost warning. But while his phone was in his hand, he checked his email for the millionth time to find his father still hadn't replied. Not that he wanted to find himself in the ratcheting clamp of his father's wrath, but the suspense wasn't all that fun either.

Scooping his notebook off the floor where it landed, he plopped back on the scratchy couch and reread, again, what he'd written the night before. It held less promise with each reading. Writing a story about a man and a kid was a little too close to home. It wasn't just what he might find if he stepped too close to that precipice. He lacked empathy for regretful older men at the moment and probably wouldn't do Arthur justice. Plus, his knowledge of cars stopped at the gas filler, and his ability to tell the tale got murkier as his outline wore on.

Skimming a list of genres and writing prompts, he settled on horror and a broken-down car. Tilting his new pen to the page, he forced his way into a writing slipstream, letting the words etch onto the page without the pesky interference of discretion.

His car broke down in the middle of town. If it had to break down at all, it was his good fortune it happened in the thick of it all, for that part of Maine was all trees and creeks, and the evening was growing cold. And so were his leads on a garage. Plopping on a bench outside a brick-front newsstand that was closed for the night, he shook his phone to make the signal stronger, but it didn't work, and he hadn't expected it to. He hadn't seen a person since the last red light he encountered, at least an hour ago, and by the look of things, this place was past the point of neglect. It was downright deserted. Not one store had a light on. Leaves and dirt collected in the doorways. Layers of wind-blown dust clung to windows, and moss grew where it shouldn't. The trash cans were empty. He strolled down the street peeking into each one. No drink cups or food wrappers, no discarded mail. Just rusty cans. It was as if everyone simply stopped being and doing.

There'd been a bar in a low brick building back at the edge of town, and the walk to reach it was long, but he warmed with the pace. There were cars in the lot, but none of them pinged. They were cool, sitting still for a while. And they were just this side of clean. Too clean to be abandoned. He could either stand outside that windowless building or escape the icy midwinter gales and go in to plead for help.

When he stepped inside, all heads turned his way. All three.

A sultry woman who said she was a librarian had a lead on a little cabin tucked in the back of the graveyard where he could stay for the night. It wasn't ideal, but he agreed to wait for Walter to bring the keys while she ran her fingers up his arm and called him sweetie. In the meantime, he took in a whiskey neat from the elderly lady behind the bar, just to keep up with the elderly man in the corner who scowled at him over last week's paper.

Two drinks in, he didn't see the bat coming when the elderly woman hit him with it. It wasn't until the back of his head banged the stairs that he realized his drink had been spiked. He couldn't even move his fingers. He could feel them, though, when the woman stepped on them. The sudden paralysis hadn't just robbed him of his ability to move, it stole from him the physical outlet of his fear. Yearning to cover his eyes, willing his arms to move and his hands to curl around his chest, he'd never known that ache of vulnerability. It spooled a hot panic in his chest that crescendoed, his ears ringing and eyes darting to follow shadows that passed around him. His senses went into overdrive, his nose picking up the cold concrete floor, the ghosts of spilled beers and ancient cigars. His hearing acute, he collected the scuffs from shoes that danced at the edges. More than three people were in that room, hovering about in the shadows, wordless but choreographed. They had a routine. They knew what was coming.

The basement floor was concrete, cold and hard beneath his shoulder blade, and his breathing too shallow for the air that he needed. A heart attack could be his good fortune, but the will to survive was stronger than his reason. He counted backward in sevens, like he did when he couldn't sleep. Ninety-three. Eighty-six.

The old man who'd snuggled up to the newspaper kicked him swiftly in the ribs. His body jolted against his will, and he rolled onto his side. The elderly woman tapped her bat against the floor, then brought it down hard on his shoulder. Hot pain spiderwebbed.

The librarian wasn't quite so sultry when she nudged him onto his back and pressed a stiletto to his sternum, begging to know why he picked this town. Something in her eyes said she had some heart left, though. One by one they came to him—the baker, the mailman, the florist—and wrenched out his fingernails, peeled off his toenails, and ripped out his eyelashes, plucking him for their amusement. In millimeters, the drugs wore off. His fingers curled at his command, his toes flexed, and his jaw clenched. But he couldn't let them know. It was the only tool he had.

In a lull in the torture the librarian knelt by his ear. He almost flinched and gave it away. She was all shampoo and laundry detergent, but her breath was sour wine.

"Shh," she said. "I know you can move. I need your help. We have to get out of here, or you'll end up like me, stuck here, living a lie. This town...it's full of serial killers."

The idea of Sandy in stilettos, foot on his throat, her lips that close to his ear sent a shiver down his arms, and he grinned despite the campy turn the story had taken. At least he got something down on paper, even if it was just an exercise. But the ticking cat clock blinked away the minutes, and he wasn't getting any closer to having a story. He was just adding to the pile of things he didn't want to write about. Clearly, he was distracted, diverted by the recurring memory of her sliding off the stool at the bar the night before, clutching her purse strap. There was that moment, that heartbeat pause that seemed to last an hour where she wanted to say something. Stuart had felt it in the air between them. But she said nothing. She smiled at the barstool and pushed it in. They could walk together, he wanted to say. He could lend her his sweatshirt. They could walk until their paths diverged. But the older woman behind the bar had caught his eye, and his thoughts turned timid. What had her smile meant? When she fumbled over her thanks for the beers, what had she wanted to say that she didn't?

Leaving the notebook and pen on the sofa, blank page facing up, he wrapped his arms around his middle and stepped onto the porch. A cold fog was pushing into the late afternoon, mist hanging low, reaching its arms around the tombstones. He could barely see the tips of the shortest markers, pocked by moss. The two wheel ruts that made up the drive were barely visible in the gray. It was the kind of weather that should have sent him burrowing under blankets. Instead, he was full of butterflies, jittery, and he couldn't get Sandy out of his mind.

Inside, he drew books into a pile—dog-eared notebooks full of useless tropes, a coffee-stained and crinkled journal, and on top the two from the library. His stomach did a little leap at the idea of returning them, finding something different, but it was just an excuse to see Sandy, and nothing good would come of giving into that impulse. He needed to get his car back, buckle down, write a damn story, and get back home to Madison.

He never should have been so open with Sandy. And he definitely should have mentioned his girlfriend.

It was almost four, and that plumber guy would be at the tavern soon. With any luck, he'd accept a few bucks in exchange for a ride. With his car back at the cabin, there'd be one fewer distraction plucking the strings of his attention span.

He grabbed the new notebook, his pen, his shoes, and his keys, checking twice to be sure his key to the car was on the ring.

The walk to the bar wasn't long, but the fog and damp coated his lungs, and before he hit the edge of the cemetery, he was reminded how out of shape he'd become. The air looked colder, somehow, beyond the graves. The mist preceded him to the graveyard's edge, and he paused at the last line of stones to zip up his coat. One old tombstone, wider than its kin, parted the wave. A ship was engraved at the top of the stone.

Degory Howland.

The name was familiar, but not enough to place it. Stuart tucked his chin in the neck of his sweatshirt, warding off a chill. The murk was still too new; it hadn't soaked into the leaves yet, so they skipped and skittered along the street, bunching up at the curb, and scraping along the sidewalk. They clawed at the ground, reluctant to go. Maybe they knew something he didn't.

Behind him a branch cracked but didn't fall. Just naked limbs complaining about the cold. Somewhere a car door slammed, and he jumped. Every noise seemed louder somehow, unaffected by the haze. His hands trembled, and he shoved them in his pocket as he rounded the corner at the park. A little tuxedo cat shimmied underneath a chain link fence that bowed its way around a yard full of lawnmowers, their handlebars sticking up here and there like vigilant pigeons in a parking lot. The cat shot across the street and, with a parting glance over its shoulder, picked up the pace.

He was out of breath by the time he flung open the tavern door. Helen put a napkin in front of him as soon as he sat.

"You want another Yuengling?" she asked.

"Yes, please." He pulled a five from his wallet. "Keep the change.

Any sign of that guy Grey?"

Two men in plaid flannel at the end of the bar leered at him, the same men he scampered from in the market. If he'd seen them before he sat down, he would have scampered away again. The shorter guy spurted the kind of chuckle that said volumes about his desire to make people uncomfortable, but Stuart gave him the benefit of the doubt and rolled tension from his neck. Maybe the guy was just misunderstood.

The larger man picked crud from beneath a fingernail and slapped his pocketknife closed. He nudged his friend's shoulder and shot him a snarling glance.

"What?" The short guy raised his hands, pleading his innocence.

"The guy's asking for Grey. You seen him? I ain't seen him."

They both spun to face Stuart.

The shorter man clutched his beer and leaned back. "What do you want with Grey?"

Stuart unclenched his jaw. "I need a ride. My car's at a train station in Colby. Wherever that is. It looks like it's less than an hour from here. I heard that Grey heads out that way, and I wanted to ask him for a ride next time."

The taller man nodded and stroked his beard. "It is. That's true. Grey goes out that way for plumbing stuff."

Helen put another beer in front of Stuart, then turned to the two men in plaid. "Dan, why don't one of you drive him over. You've got nothing better to do with your life. Sitting at this bar all the time."

She threw her hands on her hips and confronted the shorter man, leaning toward him. "Bern, you do it. You're about as useless as they come."

Helen winked at Stuart. If that was supposed to be an endorsement for the town's two most intimidating figures, it was a weak one.

Stuart swallowed his sip of beer hard, pushing it past the welt in his throat. "No, it's alright. You don't have to do that. I'm happy to wait for Grey."

The trap Helen set had snapped, and the two men shared a glance that sent an icy chill down Stuart's spine. The trust he'd placed in her fizzled with the beer foam.

The tall man Helen had called Dan stroked his chin, his face lighting and beard flaring with a grin that would be jovial under ordinary circumstances, but these weren't ordinary circumstances. Nothing about this felt safe. He was alone in a town he didn't know, surrounded by people he didn't trust. He had no car, his cell phone reception was spotty, and they had more than three weeks to bury his body before Madison would even miss him.

The man's voice boomed. "Well, I don't see it's a problem for Bern to give you a ride. Name's Dan."

"Stuart." His second sip of beer did no better at wetting his throat.

Dan smoothed his beard back into place. "How'd your car get to the station without ya?"

"Girlfriend had to leave early. She parked it there. I figured I'd get a taxi or Uber or something, but there isn't one."

Dan nudged Bern with his elbow. "Bern's only had two beers. He'll take ya. We won't take no for an answer."

Helen wiped the bar in front of Stuart. The rag left behind a milky haze. "They're good folks. Don't let their look fool ya."

Bern stretched. "Hear that? We're *good* folks. Nothing to be afraid of. Let me take you for a ride."

A ride was exactly what he was afraid of. But he couldn't turn it down tactfully, having already admitted to having no other arrangement. And he couldn't exactly leave the car in another town forever, either.

Stuart lifted his wallet from the bar. "I can pay you for the ride."

Bern tilted his head back and downed the remaining quarter of his beer. He ran the back of his hand across his mouth and wiped it on his shirt.

"Ain't no need to pay me." Bern stood and his stool clattered. "Guzzle that, city boy. My Jeep's outside."

CHAPTER FIFTEEN

"You sure you're okay to drive?" Stuart fumbled the seat belt until it clicked.

Bern's Jeep smelled like stagnant water and fertilizer. Gravel and mud coated the floor mat, and stuffing fought its way out of the seat, exploding like dough that overproofed in its container. The soft top crinkled when Bern slammed his door shut, and the plastic back window flapped, a foot-long slit cut through it.

"I'm fine to drive. Just hang on." Bern pointed at the dash in front of Stuart. "If we hit something, don't grab that bar, though. Break both your arms."

"Does that happen often? Hitting things?"

"Not in a while." There was no humor in his voice.

Bern wasn't a young man but wasn't an old man either. Judging by the look of him, he could be thirty-seven or fifty-eight. He was one of those men who didn't carry his years or his worries, and he didn't look at all as if he cared what anyone thought about it. He was the kind of guy who pushed himself beyond his natural boundaries, taking up more space than the universe gave him, daring you to have an opinion about it.

Stuart made a silent vow to keep his mouth shut, knowing that he wouldn't keep it. His tendency toward rambling when he was nervous always got the better of him.

The Jeep shimmied when the engine started. It reminded Stuart of an old school bus, the way the gears engaged, and it churned to life. Pulling out onto the road, he expected Bern to accelerate. Instead, the Jeep lumbered along, as if hauling its body down the street was an act of desperation.

The last time he'd been on that street, he was with Madison. She was talking about the shoulder of the road, how narrow it was, and how scary it must be at night. She hated driving where there weren't any streetlights. Always a city girl. He'd been looking at the GPS on his phone, hoping the estimation was right, because there was no signal. He hadn't known then that the red light ahead was the only one for miles.

A shiver ran down his arms. What if Bern left him out there?

"Ain't got no radio." Bern answered a question Stuart hadn't asked. "Don't work."

He thumped the dash with his hand.

"It's okay. So, do you work in Ramsbolt?" He rolled his eyes. Of course, he did. Small talk wasn't his forte.

Bern scowled at him, his gaze lingering just a little too long, the Jeep drifting toward the ditch then lurching back to the road again. "No. I work in Los Angeles as a movie star, but I drive home to Maine every day in time to get a beer at the bar before bed."

"Dumb question."

"You said it, not me."

Stuart cleared his throat. They were going thirty-two miles an hour. The speed limit was fifty-five. "What do you do?"

"Farm stuff. Stuff you ain't got time for." Bern twisted a knob and tried out the heater. A blast of chilled air hit Stuart in the face. He pushed at the vents, closing them, but Bern turned it off. The Jeep went silent again. Just the school bus engine and the pounding of his heart.

"We have farms where I'm from."

Bern looked him up and down. "I didn't say there weren't farms wherever you're from. I said you ain't got time for it."

"What's that supposed to mean?" Pinching the bridge of his nose, he didn't bother to hide his regret. Picking a fight with a guy who barely kept the car on the road after vowing to keep his mouth shut was not a good survival strategy. Keeping the conversation going might lower the tension, but the onus was on him to keep it peaceable.

"I mean, you're some office guy who don't care about farm life, and I ain't got breath to waste telling stories."

Bern's words hit him in the gut. If the man thought stories were a waste of breath, he'd gain no respect by defending himself. As slow as the man was driving, the last thing Stuart needed was to drag things out and make them less bearable.

Stuart wrapped his arms around his middle to hold in the warmth. A dull headache he attributed to whatever fumes the Jeep was spewing began to push at his temples. This wasn't a part of the world with a mileage marker every tenth of a mile, and he hadn't seen any signs indicating they were going in the right direction. He'd already lost track of time with no way of knowing when he'd arrive at his car. Putting his life in the hands of a random stranger was starting to look like a leap of faith into thin air.

Outside his window, grasses swirled in the headlight's periphery. He pictured a quick tug of the door handle, tucking and rolling into the field. He'd probably end up covered in ticks. He'd deserve it for hopping in a car with a stranger when his gut told him to run the other way.

Bern reached around, his arm flailing behind his seat. The Jeep swerved into the other lane, then back toward the shoulder, narrow as it was. Stuart gripped the foam that purged from his seat, holding his breath. Bern twisted back and settled behind the wheel, shaking out a pair of gloves. Leaves and pine needed fluttered into the man's lap. He shoved his fingers in and pulled a blue knit cap down over his ears.

"Hey, you said Colby is a half hour away?" He fiddled with the vent, praying for warmth. He should have waited for that Grey guy.

"About that. Half hour or longer. Maybe more. What are you poking around town for, anyway? We don't get visitors. People think you're creepy. You know that?"

Stuart leaned against the door. His breath made little puffs of fog. Eyes fixed on the road, he tried to read between the lines. Was Bern just trying to rattle his cage? Whatever his objective, Stuart's best bet was honesty.

"I'm a writer. I tell stories. I'm staying in…in town. Like a writer's retreat, I guess. Just looking for some peace and quiet."

"We got plenty of peace and quiet." Bern adjusted his hands on the wheel, straightening his elbows as he pushed his back into the seat. The Jeep picked up speed. "We don't like it disturbed, if you know what I'm saying."

Stuart searched the man's face with his peripheral vision, careful not to seem confrontational. Luckily the shadows offered him plenty of cover. Unsticking his tongue from the roof of his mouth, he said, "I'm just a college professor, here to work on a book. That's all."

Bern laughed, a sinister crackle that sparked through the dry air. "I ain't got tolerance for academic types. People running around trying to get paid for thinking. Like their thoughts are better than anybody else's."

Stuart rubbed the back of his neck. "It's not quite like that."

"Sure as hell feels like it from here."

Every muscle in Stuart's body tensed and flexed. He dug his fingers into his biceps until they ached. He couldn't unravel in this guy's car. He wouldn't allow his voice to rise, for his defenses to unfurl. That's what the man wanted, to make him uncomfortable just for the fun of it. Keeping his cool and staying calm meant being quiet, so he counted his breaths and took them slowly, letting the oxygen linger in his lungs.

Bern barreled down the darkened street, taking a right curve a bit too sharp. Stuart tumbled to the side, his arm brushing Bern's. He gripped the handle on the dash to straighten himself, letting his heart settle while Bern cackled. Eyes focused on the dash, Stuart waited for the flush of adrenalin to subside and his pulse to steady. Surely Bern wouldn't put himself in harm's way and damage his car just to scare a stranger.

There was no way he'd let this overgrown schoolyard bully get the better of him. Instead, he made mental notes about Bern's nature, the way he stiffened when he laughed and how his belly rose and fell, the muscle at the back of his jaw, tight and round like a little knot. It was the stuff vivid characters were made of. He could use all of it—if he lived long enough to write a book.

Bracing himself as the Jeep bumbled around another corner, gravel pounding and pinging off the underside of the car, Stuart couldn't help wondering just how dense that forest was as pines and bramble crowed and reached into the road. No one but those people at the bar even knew where he was.

He wiped his sweaty palms on his pant leg and tried to focus on the road, on the lefts and rights and the landmarks they passed, but his mind raced with possibilities, being stranded in the woods, in some unfriendly town, or being picked off by a bear. He lost track of the few natural features he could see, little clearings with tiny ponds, ruts in the road and mounds of stones. Every inch they careened down the road, though, was one inch closer to his car, to getting back to the cabin where he could relax. If he could get through this ride, and if he wasn't dumber for the exhaust and gas fumes, he'd be fine. It would just be another funny story to tell Mohl.

He counted his breaths, but lost track as the trees grew further apart, and lights burned on the horizon. The Jeep steered into town and past darkened shops before pulling into a long parking lot. The Subaru was under a light, just like Madison said it would be, the only other car for miles.

Bern stopped the Jeep just inside the lot, a football field away from the car. The engine idled, still in drive. In the momentary tug of war, Stuart paused, his hand teasing the belt latch, and Bern's fingers drummed the shifter. Trusting he wouldn't pull forward, Stuart tumbled from the Jeep. He uttered a few words of thanks that came out jumbled, but Bern laughed, churned the gears and steered back the way they'd come.

Stuart took a straight shot to the car, playing connect the dots with the pools of light. He unlocked the door and slipped into the cold stagnant air. An envelope sat on the passenger seat, his name on the front in Madison's handwriting. She'd recycled the envelope his car registration had come in the summer before. It sat in his hand the way bad news does, a ticking bomb that would go off no matter how long he spent considering the wires. He could pluck the yellow one, shove the envelope in the trash and say he never saw it. He could pluck the green one, rip the whole thing to shreds and throw it in the fireplace. Or he could choose the red one, brace for the explosion, and untuck the flap.

She wrote her note on the back of an expired insurance card, small and scribbled. He held it up against the steering wheel where a ribbon of light fell on her words.

Waiting for this train. It finally hit me that you're right about Ed. There is intimacy there. The emotional kind. I talk to him the way I can't with you. Maybe it's because we live in the same world, we keep the same hours, like the same stuff. With you, maybe familiarity breeds contempt. I don't hate you, though. And I don't love him. Not like I love you. But you play different roles in my life. And the longer I live this way, the more obvious it is that I can't have both of you. You'll demand I give you what you deserve. And Ed already wants more. Sometimes I want more with him, too.

There was no surprise at her words, no shock or emotional jolt. They took from him far more than they gave, ripping from him his fear of the drive, his discomfort with Bern. They left him hollow.

For months, in the quiet moments, he'd been preparing himself for just this thing, for the moment when she finally told him the truth. He'd walk through their apartment and take stock of what was hers, what was his. Long ago he'd given up on the idea that anything in their apartment was truly *theirs*. The end had been nearing for quite some time, but he could have sworn that the wake of their passion would be rough, explosive, full of the raw emotions of ending things and closing doors and finishing chapters that had started off with promise. Instead, the waves rolled on. He was hollow.

I try to talk to you, but I never get the words right. Every time you talk about Ed, I get defensive because you already know the truth. This letter made the hard part easy for both of us.

I'm not sure where we go from here, but I have to figure out what I want. So do you. Call me when you know. ~M

He folded the note back into a rectangle and shoved it in his back pocket. It was as if a giant swarm of bees all took off in his brain at once, bouncing off the confines of his wit. If only she'd broken up with him instead of putting it on his plate. If only she'd done it before they came to Maine. Here he was feeling guilty about a friendly conversation with a librarian while Madison was free to do as she wanted. In a way, he wished she'd waited until he got home. If he'd come for the car sooner, he would have known. Of course, he wasn't sure he was ready to face the truth now. Or maybe he was relieved.

His stomach wound itself into a ball, and he squeezed his eyes tight, wishing himself back to a moment before it all went wrong, back to Philadelphia and a winter when they made a snowman on the sidewalk outside a Center City restaurant. The streets had been empty then, just the two of them and the city. Since, the smell of snow and the whistle of winter as it swept between buildings took him right back to their early days of passion and promise. But when Stuart opened his eyes again, the windshield was still there, the little pools of light in the parking lot. And he still didn't know what to say to Madison.

It was hard to see this trip as anything other than an orchestrated hit. When she saw her chance to drive him away, she leapt at it. Not only was he dumb enough to think it was a great idea for their relationship, but he was also so inept as a writer that he thought he needed a change of scenery to conjure words out of the thin air between his ears.

"I've been so dumb. How did I get so mixed up?"

Part of him wanted to drive straight back home and fall on his knees, beg Madison to turn her back on Edward and make it all work, but clinging to the hope of feeling something again wasn't the same as feeling it. And he still wouldn't have a story. And he could still lose his career.

Squinting out the windshield, he tried to make sense of the scene before him, but there was too much fog both on the window and in his head. A gust of wind blew leaves across the parking lot and they piled against a chain link fence.

"It's all on me, isn't it? It's always about me figuring out how to live with you."

CHAPTER SIXTEEN

The sun had set. Stuart struck a match, cutting off his breath before he took in the sulfur. A flame sizzled to life, licked at the corner of a twisted newspaper page and flared. He stood, Madison's letter crinkling in his back pocket, and brushed kindling chaff from his hands on his jeans. It sprinkled the cabin's hearth. He turned his back on it and plopped down on the sofa with a sigh so deep it could have come from his toes.

He couldn't create in his heart what he wanted. He couldn't flip on a switch and shine light in the darkened room or unbox his perfect life like it was something he could order on the internet. If only it were that easy. But he could craft the cabin into a cozy place to make sense of the past. Or avoid the past and the future by writing something better instead. That is, after all, how he got in this mess. Writing was the best avoidance. He could hold a notebook in his hand, laden with ink and heavy with words, having forged something from nothing, and he could call it progress, but avoidance was all it ever was. He'd made a career of it, clung to it, and all of it was slipping away.

His silent war with his father, his giant rift with Madison, his career on the brink, the dean on his tail, and an entire town of people convinced he was some kind of maniac all screaming in his head like the world's worst dinner party. If he didn't cut through the mental clutter and sort his chaos into easy-to-chew pieces, he was going to choke. The only bright spots were his encounters with Sandy, who smelled like heaven and kept tugging his imagination away from anything productive.

He drew the notebook onto his knees, hunched over the paper, and twirled the pen around his fingers. There had to be something fun to write rattling around in his brain. Not something that reminded him of his father or some trite romantic disentanglement that played out in the shadows of his life with Madison. Something new and light and fun.

Bennett spent his whole life waiting. Waiting for time to sow the seeds. Waiting for the corn to grow. Waiting for the rains to wash him clean and draw plants from the earth. He whiled the hours alone, peering out windows and down at the ground where his shoes met the soil, where grains and seedlings would sprout in the spring. But he was a linear man in a cyclical life. With every season he grew more agitated by the past and aroused by a future where the land didn't win.

In between, he sat at the bar, feet on the rungs of a chair that took the wrong form. One day it would have made a better straight jacket. The next, a better suit of armor.

They were a lot alike, Bennett and that chair, the way they wore the wrong skin, how people used them up the way they were intended with no consideration to what they sought to be.

The animus of a life unlived swelled within him, a tumor of hair and teeth. It had a heartbeat all its own, a mind and a will whose bidding must be done. The longer Bennett refused to yield, the more it pushed against his husk, throbbing and stretching until his bile was no longer enough to feed it.

It spilled out on the town, breaking the skin, erupting in sores. Maybe he would have been forgiven for the pus he spewed in a larger town, one where he could build a nest and hide among the branches of a million family trees. But in this town, this too-small town, taunting people to feed the beast, drawing from them all the anger and disappointment and grief a destitute town could feel, left him unfulfilled. The town pulled away, taking their food with them.

Linear lives are like that. Once the fuel burns up, there's nothing left to feed the machine. Nothing grows in a barren field.

Alone, in the dry ground, he kicked at the dust until it muddied. He dug in the mud until it drained. Ice was coming. And he would stomp it until the fistula formed beneath his feet, ripe to swallow him whole.

The fire that raged while Stuart was writing dwindled to cracks and pops as it thawed. Sucked into the story, floating on the words, he'd missed the fire's demise. A gust of wind howled over the roof. His head snapped up at the sound of breaking branches outside.

"Cozy turns to creepy real fast around here."

Dropping a new log on the fire, he nudged it into place and stretched. The windowsill creaked when he rested his weight on it, his palms flat on the polished wood. It was far too dark outside to make out shapes or forms, to figure out who was doing the clomping through the leaves. Squirrels, perhaps. Foxes. That black dog.

He grabbed a beer from the fridge leaving only two behind, cracked it open over the trash can and guzzled half on his way back to the sofa. Everything felt lighter somehow, and he found himself smiling down at the story without realizing it.

Somewhere outside, the cackle of boyish laughter, too young to be out this late and too bold to be up to anything good, washed over the cabin, sending goosebumps down his arms. He brushed it aside, too eager to get back into the story.

Notebook on his knee, he wiggled back on the cushion where he could float among the words. No matter how easily they came, they weren't a whole story, though. As a character, Bennett had depth and potential, but it wasn't the place Stuart wanted to spend his days. He flipped to the next blank page, scribbling a bullet point, a launch pad. His hand could barely keep up with his racing thoughts.

What if he could drop Bennett into Arthur's story? Every hero needs an antagonist, after all.

Taking a breath deep enough to hold, he bit his lip and dove in.

Arthur wore grease the way some women wore pearls. It had been on him for so many years, he felt naked when it wasn't there. He'd smelled it in his sleep long after the smell of her had gone. Every molecule of oil and grease and gasoline held a memory of her.

"Were you a racecar driver when you were my age?" Noah asked, pushing a toy car across the floor of the garage.

"Goodness no, boy. I didn't race cars until I was nearly twenty-five. Before that,

I was a mechanic."

"Were you a mechanic when you were my age?"

Arthur cleaned his hands on a worn red rag. Dark oil etched into the lines on his fingers and in the tiny snowflake creases of his knuckles. "Being a mechanic is like being a painter. You either are or you aren't. You can learn the details, but your brain's got to think the right way."

"And what way is that, old man?"

Bennett leaned in the door of the garage, picking his thumbnail with a pocketknife. When it came to neighbors Arthur had lost the lottery. It didn't matter whether Bennet was growing more annoying or Arthur's patience was wearing thinner. With each passing year, their relationship became more strained. For years, Arthur had put increasing energy into avoiding the man, peeking out windows through peeled-back curtains to be sure the coast was clear, shopping for dairy when he needed fruit just to skirt the man in the market.

But Arthur had been taking his life back lately. Standing taller when the wind pushed in.

"We don't need your hot air, Bennett. Go on, now. Back home with you. No one invited you."

Noah giggled, and Arthur rustled the boy's hair, forgetting the stern warning he'd received from the boy's mother not to let the child get too dirty.

"Be careful where you learn your lessons, kid." Bennett waved his knife. "If the old man had ever been any good with cars, at least one of them would be running. Got six in the driveway collecting more rust than miles."

Stuart scratched behind his ear with the pencil's eraser. It wasn't great prose, but it did set a scene. Just like the man who inspired the character, Bennett felt right as an adversary, someone to pluck Arthur's feathers. His name didn't feel quite right yet, but the right thing would come to him. The excitement charged within him, like static.

His fingers tingled looking over the words. There was magic in there. A man who'd given up on life being dragged back into it by an innocent boy, forced to confront his fears and failures in a town that refused to understand him. If he stuck with it, he could make something of it. He just had to keep writing.

A bang thundered at the door and shook the window. It was way too loud to be the dog. Not unless the dog had built a battering ram. Stuart jumped to his feet, the notebook tumbling to the floor, pencil rolling toward the fire. Palms spread for the sense of balance, he strained to hear past the pounding of his heart. Every hair on his body raised, he ran his hand down the back of his neck, slinking to the kitchen for a weapon while keeping his eyes glued to the door.

He white-knuckled a ladle like a sword.

What are you going to do, scoop them to death?

Back to the wall, he inched along until he reached the door, then he gripped the doorknob, holding his breath, listening for the earth to pulse, for crunching leaves and cackling men, but it was just his heart in his ears. His hand was clammy, and the knob was slick.

Cracking the door open just a millimeter or two, the smell hit him before he could see. Slamming the door shut again, back against the wall, he covered his mouth against the wretch. Spoiled milk and old meat. Yanking his sweatshirt over his mouth, holding his breath, he inched the door open again.

The contents of a trash bag had been sown across the porch, seeds of teenage discord. Grey clumps of cat litter mingled with yogurt cups, expired lunch meat, and a thankfully still-closed plastic soda bottle that appeared to be full of piss. Stuart had no intention of finding out.

His eyes watered, and he swallowed back a rush of saliva. Sweeping it into a pile with the broom from the kitchen and pushing it off the edge of the porch, he scanned the graveyard for movement, but the only shuffling was the leaves still clinging to the trees as a breeze raked across town. A storm was coming.

"Kids." He consoled himself under his breath. It wasn't personal. It was just mischief.

"Creeper! Go home!" Their laughter chaffed like sandpaper. The names and slanders hurled like bombs that landed flat. They preceded the clicks and grinding chains of bicycles as the boys rushed past, whizzing through the graveyard.

Stuart ignored them, mentally giving them the finger, and lifted the broken black sack of garbage with the end of a broom. Grey sludge dripped to the grass. He'd touched some gross things in his life. Fish. Slugs. That bowl of skinless grapes at a Halloween party when he was a kid. But there was no way he was touching that pile of rotting garbage until he had a pair of gloves. It could sit there until morning.

The kids whizzed by again, looping back, circling him at just enough distance to remain cloaked by the dark. One of them lobbed an old dodge ball that hit the back of his car with a springy overfilled boing. They must have given it air just for the occasion. Little did they know it would take a lot more than a kid's ball to harm a car that survived

Philadelphia's roads. But the boys' arsenal wasn't empty. Crunching leaves and churning gravel surrounded him. Something hurled past him, landing sharp and splatting on the porch. An egg. Being cut by shards wasn't on his agenda.

He made a fist, nails digging into his palm, and made for the safety of the cabin.

"Go home." He lobbed the parting shot over his shoulder and slammed the door. The painting of the ship shuddered and fell down the wall, landing facedown on the floor. He strung its wire over the nail in the wall and cracked his knuckles, double-checking the lock.

"Geez, this town is unfriendly."

Stuart leaned the broom in the shower and made a beeline for his writing. He wasn't the man who dwelled on these things, who let adolescent mischief jab a hot poker into an already festering wound. No, he was the kind of guy who shook it off, who got back to writing. Embracing the fog for the dense cover it was, he sat and cracked his neck, happy to finally feel like the teacher his students expected him to be.

Crippling writer's block, imposter syndrome, and fear of the pen were all just fancy diminishing terms that he'd used when he hadn't yet realized his brain was busy sifting through ashes and digging up truth. He had it now; it was in his grasp, and nothing would stop him from getting it down.

His affinity for Arthur had a taproot drinking straight from his well, soaking up his groundwater to feed a character who wanted so badly to belong, who had lost it all and found himself at the very last moment. Noah was more than an innocent foil for the older man who'd seen it all. The child was the guiltless unimpeachable soul that Arthur wanted so badly to be, that Stuart wanted so badly to be.

The fire popped as it started to die, and sparks sprayed up the chimney. Sandy and Helen had been right about finding his truth and putting it on paper, but it had all been a trope at the time. Of course, a writer would hunch over a typewriter in a cabin at the edge of a town, cranking out a story fit to heal his wounded soul. But he hadn't expected the truth to be so elevating. He hadn't expected growing pains to hurt so good. In some strange way, he didn't want resolution with Madison. He wanted the uncertainty to fuel his creative hunger. He'd been starved for so long.

The fire shot another spray of sparks, and a glowing ember settled on the brick hearth. He bent and stabbed at it with the poker, tossed on another log.

Notebook poised on his knee, pen in his hand, he waited for the fire to flare before returning to the story. When he'd left off, Bennett was trying to rile Arthur, pointing out the obvious fact that every car in his driveway was broken.

Arthur wiped grease from the wrench, scrubbing harder than he needed to. Bennett had no right to say such a thing, to scratch at the surface and pick at the scab. Every one of those cars had a memory in its upholstery. Drive in movies with Rachel at his side. Her tugging at bolts and dislodging the ache that kept him fixed to engine blocks, immovable. She loosened them all in her own way, with long breaker bars and gentle penetrating oils. Every broken thing in that driveway was just the way she left it, and they were perfect as they were. One man's rust was another man's glue. Without those scars, Arthur would have nothing left of her, and even less of himself. Late at night when the house was quiet but for the pops and creaks of life settling, he clung to the dream that one day those engines would crank over and her voice would come through the old radios, guiding him back where he belonged. And he'd steer toward her, to tell her all the things he never could when he had the chance.

Stuart rubbed the back of his neck. He should have told Sandy about Madison. He shouldn't let her think that his heart was free. As for Madison, she could never know about Sandy, but she had to know his heart wasn't hers, and it hadn't been for a while now.

Slouching over the notebook, shoulders aching from the slump, he was hit with the liberating realization that there was no moral in the end of his story with Madison. Neither of them would come out a hero. She'd driven him away, slowly over the years with her distance and anger and quickly at the end by abandoning him in Maine instead of bringing up her feelings while they were still in Philadelphia. He was equally to blame for letting it fall apart around him and not walking away before it got like this. It had been over for so long that there was nothing left to mourn. He'd stopped sharing his life with her as much as she'd started sharing hers with Edward. Everything else was a consequence.

A tough conversation was on the horizon, first with himself and then with Madison. And Sandy's feelings could still be hurt if he didn't rectify his omission of truth. And he was lighter for having a path.

There was nothing left to do but clean up the mess he'd made. It was time for a fresh start.

He collected his notebooks from the kitchen table: the one he kept in the car that still had a few blank pages left and the two from home he'd finished off with garbage missives and bad thoughts. He tossed on top the one he just bought, with Arthur redefining himself in a world that went on without him, young Noah finding his way in a world that wasn't yet ready for him, and Bennett who was angry at it all.

He threw them onto the young fire, which darkened, smothered, popped and spit, fighting for air. Tiny tongues licked at the edges, and the fire roared to life.

CHAPTER SEVENTEEN

"Oh my God. What have I done?"

Stuart fell to knees before the fireplace, pushed his sleeve up his arm, and reached into the fire. He plucked at the corner of his composition notebook until it fell to the hearth. One by one, he saved his words, pushing them away from the heat, spreading them out on the bricks where they smoldered and smoked.

The covers were damaged, the corners charred. The first and last pages were reduced to ash. His fingers were already forming blisters, but he'd saved them. After wiping soot and cinders from his hands onto his sweatpants, it seemed mere minutes had passed, but as the last embers of the fire surged, their dying light pulsing beneath the cooled ashen surface of charred wood, he sat on the floor as his reeling mind unspooled as his feelings unraveled. He couldn't count on both hands the years that had passed since tears last sprung to his eyes, but he let them.

The hours had stretched on too long, and it was too late to call Madison now. In the morning he would ring her. Tell her that he may not know what the truth is anymore, he didn't know when things got so muddy and gray, but the passion was gone. Or something like that. It was just as well that the night had dragged out so late. In the morning, with a clearer head, he would know what to say. Tonight, the words would only be choked out, incomplete, doomed for regret.

He wiped damp from his cheek with the back of his hand. His father would never have burned his work.

His mind drifted off to Sandy. Somewhere in this tiny town she had a home, a cozy place with a cat, tidy little kitchen that smelled like fresh bread and hearty soups, and a shelf of tablet readers because she hated to break the bindings of books. And here he was, burning his work.

He checked the covers and charred corners of his notebooks. They were cool and out of the woods. He spread them out on the hearth, turned off the lights, and flopped down on the sofa, hoping that either sleep or direction would come to him, but certain both were far off. Turning the brightness down on his phone, he checked his email, waiting for them to load. Spam, retailers. A restaurant. A rant from Mohl about the college's new health care plan. Nothing from Madison, thank God. And nothing from his father. There was a reply from Markus.

I ran into Mohl at Kung Fu Necktie. He was drinking his way down the shelf of shame, halfway through a can of Boxer. He said you were up in Maine on sabbatical, working on a killer novel. He must have been the one who told you. The book I sold...I made it from the short story prompt you gave us in that class my sophomore year. I told my agent about you, what a great professor you are, and he's dying to read your work. When you finish that mystery you're writing, submit it to him. His info's attached. Tell him I sent you. You inspired me a lot. Thanks for everything. Signed copy coming your way for that shelf of yours.

He let the phone fall onto his chest and unclenched his jaw. He could focus on the upside like a normal, rational person, and be proud of his student and not the least bit jealous that the guy got a book deal after building it up from a short story writing prompt. He didn't have to think *those who can do, and those who can't teach* every time a student got a good bit of news. If he were a bit more mature about it, he could even be excited that he got a referral to a great agent. Most writers never got opportunities that sweet. But the sentiment soured, considering how far he was from the finish line.

Holding the phone above his head, he typed his reply.

Great to hear from you! It's also great to hear about your success. You were a fantastic writer as a student, and I'm sure you'll achieve so much more in the years to come. Thank you for the agent referral.

It wasn't worth mentioning that the story he was writing wasn't a mystery, that he'd burned his enigmatic notes, or that he'd spent so much time puzzling with pieces and useless words that he would be lucky if they fit together into a book when he was done.

I'm a ways off from being ready to submit, but I may take you up on it. Keep me posted on publication progress!

The email swooshed off to bounce between satellites. Stuart closed his email and silenced his phone. Wind pushed against the western wall of the cabin, shuddering the windows in their frames, and rain began to pound the roof. Stuart shifted the pillow behind his head and let the white noise lull him to sleep.

* * *

Stuart's dream began the way odd ones do. It was normal at first, just the ding of the bakery door as he walked in. It smelled like heaven, like blueberry pie and cinnamon rolls and fresh baked cookies all at once but separate somehow and not even a little bit nauseating. And then the scene tilted toward the surreal. Ice hit glasses and laughter washed overhead like flocks of geese, heading out of town on a route they knew well. Stuart was drenched in the uneasy feeling that he hadn't been invited.

It was too dark to make out faces, but the forms were there, the round of human shoulders and soft waves of hair. Stuart knew somehow that the table was his as soon as he stubbed his toe on it, before he saw the reserved tent card with his name in cursive. A notebook and pen had been laid out for him. His job was to write it all down in the time allotted, all the little logic problems and recipes he could think of. Ninety minutes, then a break. His stomach growled, calling out for a cookie, but it would have to wait. If he failed, if he couldn't write down enough to satisfy the proctor, he would never satisfy his craving.

The room was dark; his writing was hard to see.

Halfway through a recipe for banana bread, someone switched on a lamp. A pair of hands landed palms down on the table, and a set of eyes peered into his.

Sandy.

Relief washed over him, like a rubber band stretched too long had finally snapped. Pen down, he leaned back, and she fell into a recliner across from him, pipe in one hand, the other in her lap.

"I'm glad you're here. I have to tell you something."

He wanted to tell her about Madison, about the last few years and how distant they were, how he wanted so badly to feel something for her that wasn't resentment over Edward. He wanted to tell her about the letter and talk about his feelings, but she leaned forward, cutting him off, her eyes blazing with urgency.

"I need you to see this," she said.

His heart raced. She held out the pipe, and it fell to the floor, a careless mess in the shadows.

"Can I get some light on this please?" She looked up into the darkness. "Lights? Please?"

The spotlight widened, jiggling and jolting until it pooled around her.

"I didn't know this was a play." Stuart squinted, peering into the darkness, but there were no signs of an audience. "I thought we were alone."

"We are. Look." She pointed to her lap, and he leaned forward, coming off his chair to see what she was holding. His pulse raced the closer he got, her perfume washing over him. On her lap was a stack of old books with earth-tone covers, softened and faded by the years. In her hand, she held a giant knife which she used to cut the books into wedges, soft as cake. Looking up at him, she sank the knife in and let go, holding her hand over her heart. There'd never been so much perfection in a woman, in the shape of her ears and the delicacy of her fingers. It wasn't at all in her chemistry or shape, for she truly was no more and no less remarkable than any other woman. It was her air, the way she occupied her space. She gave off an energy that drew him in. The table dissolved before him, and he slid his chair closer.

"If you eat a slice, you'll find your story," she said.

"Like *Alice in Wonderland*?"

"Bigger and smaller than that." She handed him a triangle slice of covers and pages. "Eat it fast, or it will melt."

His stomach growled, and the deepest hunger burrowed into him leaving nausea in its wake. It would only end, he knew, when he took a bite of pulp and paper. Tears welling in his eyes, the swell of gratitude for life, he brushed away what he could, blinked back what remained, and faced her.

"Thank you." She held out a hand, and he took it. He squeezed. She squeezed back.

On his lap, the books were melting, the edges weeping like ice-cream cake served slow on a hot summer day. It wilted in a puddle of cherry-red blood.

"It's all wrong." He blinked at her. "It doesn't work."

She shrugged and shook her head, sympathy deep in her eyes. She'd tried. She'd done her best, he knew. But there was nothing else that could be done.

With a crack, the ceiling webbed like lava, cooling on the outside, molten in the middle. Bright light shined through, blue as lightning, and the cracks widened in an instant that felt hours long. The light expanded and his sight was gone, like staring into the sun. And when his vision faded back to focus, the bakery was there in its pastel glory,

Marissa behind the counter, people clustered at tables drinking wine from horn mugs, and the room was full of plants.

* * *

Stuart bolted awake, sitting up straight, his heart pounding. Rubbing the fog from his eyes, he took stock of where he was, the panic of unfamiliarity fizzling as the cabin came to reason.

"*That* was a dream."

Mouth dry, he fumbled with the kitchen sink, filling a glass with tap water.

If he were the kind of guy who looked for meaning in nightmares, he would think his subconscious was telling he was losing his mind. It didn't make a lot of sense, and he couldn't quite make the connection between Arthur and that dream, but he knew that Arthur's story was the one he wanted to write. He couldn't let it go.

Rain spattered the window, and a short gale whistled across the chimney.

"Sleeping weather." He dumped the last of the water in the sink and crawled into bed, pulling the covers up under his chin.

For the first time in a very long time, he was excited to get up in the morning to open his notebook to a blank page and start to write. Not to figure out his characters this time. He knew who they were, where they'd been, how the world had beat them down. He was ready to bring them to life, ready to force them to confront the ultimate power in their lives. He'd find his own along the way.

A squall of rain battered the side of the cabin. With any luck, the rain would wash off some of that garbage by morning.

CHAPTER EIGHTEEN

The sky opened with a crack and a flash. Broken wood and sprays of dried leaves, wet from rain and cold from wind, splintered down on Stuart. He winced against the sting of a cut on his right cheek. The bed jumped, and his back slammed down against the hard mattress as a beam from the roof missed his head by a narrow margin. His breath caught in his throat, and the sharp pain of being startled awake drove into his chest, throbbing against his ribs.

He clutched his head, drawing his knees up, and with broken breaths, he pieced the room together. The cabin. The fireplace. His notebooks. He was in Ramsbolt. Writing a book.

He wiped a trembling hand down his face. It came away wet, not sweat, not tears, but cold. His fingers tangled in knots of leaves.

"What the hell?"

He couldn't sit up. Branches were in the way. A wood beam that was once a part of the ceiling had missed his head with a narrow margin.

The sky lit up in the brightest, whitest blue, the imprint of crooked fingers of branches and the raw yellow of shattered wood etched on his eyelids when the flash went out.

A wall of water pushed by wind pelted him, beads sharp like ice.

"Hail. Oh my God."

He scrambled, scraping away the blankets, kicking at the sheet. The tree creaked, and the walls cracked, settling into their new groove. Covering his face with his hands, Stuart prayed to a God he never knew that the beams would hold, that they wouldn't break him into pieces.

"Get me through this. Please. I don't want to die like this."

Hot sweat broke through cold rain, the water mixing with blood on his hands. Feeling for the cut, it was just his cheek. A scratch. A scrape. It could have been worse. It could still get worse. Testing the mattress, he inched his way up, wiggling his legs from beneath the tree, begging it not to budge, to hold the breach of the walls.

Skin tingling with the adrenaline rush, he gasped for air and clawed his way out, under and over and between the branches and trunks, moss and lichen clinging to his skin. Leaf mold and splinters filled the air. He clutched his chest, his breath short.

How could so much tree fit inside such a small cabin? How much would it hold before the floor caved in?

Inching along, his toe found the edge of the table. Groping in the dark, he found his phone and car keys, and he gripped them to his chest. His wallet wasn't there, though.

The notebooks. All his writing. The torso of a giant tree, immovable for its might, stood between him and his work. He pushed with his hip, but it wouldn't budge. He hadn't expected it to. There was no climbing over it, not with the branches rising from it, broken at angles. Tucking his keys and phone in his pocket, testing the branches, he pushed and pulled. The floor groaned under the strain. The last thing he needed was to crash through the floor.

Shielding his eyes from the stinging rain, the only path he could make out clearly, the path of least resistance, led to the front door.

Breaking limbs and snapping branches, he fought his way out. His pants snagged by wooden claws. He pushed the door, and it wouldn't budge, wedged shut by the twisted frame. Shoving with his shoulder, he broke it free and stumbled onto the porch, head down against the driving rain, catching glimpses of destruction through lashes that fluttered against the pelting sting.

He passed garbage soaked and flattened against the earth, and his foot caught on the burst trash bag.

Kicking and flailing his leg, he cursed. "Stupid kids and their rude parents. Why doesn't anyone raise their kids anymore? Who does this? Who throws trash at someone's house? What the hell is wrong with this place?"

The bag unfurled from his foot; celery tops and eggshells stuck to his socks.

He curled his cold toes in the mud, shoved his phone in the pocket of his sweatpants, and clutched his elbows.

The giant tree outside the kitchen window had been the intruder. Its roots peeled up the earth and jutted out at the sky, craggly fingers grasping at the air. Mud streamed from the hole, past the house, toward his car. He slipped in it, mud squishing between his toes, and his knee landing hard on the earth. Using the bumper, he hauled himself up.

There was no use climbing in. He was already soaked to the bone, sweating like a marathon runner in July despite the cold rain. He sat on the hood instead, water oozing from his saturated pants, leaning back on his elbows. He really ought to care about the rain. He could hear his mother's voice warning him that he'd catch a cold out here, wet hair and no coat. If this wasn't the thing that would do him in, maybe it would be the thing to finally wash his slate clean.

Metered steps sloshed in the puddles and stopped next to the car. Stuart blinked down at a black lab who stopped by the fender, head tilted to the side, considering the carnage with canine curiosity.

"Aren't you the guy who knocked the chair over?"

The dog shook his whole body, head to tail, and water sprayed the side of the car.

"What do I do now, huh? All my clothes are in there."

More than that, he lost his notebooks. All his ideas were gone. Maybe this was the universe's plan all along. Maybe the forces of nature were trying to tell him that he had no business being here, and he was on the wrong track. That he'd wasted all that time and all those years, and if he'd been a little bit smarter or a little bit less dense, he would have realized his true destiny was to plow snowy roads, be an air conditioner technician, or sell pretzels from a cart. He'd be warm and dry somewhere, not sitting on the hood of his car in wet socks, a target for stinging hail, cursing his own brain for not being good enough to make a decent living at the only thing he thought he knew how to do.

The dog took a few timid steps, sniffed at the ground, then

sauntered back the way he came.

"Not a bad idea. What next?"

Stuart pulled his keys from his pocket and twirled them around his finger.

There was nowhere else to go. That hotel, maybe, across from the tavern.

His head started to throb as another band of rain swept over him. Water dripped from his hair. The cut on his cheek stung.

Bouncing orbs of light appeared at the edge of the cemetery, growing larger and closer. Voices cut through the distant rumbles of thunder. A beam of light landed on him, and a man's voice called out his name.

Stuart shielded his eyes. "Warren? That you?"

The party of a dozen people picked up their pace. Clad in plastic jackets and ponchos, he didn't recognize them, but Warren was leading the way, a knotted-up grocery bag in his outstretched hand.

"One of the neighbors up the hill saw the tree go down. We brought you some dry clothes."

Stuart accepted the bag and pulled it onto his lap, hugging it to keep it dry. "Thanks."

"I have an apartment over the post office. It's not much, but the heat's on."

The wind picked up. Stuart shouted to be heard. "I appreciate that. It's kind of you."

A woman peered around Warren. "Did you lose anything in there, other than your clothes? You didn't have anything of value in there, right?"

Her words struck against his flint. "Oh, no. Nothing of value. Just my entire life."

The woman peeled back, shrinking behind Warren, whose eyes widened as his frame stiffened. The man started to speak, but there was only enough air for Stuart, and Stuart wasn't sharing.

"All my work is in there. I didn't even want to come here. I didn't ask for any of this." His voice echoed back at him off the tombstones. "I wanted to write a book, but no. For some stupid reason I'm the only writing professor on earth who has writer's block as a personality trait. And you…" He spun and hurled the bag at the Subaru's windshield. The splat was satisfying, and it hit the wipers with a thud. "Stupid car. This whole damn town with its rude kids who throw trash at my door and stinking milk garbage and dogs that scare the crap out of me. *You people* are creepy. You stare at me everywhere I go, my father's a dick, Madison's gone. I'm about to lose my job. I'll have to move when I get home."

He flung his arms at the sky.

"I have to find a place to live, because my girlfriend would rather date that slimy Edward guy with his slicked-back hair than spend another day with me. She dragged me up here to this godforsaken town to get me out of the way, and now she's down there making out with the guy she swore she didn't love. Why is everybody lying to me?"

He turned, his feet slipping in the mud, his arms failing to keep his balance. He found the woman in the crowd, the one who asked the stupid question, and pointed a finger at her. "Know what I lost? Huh?

You want to know? I lost notebooks. Years of ideas and notes and stories. The only damn good ideas I've ever had are in there. My career is over. My shoes are gone. I lost my wallet." He gritted his teeth, the anger shaking in his head. "And I got a cut on my face, and it stings a lot."

A small voice from the back of the crowd cut the silence. "The outdoor store opens at eight." She cleared her throat. "It's across the street from the post office. Come in when you see the light on, and I'll sell you new clothes and shoes at cost. You can pay me when they dig your wallet out."

He uncurled his fingers from the fists they'd clenched in rage. "I appreciate that. It might not look like it, but I do."

Warren adjusted the hood of his dark blue raincoat, blinking up at the sky. "This looks to be lightening up. We'll collect your stuff and bring it by. I'll put in a call to some guys, and we'll get it straightened out." He carried himself like a man who solved a lot of problems, the kind of man who just kept at it even when no thanks were offered. It wasn't Stuart's fault he added to the burden, but he regretted it all the same.

"I don't want to put you out." Taking help, having no other option, dug the pit of his helplessness a little deeper.

Warren shook his head and rain streamed off his head and down his hood. "You're not putting me out. I gotta clean it up anyway." He held out a key. "The door to the apartment is next to the post office. It's blue. Can't miss it. You can park out front if you want."

Stuart shot a look at the car. It had a lot of miles on the engine, and it had suffered its share of city scrapes, but its seats were still in good shape, and it didn't deserve to wear his mud.

"I'll probably walk, if that's okay. Leave the car here."

"I don't blame you."

He'd never been much of a runner. As a kid he'd rather have been reading than trying to keep up in gym class. He never understood the compulsion to pound away at hard pavement, jarring his joints and straining his muscles, not when he could sit and read or think. But for the first time in his life, he wanted to run as fast as he could from all of it. From the storm and the tree, his job and Madison. She'd been the only adult relationship of his life that had been worth pursuing. He'd loved her until there were no spaces between them. He'd loved her until the shine wore off. He'd loved her long after she stopped loving him.

He needed to run from the father whose name he couldn't live up to and from the universe that didn't want him to.

He needed to run from the book he couldn't write and all his failed attempts. His notebooks, the last good ideas he'd had, were now bleeding into the bad ones in the ruins of the only shelter he could claim, even if it was just a holiday rental.

Maybe he had to lose his breath to catch it. And a good, hard run in the pouring rain might do the trick.

Bag of clothes in one hand, he accepted the key from Warren with the other. "Thanks."

CHAPTER NINETEEN

Sunlight limned the walls of Warren's apartment above the post office in a brightening shade of gold, and Stuart sat on the end of the twin bed, hands on his knees, waiting to go up in flames, as strange as the last two days had been. He was covered in mud and chunks of dried leaves, but with no towel or a washcloth, he could hardly make use of the tiny shower. He sat, weighted into stillness by the fear he'd leave a mess behind.

This wasn't his first impossible sunrise. It wasn't the first time it rose when it shouldn't. The earth went on turning. The sun insisted on lightening the horizon, and every inch it crept, the more it sucked the hot anger from him, leaving behind a painful aching cavity that he slowly filled with an inelegant to-do list. Call the credit card company. Tell the world he'd escaped a brush with death barefoot, wearing sweatpants with holes in them, and a Dropkick Murphys T-shirt.

He pressed the button on his phone. It only had twenty-three percent of its battery left, but a new voicemail he'd missed in the storm enticed him to check his call list. His father.

"Stuart. I ran into your dean at The Rosenbach. They recently acquired another lovely old Chaucer. But you wouldn't care about that."

The usual condescending tone sailed further than usual on the wind of dramatic lilt. Of all the things Stuart longed to endure after his sleepless night and the loss of everything, his father's bite hadn't made the cut. He put it on speaker phone.

"I only mention this because Hessel may mention it, and the rest of the world need not know our division. He iterated to me what I'm sure he's tried to impress upon you for some time now, that if you hope to continue to enjoy the benefits of being a professor, you will need to earn your stripes with something other than editing a quarterly journal of freshman fiction."

At least the condescension didn't stop at Stuart's door, if those punctuated words were to give him any relief. Unlike Stuart, the freshman who revered the man would be spared knowing about his low opinion of their work.

"More to my point, Hessel seemed to look to me for some reassurance that you were achieving greatness during your sabbatical. You'll be pleased to know that as a result of having nothing nice to say, I opted to keep my mouth shut."

Stuart leaned back on the bed. "Here it comes."

"This time. I will no longer pull weight for you. If you want to make it on your own, that's exactly how you'll do it."

There was no click at the end of the call, no goodbye, no lift in his tone.

His phone beeped, begging for energy. He threw it down on the bed, hauled himself to his feet, and paced. He couldn't do anything about his father. That relationship had been in tatters for years. It would mend itself like it always did, either into civility or something that resembled it.

He shuffled to the tiny bathroom, bending his joints as little as he could, not wanting to leave any graveyard mire behind. He winced in the mirror at the vision of his father. Same nose. Same jaw. The cut on his cheek, a smear of beaded blood and sweat. In the absence of a washcloth, he reached for toilet paper, but there only a few strips remained on the roll since God knows when. He wet his hand and dabbed at the cut. It wasn't deep. It would heal and leave a lasting reminder of this strange trip and this weird little town. With any luck he'd look back on it all as some marvelous adventure that changed his life and turned him into the man who could conquer the world.

He turned from the mirror.

Hands on the windowsill, he peered down at the street. The Outdoor Store wasn't open yet. Maybe they would have cell phone chargers. He'd need a new razor, too, and some clothes to get through the next few days, towels to wash the mud off his body, and a toothbrush. Then he could hop down the street, buy another notebook and a new pen with something less judgmental than a bobcat in it, and finally get down to business, assuming Warren would let him stay.

He owed Warren a lot of thanks. If it weren't for his kindness, Stuart would still be sitting on the hood of his car like a lost pigeon in a parking lot, scanning the skies for a sense of direction. At least he had a place to hold his life together in private.

And he'd have to call the bank and get a replacement debit card. His driver's license was shoved up a tree somewhere, along with the rest of his wallet.

What if he'd never come here? What if Madison hadn't left? Would anything be any different if he'd never bought those notebooks or tried to write those stories? Could one tiny change in the last week of his life have altered the ripples that made this giant tsunami of garbage? Could any tiny gesture or nod that differed have prevented his work from ending up in a soggy puddle in a derelict cabin in the middle of a Maine graveyard?

A door slammed and someone plodded up a flight of stairs down below. Someone at the post office perhaps or one of the shops downstairs. The world was waking despite him. Or perhaps to spite him, depending on how his day went.

He ran water into his hands and splashed it on his face, gasping for air as the cold constricted his breath.

A knock at the door by a delicate hand made him jump. He tugged his T-shirt over his face and dried off as much as he could.

"Stuart?" The muffled voice belonged to a woman. "Are you in there?"

"Coming."

He crossed the old tan carpet in his bare feet still streaked with mud and opened the door. On the other side, the woman from the bakery held up a cardboard box.

"I have some of your things. And Warren sent over a towel in case you want to take a shower."

"Your timing is perfect." Holding the door wider, he nodded her in. "Sorry, I'm a mess. I must smell like I crawled out of a grave."

She left the box on the little kitchen table and unfurled her scarf, knotting it in her hands. "Not at all. And it's understandable."

"Thanks." He rubbed at his chin and accepted the box. "I guess the whole town heard about the cabin, huh?"

"Yeah, they're all down there. Just about wrapped up now."

"I guess they heard I had a temper tantrum, too?"

She shrugged, but he could tell he'd been the topic of at least one trip around town in the gossip wagon.

"I'm sorry if I was a bit unhinged," he said. "Thanks for this. It's nice of you. Of everyone. Can I do anything to repay you for bringing this stuff by?"

"All I did was bring it up. I had to pass here anyway. Don't worry about it." With a narrowed brow and a glance at his feet, she seemed as uncomfortable as he felt.

"I should be down there helping clean up, shouldn't I?"

She leveled with him. "You don't even have shoes."

"Right." Helpless, as usual.

"I do owe you an apology, though." She knotted the scarf.

"What for?"

"What I said. Warren and Helen told me the truth. I should have learned my lesson about spreading rumors a long time ago, but I've got a thick skull. In a town this small, walls are pretty thin, if you know what I mean. I get carried away sometimes."

The pieces weren't lining up for Stuart, and he didn't have the energy to tease them out of the tangle.

"What do you mean?" he asked. "What truth? What rumors?"

She spoke slowly. "I thought you were creeping on little kids when you were looking out the bakery window. I might have warned some people you were up to no good."

"That explains some of the dirty looks I've been getting." The kids had called him a creeper when they threw trash at his door. A small town in the middle of nowhere could be forgiven for their suspicions. It's not like he hadn't arrived with preconceived notions of his own. "It's a hell of a leap, though, isn't it? I was just sitting there, writing. I didn't do anything wrong."

"No. No, you didn't. My imagination got the better of me. I *am* sorry."

Dizzy from hunger and the scattered flitting of things yet to be done, he leaned on the table, gripping the edge of the box. There wasn't enough energy to expend on his reputation, especially among people he'd never see again. Not when he had so many characters to rebuild and stories to form if he intended to save his career. It was a big if.

"Is my wallet in here, by any chance?"

She shook her head. "I don't think so. There's a bunch of notebooks in there, though. A little mangled and waterlogged."

He peeled back the flap, and the stench of wet paper unraveled out at him. Ink had bled from one sheet to another. He shoved the box across the table, and one corner left a wet streak as it slid.

Plopping into the chair, he rubbed at that spot in his chest with the heel of his hand.

Marissa shuffled. "Some of your clothes were dry, but most were dirty and really wet. They're in my washer."

"You washed my clothes?"

"Yeah. I mean, they were pretty gross. I figured the laundromat takes a lot of quarters, and it would just be another thing you'd have to deal with."

With his thumbnail, he dug a trench through the dried grit on his sweatpants. "I appreciate that."

"You can come get them from the bakery around noon, if you want."

There was no way his smile reflected his insides. No smile could. It was a hot casserole of gratitude for help he didn't deserve and anger at words he hadn't earned. He picked at the label peeling off the cardboard box.

"You guys dug through that house to find my stuff. You're doing my laundry. That's a lot. Thanks."

"I didn't do much. Warren and Grey crawled through it to get your stuff. Adelle and Kyle cut branches out of it, and Jaleesa used Penny's Jeep to pull the tree out of the house. It was a whole town thing."

She turned to leave. He pulled the box onto his lap and peered inside.

"I forgot to say…" She coiled the scarf around her neck like frosting stopping a cupcake. "There are two library books in there. They're wrapped in a trash bag to keep them dry."

"I forgot about that."

She smiled. "Sandy would have killed us all."

"At least she's consistent. Hey, did you find a woman's sweater with the clothes?"

Brow furrowed, she shook her head. "No. I don't think so."

"I'll go back down and take a look around."

"There's not much left to see. Once Jaleesa pulled the tree out, the whole thing collapsed. You might be able to get to the fridge, but that's about it. You were lucky."

"Lucky." Water soaked through the cardboard, through his pants. He'd have to spread all this wet paper out and hope he could still read it when it dried. That story had been heading in the right direction, and it felt good for the first time in a long time. "Somehow, stuff always works out the way it's supposed to."

Madison probably didn't expect to get that sweater back anyway.

CHAPTER TWENTY

The water was hot enough to melt the skin from Stuart's back. It stung his side. He ran the thin washcloth down his ribs, tilted his head back, and let the water wash the blend of mud and blood and sweat from his face. He'd been tense for so long, all the muscles bound in knots. As they unclenched, he unraveled with them.

He couldn't scream, no matter how badly the primal urge coursed through him, in case someone downstairs in the post office freaked out and called the cops. He couldn't punch the walls or stomp his feet. His anger at Madison, and his stupid brain that couldn't write a story, and at the dean for not understanding he was trying, all frothed and foamed and stung his eyes. There was no soap, no shampoo, but he tilted his head back and let the dirt drip down his back and into the tub where it formed a puddle of thin mud that swirled around the drain.

If he were lucky, if he were really lucky, when he opened his eyes he'd be home again. Madison would be banging pans in the kitchen. There'd be a morning traffic jam outside. It would be spring, and his walk to campus would be warm and uneventful.

But he wasn't that lucky. And maybe he didn't want to be.

The thought of Madison at the end of the hall didn't fill him with warmth anymore. They'd been little more than roommates for quite some time, her going one way, him another. He didn't want the loveless thing it had become any more than she did, and nurturing something that had long been dead just because the timing wasn't right for a dramatic funeral wasn't the kind of living he envisioned for himself. Not like going out and grasping a thing, manipulating fate in his favor was his way of doing things either. He'd always been the kind to go with the flow. But was it worth being swept up in the tide?

He threw his foot on the edge of the tub and scraped dirt from his toenail.

Maybe he should just stay in Ramsbolt forever. Never call Madison, never argue over whose apartment it was and who got to keep the furniture. At least the car was his. He could drive it to the end of the earth if he wanted to, just to get away from all this.

But that wouldn't solve anything.

He wrung out Marissa's pink washcloth again and again until the water went clear. Then he climbed from the shower, tossed the rag in the sink, and wrapped himself in the fluffy yellow towel.

He'd never dry off with all that humidity saturating the air. He cracked the door open, and the steam poured out.

Balling his old clothes into a wad and shoving them into a plastic bag, his cell phone fell from the pocket of his sweatpants and landed on his toe. Cursing the pain, he checked the time. He had to get across the street in his bare feet and buy some shoes. The battery was almost dead. There had to be a charger in this town somewhere.

Sandy came to mind.

His fingers placed a call to Madison before his brain had fully engaged. He jumped at the beep, at the near death of his lifeline. With each ring, his resolve deepened like a red wine stain spreading on a white cloth napkin. What started off as a tiny drop saturated him by the time she picked up.

"Why are you calling me at this hour? You know I work late." Her voice wasn't pleasant. Par for the course.

"You left me a letter in a car. You don't get to ask me why I'm following up with a phone call. You told me to call you, anyway."

She was sitting up. The bed was creaking. He could picture the sun coming through the blinds, striping the gray duvet cover. Was Edward there? He didn't want to know.

"So? What do you…" It was perfectly fine that she trailed off, because he didn't really have an answer. He knew he wanted more for his life. He wanted not to second guess every decision he made. He wanted to be a confident guy who walked into a room and was accepted on principle. He wanted to be one of those professors who commanded authority in social circles. He wanted to be respected, for someone to trust him instead of needing a leap of faith just to rely on him, and he wanted to prove them right.

"I don't want to do this anymore. That's all I know right now." He ran a hand over his head. His hair was starting to dry already.

"Are you coming home today?"

"No. I lost my wallet."

Madison huffed. "Where'd you leave it? Third shrub on the left? Behind a thirty-year-old can of Crisco in the market?"

"Don't be a bitch."

"I'm not. Why do you always think the worst about me?"

"Maybe because you don't give me your best anymore. Look, the lady who runs that bakery is doing my laundry. I have to go buy some shoes and call the bank. Just…"

"Just what?"

Was there room for a demand from Madison? Did he have to defer to her. "I'll talk to you later. I just had to get that off my chest."

"Are you even sad? I mean, don't you want to yell this out?"

"What the hell, Madison? No, I don't want to yell this out. I know that's what you want, some giant argument that you can hash out with Edward until you've convinced yourself you've won." He put the call on speaker and tugged on the navy sweatpants that belonged to some guy named Kyle. He pulled the T-shirt down over his head, shaking into it. "There are a lot of things going on right now, and for once I'd appreciate it if you would cut the shit, be upfront with me about not wanting to be part of the solution, and stop being part of the problem. Every time you see me on my knees you kick me in the chest, and I am done. This is me, walking away. I'll be back at some point to get my stuff. Just leave my shit alone."

He had to stop clinging to things.

And then he had to write Arthur's story.

CHAPTER TWENTY-ONE

Jeans that fit, an oversized hoodie, socks and boots, and a camping pillow set him back a little more than a hundred bucks, a bill he promised to pay when his new debit card arrived, but the nap he woke from on the hard twin bed was priceless. Sun still saturated the room, throwing its light on buttercream walls, and he wiped the slumber from his eyes, gritty remainders of a deep, if not slightly plugged-up, sleep, and checked the time on his phone. The charger he borrowed from the kid at the market was just long enough to reach the bed. Three hours had passed since he fell asleep. Two more before he could collect his laundry.

A knock on the door, soft but assertive, set him up straight.

"Stuart?"

It wasn't Marissa this time. He'd know that voice anywhere. And for the first time since he'd met her, she was the last person he wanted to see.

Joints stiff, he shuffled to the door and cracked it open to face her. His hand flinched and grasped the edge of the door, a defiant clutch against the instinct to shut her out. She had this way of seeing through him, and so much had changed since they last sat at the bar, none of which he wanted to face or explain. He didn't want to justify his distance either.

She held up a paper cup of coffee and a pastry box. "I brought you something to eat. I just heard."

He held the door open, and she accepted the silent invitation.

"You must be the last one to know." He plopped down at the table and peeled back the pages of a drying notebook to make room.

She set the pastry box down. A stack of pastel paper rested on top.

She lowered herself onto the seat next to him. "I print a lot of flyers for kids' programs and stuff like that. I hold onto them to use for scrap paper. I figured you could use some to write on. I got a pen for you, too, so you can keep going. Things were going well before…" All the wet paper must have registered because her shoulders fell. "Before the cabin fell down. Did you lose it all?"

"Not sure." He tapped at his temple. "It's up here. I can make it again. I appreciate the paper. I'll definitely use it."

"I stood at Marissa's counter for ten minutes trying to decide between bagels and muffins. I went with muffins. Her chocolate chip are legendary, but all she had left were lemon poppy."

They smelled fantastic, and his stomach growled. He hadn't eaten anything in what seemed like days. The last food he even thought of had come to him in a dream. "I bet they're delicious. I'm glad it's not cake." He brushed off her puzzled look. "Just some dream I had. We were at Marissa's and you had a cake. Then the place filled up with plants, the cabin fell down, and I woke up."

"You dreamt about me?" She blushed and grabbed a muffin, peeling back its oily paper. "I'm glad you weren't hurt. I walked up there. It looks bad. The ceiling caved in. Two walls collapsed. I can't believe you dug out of that."

He shrugged. "It wasn't that bad when I climbed out. Must have happened when they pulled the tree out of it."

"Probably. I can't imagine what that was like." Concern chiseled her, making angles of her arms, her stiff shoulders. The late morning sun lit her high cheekbones. Tips of her dark hair strayed from the strategically messy knot of hair at her neck. Everything about her was effortless, immaculate without excessive polish, as if she woke up perfect every day. By contrast Stuart might as well have been a lump of clay.

She put a hand on the table. "Is there anything I can do? Give me a list. I can make a place in the library where you can work. There's a little kitchen in the basement, and you can have the whole thing to yourself if you want. You're probably most worried about your notes, though, huh? I could try to replicate any of them for you or make some photocopies if that would help."

Dark blue ink had bled through the paper, running his words together. Last June was bleeding into last Thursday. They might as well have been written by fifteen different men. The reluctant professor, the distant boyfriend, the utter failure.

"I don't even know how much of this is worth keeping, to be honest. It's barely even first draft material."

Stuart had faced down more than his share of horrible word choices and bite-sized plots alongside cringe-inducing emotional buffets. They never got better on their own. The paper never healed itself. Like he told his students, the recoil from a first draft was just a reaction to be fought through. The real art happened in the response. And there was no other way to arrive at a finished product than to get it down on paper, tear it up, and move on.

This time, he had to face down more than just some scraps of paper. He had to confront the man he used to be and figure out who he would become.

Laying a hand on a crunchy page of blurry writing, he was ready.

"This stuff isn't worth much, but I am looking forward to digging in. All of this is destined for the recycling bin, anyway."

Sandy's eyes were fixed on his hand. "No, they can be saved. They're not all bad. But your hands don't look great."

He hadn't noticed before how scratched they were, covered in little cuts starting to scab over.

"It's not that bad." He cleared his throat and tucked his hands between his knees. "And all those notes? They're just part of the process. What's the use in carrying all this stuff around, huh?"

She picked up a notebook with a reluctant hand, bringing it closer, inspecting it. She flipped through pages, turning them as if they held some mystic key to a new universe in an alien pen. Stuart shrank, hunching over his hands, a reflex to protect the secrets he'd placed there. He never would let Madison look at his work like that. She would have come back with some sarcastic snip. He would have grabbed them out of her hand, made excuses for them, scampered away to some coffee shop or library reading nook.

"I think you should hold onto these," Sandy said. "Spread them out and let them dry. Don't do anything too rash."

"You're probably right. It's a bit of a security blanket, knowing they're around."

She set the notebook down and faced him, folding her arms. "So, what are you up to today?"

He ran a hand through his hair, leaning back. "Get some writing done. I should get that Arthur story down while it's fresh in my mind. Maybe go over to the cabin and see if I can find my wallet, and I have to pick up my laundry from Marissa. She's really nice. I think I underestimated this place."

"I love living here." Sandy turned to the window, sunlight constricting her eyes and bringing out the hints of gold and green. "I've always thought the people were nice. I went to New York once with friends from college, and it was so cold. Everybody looked so angry to me. It's not like that here. People become what you tell them they are, they turn into the thing you treat them to be. Treat people bad enough and you can turn them mean. A town this small full of mean people wouldn't last for long."

"Philadelphia has a reputation, but it really isn't that bad. You should see what happens to someone who steals parking spots after a big snow, though."

"They don't call them mean streets for nothing. I kinda like how we don't hold grudges either. I can go in the market, grab what I need, and run. I don't have to make nice if I'm not in a good mood. You have to be forgiving in a town like this, or you'd run out of people to trust."

"I appreciate the forgiveness, frankly. I didn't realize I was coming off as creepy as I was. But returning it is the hard part. Kids threw trash at the cabin door. People spread rumors that I had some ulterior motive. Everywhere I went, people were leering at me. Maybe I don't deserve as much kindness as everyone's shown me today, but I really do appreciate it. The Outdoor Store sold me this stuff at cost. And I don't have to pay them until my bank card shows up tomorrow. Marissa apologized. Said she thought I was weird and told people to steer clear of me. Maybe I could have done something different. Maybe I did something that made me seem suspicious without knowing it."

Sandy shook her head. "No. Don't take it personally. It's just the small-town rumor mill."

"I'm sure I didn't help anything by taking notes everywhere I went."

"Creative people can seem that way sometimes. You live in your heads. It's not your job to change for everyone else." Empathy came off her like a weighted blanket he wanted to snuggle with. Why did she have to be like this, radiating this warmth that drew him in? Their hands were close to touching, her fingers inching toward his.

She broke eye contact and jumped, looking at her phone. "I have to go. I'm supposed to open the library."

He stood and stepped forward. Toe to toe, they almost touched. His hand reached forward without his consent, willing the rest of him to draw her into a hug. Maybe it was the closeness he needed most, just to feel that human connection where so much of himself had been lost lately. He yearned to hold her to him, to beg her to stay, to have a muffin and finish their coffee and talk about small towns and big cities and every mile that spanned between them. Instead, he winced and faked a smile.

"I have good news." He pointed to the kitchenette tucked in the corner, where the book rested by the sink. "The library books survived. You can take them with you if you want."

She glanced over her shoulder. "That's the second-best news I've heard all day."

"What was the best?"

She opened the door and swung into the hallway, clutching her cup. "You weren't hurt."

The door closed behind her. She left the books behind.

CHAPTER TWENTY-TWO

Caution tape webbed the cabin's hull and draped over branches that sat in a haphazard pile by what used to be the kitchen wall. Someone had chainsawed branches and limbs, setting them off to the side. Mud filled the hole where the tree once rooted. He scanned the tree line for the black lab, but he wasn't around. He probably had important dog tasks to tackle. There were no signs of the squirrel who had rustled the leaves or the crows that had marched between the tombstones days before. Gone, too, were the sudden bursts of sharp, sweet songs from migrating birds. It was as if the house collapse had sent them all running. He couldn't blame them.

His Subaru was right where he left it. The far wall with the chimney hadn't changed either. The porch roof was intact, though it had lost one support and sagged on the end, and the kitchen wall seemed to cave in and fall outward all at the same time, smashed by the trunk of the giant tree. The front door was open, inviting him to test the porch, which groaned under his weight.

If it weren't for his sense of self-preservation and the questionable structure of the floor, he could have walked right in. The kitchen counter had been snapped into pieces, the sink reduced to a dented tub and tossed aside. Shards of the cat clock were scattered through the rubble like sprinkles on a cake. Excepting for the missing kitchen wall and the giant hole in the roof, everything else looked much as he'd left it. The bed was on the far wall, covered in the blanket he'd been sleeping under. The fireplace still stood, full of ashes. Using the flashlight on his cell phone, he scanned the room and found his wallet under the sofa. It must have fallen out of his pocket when he was sleeping. There was little time to feast on the relief, though, not with the book looming over his head and the impending doom of a porch collapse. Wiping the sweat from his forehead, he hopped to the ground and kicked at branches until he found a sturdy one that might reach. Bracing himself in the doorway he doused beneath the sofa for his billfold, snagged it as soon as it was within reach, and clutched it.

Only slightly damp from the humidity of the storm, his life was intact. His cash was still there, as were his bank and credit cards. His school ID and his license were there. He even still had one of his father's old business cards. It was scratched and greyed, the corners rounded by years of wear. There was no real reason to have it anymore. He hadn't taken it out in years except to shuffle things around. The only reason he started carrying it all was to prove to people that he really was the son of the great, beloved Stuart Dolan Sr.

Balling it in his fist, he threw it into the muddy pool, hopped in the Subaru, and let the engine idle settle while he called the bank and canceled his new card.

Parking his car in front of the post office, he couldn't help but notice how much more life there was downtown. A young couple left the bakery holding hands, nodding to him as they passed, and he recognized the woman from the bar. Two women stepped out of the hardware store and shared a quick embrace and gentle kiss. A few doors down, an older man swept leaves from his doorway, the metered scrap of the broom's bristles echoing off the town's brick walls.

It had a life to it, a heartbeat he found familiar, and as he climbed the stairs, for the first time in a while, he ached to write, to open the gates and let the words flow. They streamed from his pen as he sat at the table, surrounded by the warbled panes of his old notebook scribbles, flying onto the back of orange and hot pink flyers that promoted last summer's elementary reading challenge. Brushing away the occasional muffin crumb, Stuart found his way to Arthur.

* * *

Arthur's knees weren't his best feature. The years had taken them along with everything else that had been good. The grimace on his face as he lowered himself from his truck accounted for all of it. If he could go back and warn his thirtysomething self that Maine wouldn't be the best place to live once arthritis settled in…who was he kidding? It wouldn't even have been near the middle of his list of regrets.

His feet landed on the Main Street curb outside the hardware store. Inside, behind the counter, sat Clara.

"You need any help finding things, Arthur?" she asked, peering over the top of a magazine.

"I would if you ever moved anything," he barked back. Passing cans of paint

and a display of colors in a disgruntled rainbow, he muttered to himself. "Half this stuff is older than me."

He grabbed a spool of ten-gauge wire and a little tube of dielectric grease. Throwing them down on the counter, he listed to the left, digging his wallet from his pocket.

"They say carrying around a big wallet can be hard on your back. Sitting on it all day. Course I'm too poor to know what that's like." Clara smiled, forever amused by her own self-deprecating stabs at humor.

"I wouldn't know either, Clara." He held out his hand, waiting for his change.

She counted the coins as if they were foreign. "That tube looks older than this town. You sure it's not expired?"

He clutched the yellowing silver tube. "Never expires. It's grease."

"You want a bag?"

Already at the door, he declined with a grunt. Back at the truck, he tossed the spool of wire on the dash and took the corners slowly so he wouldn't lose it beneath the seats, the tube of grease warming in his left hand. The last time he held a tube like that, television shows were filmed for square televisions, most of the good shows were in black and white. You couldn't see most of them in Europe, though. Not the good American stuff. He'd still been driving that old Citroën, volleying between cities and taking orders from his racing boss. Last time he held that little silver tube with the crimped end, he'd grabbed it off a table and tossed it to a guy on his pit crew. There'd been mere seconds to spare before the lineup. Before the lights went green. Before his career ended. Before his life took a spin and he hit the wall.

A lot of things had changed since he last held a tube of that grease.

Sitting at the turning circle at the park, waiting on traffic to clear, it all came back to him. The pat on the back. Hopping into the race seat, settling in.

"It's all fixed now." Greg slapped him on the helmet and adjusted the collar of his race engineer jacket. "Don't get too punchy out there. We need this car to last. I'm warning you."

Then the light went green, and he raced down the straight. He picked up four positions going into the first turn, but he lost traction and spun. Green and blue, green and blue, the world swirled by like one of those carnival rides where the floor falls out, but you stick to the wall. It wasn't his first time or his hundredth. He hummed the chorus of "Can't Buy Me Love" while he waited for the spin to stop. It had been stuck in his head since that bar in Paris the week before. Since she sat on his lap and risked blowing their cover. The force of the whirl pushed him back in his seat.

And crash. The car hit the barrier at the front right corner, shearing off the nose. He slammed his eyes shut at the impact, an indulgent instinct against the flying debris. He got used to the sound of the smash years before. He'd walked unscorched through enough fires not to fear them. None of this would give him nightmares. Not like it did the first few times. He didn't want to hear what the peanut gallery in the pit crew had to say, though. They got all twitchy when they had to make big repairs.

He wiggled his toes as the car shimmed and shuttered, hissing and spitting.

It would be a long walk back to the pits from where his car came to a stop. At least he'd be able to steal a few moments alone with her. Run his hands through her hair as he dove between her lips. She always smelled like fruit and perfumy shampoo. They'd find a spot, behind a wall, in a corner, a locked car at the back of the lot. Anywhere he could get lost in her smell.

Smoke.

He brushed debris from his arms and shoulders, yanked at the steering wheel to *free himself from the collapse. Arms lifted him to his feet, and he scrambled to find his footing, stumbling and tripping over a car body part in the thick black smoke. He stubbed his toe. Men rushed the other way, pointing canisters into the fire, whooshing foam at the inferno that helixed into the sky. Greg would be pissed.*

Hands pulled at him, yelled at him, as if he could hear over the roar and the helmet over his ears.

Ambulance.

The hospital had been far worse than the crash. Always was, but this time was different. A quick system check when he woke in the brightness told him his leg had been broken. Stiff white cast was still hardening at his knee. His hands hurt like hell, nerves screaming at the burns, wrapped in gauze. Some guy in a lab coat shoved a needle in a tube, said it could have been worse in a Southern American drawl. Worse for the hospital, maybe. Worse for his leg. Not worse for his career. The fact that no one waited in the corner told him all he needed to know about his status with the team.

"I thought I was in Germany."

"We're both in Germany," the lab coat said as he left the room. He bumped into a woman on his way out. Not just any woman. Her.

"It's August. Hot as shit. What are you wearing?" His voice cracked, emerging from his anesthetic haze.

Bundled up against weather that hadn't hit the country since the last ice age, she fell into the chair.

"Huh? Why are you wearing that?"

She fell into the chair at his side and unfurled a winter scarf. "I did not want to be seen," she said in her thick French accent, cutting off the end of each word in a delicate termination.

"You shouldn't be here. At all. You should go back to Lucien before someone finds you here."

"That's why the outfit." She pulled gloves from her hands.

"This is the best you could come up with to keep from drawing attention to yourself?"

She swatted him, playful. "Silly. You do not evade by hiding. You make it impossible for them not to see you. Then you convince them they saw something different."

The raw nerves of his hand sent fire up his arm. He couldn't touch her or clench a fist. Both seemed utterly necessary and thoroughly impossible. He turned to the window where a setting sun blazed the sky.

"You need to go," he said. "You have to go back to him. I mean it."

"He thinks I am looking for coffee. We have a little time."

"I mean forever, Aveline. We have to do the right thing. Lucien is my best friend. He's your husband. This isn't right."

Tears welled in her eyes. "You destroy me. I will not. You love me. You say so all the time. You are my true love, and it is too late to take it back."

"I'm serious. This is over. Now. He can't ever know."

"No. It is too late. You sleep. I see you in the morning. You save the fight for your leg."

She patted his arm, and he accepted the comfort.

When morning came, she was at his side again, in another garish outfit twice her size. She was nothing if not a force of nature, this graceful thing in an obstinate world. She was a polemic against indifference, rushing into every scene demanding it bend to her dramatic will. A certain amount of his resistance would be futile, but the effort must stand as a testament to his needs. Lucien was the better driver, not for want of speed or ambition, but for consistent waving of his driving flag. Arthur could no longer live this fast life. Losing this seat would mean losing his place at the table. Aveline was distraction and disruption. She would also mean disaster for the only true friendship he'd ever know. Lucien deserved better from both of them.

She pulled a folded newspaper section from a mysterious inner pocket and held it up. The headline was in German. "I read to you, yes? It is morning paper. It says Lucien's wife has left him for his teammate, Arthur. It says she is by her lover's side, having chosen between her two great loves."

"This is a terrible joke, Aveline." He tried to push himself up in the bed, but his hands were useless.

"Is not a joke. I revealed it to that paparazzi man who puts down his camera when I ask. He shows kindness, I give him the gift of story. See?"

"See? What am I supposed to see?"

"Is on the televisions. Everywhere. Around the world."

His mouth went dry. He couldn't even hold a cup. He motioned, and she held the straw up to his lips.

"I do it so Lucien is the good guy. He is victim."

Arthur threw back his head and swallowed hard to make room in his mouth for the words. "You victimized Lucien, made me the bad guy, and put this completely fake story into the news for what? Why? I told you last night that this is over between us. Now you've destroyed him and your marriage, and what's the point?"

A nurse poked her head in at the rise in his voice. She left with the wave of Arthur's hand.

"I choose. I choose you."

"You don't get to choose, honey. You chose when you married Lucien. Period.

This is over."

"I do anything to keep you. You are lucky. Many ways lucky."

His lungs still ached from the smoke, but he filled them anyway, letting out a sigh that should have relieved his ache. "The lab coat from North Carolina said as much. But that doesn't mean you have to take a match to the whole world just because I got lucky."

She leaned in, eyes stern. She looked harsher than the German nurses. "You hear me. You lost your contract. Too many risks you take all the time. The team signed someone else for next year already. Days ago. They do not tell you yet. You're such a bullfrog of a man."

"Bulldog."

"That, too. This has nothing to do with this wreck. You do not listen."

"They can't fire me because I take risks. That's how you win. And this wasn't a risk. I didn't cause this wreck."

"The crash was electric. Something caught fire, and the fire spread and breaked up the car. Then you spun and crashed."

"I'm not being blamed for the wreck? Publicly?" That might mean the difference between finding another racing seat at some other fledgling team or filling out job applications at a lumberyard in some Midwest town.

"No. They admit it to the press. They had no choice when investigation showed the electric problem. You never should have climbed in that car."

"I pushed them to finish it. I wanted to get out there."

"It wasn't ready. Of course, they put you out on track no matter what. They're poor. They must race. And they can't afford to have someone reckless even if they win." She leaned in and grasped his arm. "They can't afford to keep the car on the track, and you keep wrecking it. That's why you need me. To make you healthy

again and grounded. You need my money to live on until they fix you upper."

She was right about the need. He could deny himself of her for the rest of his life, but he would still need her. As for the money, he'd make his own way. She wasn't the only source of cash in the world, even if hers was old money inherited that neither of them would have to work to keep.

Some cognitive shift must have passed over his face, because she jumped on it, the broad smile that said she'd come up with the perfect plan for mischief, the kind that would leave him tingling for days.

"It will be beautiful," she said. "We buy a cabin somewhere, a beautiful place. You rest. I sing you to sleep and cook you the best foods. You need me. You know you do."

The hand she gripped him with had no ring. She'd given up her marriage for him, the high-flying lifestyle of a European heiress who grew up in a castle so cold it bore no resemblance to his suburban postwar American delight. She often whispered about running away from it all, her soft tongue teasing his ear as they snaked together in the bench seat of whatever car the team set Lucien up with. Arthur knew all along the chills she sent down his wires were borrowed and belonged to another man, but she gave them freely, and he charged back in for more. Her musings were just that. Her dreams were her style of talking dirty. He'd never taken her seriously.

"Dammit. What is wrong with you, woman? You know I lost my seat. Now I'm the scourge of the racing world, and I lost my best friend. Do you know how much harder it will be for me to find another drive?"

"Maybe you find one and maybe you don't. But I believe in you no matter what. You need to heal first. You can't heal while sleeping on couches and partying across the continent. You need a home."

Hot pain seared up his leg when he shifted to face her. He wanted to grab her by the shoulders, demand she undo what she'd done, but the inferno within him was lit for her, and putting it out would mean facing the future cold and alone. He'd barely allowed himself to accept that feelings had come to him, that they'd landed on him like innocent seeds in a spring garden, and while he was denying himself the security of settling down, racing between pubs and clubs, his eye for women had settled on her. She knew him better than he knew himself, and he couldn't lie to her or to himself. He'd sabotaged everything good in his life but her, and here she was begging him to hold on, to give in.

"Where will we go?" he asked.

The eyes blinking back at him were steady. "The team is paying for your care here. The doctor says you can go home in two days. I will go to London today and rent a loft. I'll send for my things."

"My stuff is at the hotel."

"I'll take it to London, and I'll come back for you. We take a train."

"If we find a place in London, I'd be close enough to a bunch of the race teams. I could heal up. Find a seat."

"We will be a family. You and me."

"I have to race." He couldn't let the possibility of walking away leak in. He couldn't give it light. But he could tell from the look on her face that she had considered it. Whether she was banking on it or not was a question for another day.

"Every time you were at a track, you were wishing it was a different one. There was always something wrong. Wrong track, wrong suit, wrong seat. Helmet visor was wrong. You've been in the wrong place your whole life, Arthur. Searching for something else. Someday, love, you will find it. I will help you. Even if it isn't me."

But it had been her.

It had been her since the moment they met, since she fluttered her eyelashes over her drink and took long, slow drags off those slender cigarettes. Since the tips of her fingers caressed the cut glass of her aperitif and every fiber of his being begged, ached to take its place.

It wasn't just the drugs that made him loopy that morning in a German hospital. It had been her. All the way from London to the gingerbread cottage near the Cliffs of Dover then to Maine, spur of the moment. They'd sold it all and hopped on a plane, took a train to the edge of the country. She got her green card, and they bought old cars, tinkering with them in the garage as if she could turn back the gears for him on those days. She wore oil cloth coveralls and full makeup, dash of perfume behind each ear.

He could still smell her sometimes in that garage.

Arthur yanked the parking brake, and the truck rocked into its spot in the driveway. He grabbed the spool of wire off the dash and tossed the tube of grease to Noah who sat obedient on the wheelie stool.

"Clara has everything doesn't she?" The young boy beamed up at him.

"Just about." He crimped a connector on the end of the wire and held it out to the boy. "Put a dab of grease in there. Go ahead. Just a little."

"What was it like to drive really fast, Mr. Arthur?"

He dove beneath the hood of the car for the stray wire that had shorted out. It had rested against the exhaust, getting too hot and wearing through. He cut out the bad part with a pair of wire cutters.

"Driving that fast is a lot like sitting still."

Noah shook his head. "Is it just colors whizzing around?"

"Something like that. You stop seeing the world whizz by, and you only see the road you're headed to."

"Why'd you stop racing? Mom says you got tired."

Retired was more like it. Against his will. He held out a hand and took the wire from Noah, attaching the two ends.

"Life had its own plans. I don't have any regrets."

"Do you watch the races still?"

"Now I do. It's different than it was when I was young, though. I didn't watch for a long time. Sometimes you gotta take a break from the thing you love the most. Hand me that tube of grease, huh?"

CHAPTER TWENTY-THREE

The town moved past Marissa's bakery window, bikes and shoppers and people running errands. Stuart sat at a little table, his feet tucked under his bag of cleaned laundry. He bit a back leg off a sheep cookie and caught a crumb before it landed on the stack of fluorescent pink paper covered in the scribbles of his own shorthand. At least an hour had passed since he finished his outline, but he refused to check the time on his phone. The sun was only starting to cast long shadows on the street, and it was Wednesday. Mohl had no evening classes to teach, and he promised to read it over and give him his thoughts before bed. There was plenty of time to type it out and send it over, and being in the slipstream, scenes falling out of him onto the paper, was just too satisfying to step away from.

Things would change, of course, once the characters let him know who they were, as tensions unfolded between personalities. Nonetheless, the story arrived like a cannonball, blasting down the walls of his writer's block. The book seemed to have been there all along. His grandfather's blind addiction to anything greasy he could fit in his garage, muttering about grudges he'd harbored for years, played out in Arthur's hands. His grandmother's lifelong love affair with her tinkering husband, following him around, finishing his projects after he'd turned his back on them could be felt in Aveline's affections. Aveline was more than just Arthur's biggest fan and his cleanup crew, she was his salve.

Aveline's dream of a home in Maine had been a recurring one. Arthur caved when his hopes of signing with a European race team petered out. Riding in her slipstream, he agreed to a cabin in a rural town, intent on finding an American crew, but phone calls and letters were getting him nowhere, and her dream had become his nightmare.

He'd been holding in his resentment. As she flitted around him hanging curtains and fretting over where their dishes should go, it was becoming more obvious to him that he was little more than a green card, an American dream achievement for a European heiress who found his accent charming. God knows Lucien would never have brought her to the States. He made little jokes, trying to force her to admit it, but she'd run her hands through his hair, and all would be forgotten until the morning.

He spent his days growing wider on the porch, rocking in the chair she bought from the antique store across town. She'd finally noticed he wasn't in the room.

"Come inside and help me with the kitchen table." She hovered in the doorway, clutching closed the plaid shawl he'd bought her in Ireland. "It is too cold out here for sitting, no?"

Eyes fixed on the neighbor's garage door, he balked. "It's fine. It's nice out. You don't need my help with that."

She closed the door behind her and sat on the porch step, drawing her knees up tight. "So many changes so soon. Do you hear back from that New York man?"

"Did I. I did hear back from him. They're fostering younger talent, he says."

"Someone will——"

He pushed to his feet, and the chair slammed against the siding. Aveline jumped and snuggled deeper in her shawl.

"No one will, Ave. It's over. I've been turned down by everyone. Our phone bill is through the roof, I'm stuck in this insane town at the end of a road to nowhere, and none of this had anything to do with me. This is all yours. And don't make that face."

"What face?"

"That face. That one." He scrunched up his face and wrinkled his nose. "You got everything you wanted out of this deal. You got your cozy little house in Maine and your American trophy husband, and I have nothing. Absolutely nothing."

"Trophy husband? You think this makes me the envy of my friends?"

"That's what all of this is about, isn't it? I was the one making the headlines. Lucien got boring and soft."

She stood toe-to-toe with him, her eyes fierce. "Lucien did not love me anymore, and I hadn't loved him since the minute I met you. You know this is true. I did not trap you."

"I never said you did."

She stomped a bare foot, and the rocker wobbled. "You implored it."

"Implied. I implied it."

"I said that. You lost one passion. One. But you still have me. If I am not passion for you anymore, you just need to say so."

The chill in her defiance doused his fire. He reached for her, but she pulled away.

"This is not the end, Arthur." The way she said his name, with a hard t, *sent chills down his spine. How could he be so harsh to her? "You are upset. Paranoid. You lose your purpose. But this is a beginning."*

She pulled a magazine from the back pocket of her jeans and pushed it into his hands. It was open, the pages curled back, and she'd circled an ad for an old Citroën.

"What's this? A 2CV? I can't race this."

Her hands were cold on his cheeks. She pulled his face down to hers and peered into his eyes. "You silly man. This is not for racing. It's for buying. For fixing. Healing takes work, not sitting out here like you do, staring at the sky. We go in the garage, and we fix the car, no? You call this number. You buy this car. Then you fix it."

Aveline spun on her heel, the shawl furling around her hips, and she opened the door and stepped inside.

"This is lovely and all, and it's nice of you to think of it," he said. "But you don't know the first thing about fixing old cars."

"I don't need to know. But I'll have fun all the same."

Marissa poured coffee into Stuart's empty cup. "I hate to interrupt you, but I'm dying to know how it's going. You've been sucking down coffee for four hours, and I'm starting to worry about your kidneys."

Stuart blinked up at her, his eyes adjusting to the pastel walls after staring so long at the neon paper. "Are you closing soon?"

"No." She rested the carafe on her open palm. "I'm here until seven. It's going well, I guess?"

He stacked the pages. There must have been twenty of them covered in tiny print meant to conserve paper. "The outline's done.

I'm just writing scenes now. Did you say four hours? Is it that late?"

She craned her neck to check a clock that hung above the kitchen door. "It's just after five, yeah."

He wrapped the last of his cookie in a napkin and pulled his papers into a pile. "Crap. I gotta get this typed up. Marissa, this is the best cookie I think I've ever had. I'll take two more, to go. And do you have any sandwiches left?"

She squinted and inspected the cabinet. "Chicken salad on rye."

"I'll take that too. And are you sure I can't pay you for doing the laundry?"

"No way. You'd deprive me of my apology."

"Well, it's very nice of you. Above and beyond for a stranger."

"Not worth worrying about. I'd want someone to do the same for me." She carried the coffee pot back behind the counter, Stuart on her heels. She dropped two cookies into a bag and ran his card through the machine. "How does it become a book from here, that thing you're writing?"

He tucked his card back in his wallet. "I have to finish writing it and edit it a hundred times. Then ask a bunch of agents if they're interested. It's a long process with a lot of rejection. It might never become a book, or it might take years, but I'm enjoying writing it. Tell you what. I'll name a character after you."

She beamed and handed him the receipt and his bag. "That would be the nicest thing anyone passing through this town has done for me. I had a friend once I met on the internet. He wrote a book. Said it was the hardest thing he ever did. You're making it look easy."

"If only you'd seen the last few years." Stuart rushed to grab the trash bag that held his clothes. He folded the pages in half and held them tight. "No compromises this time. This is the one I want to write."

"What's it about? Too soon to ask?"

He paused with his hip on the door. It was the question every writer dreaded most. After so much work threading layers into the story, focusing on tiny details and rich symbolism, mashing the whole thing into one sentence seemed harder than writing the book itself. At least he wasn't in too deep yet and could see the forest for the trees.

He tightened his grip on the trash bag. "It has a lot of layers to it, but it's about a guy staring down his faults and regrets, redefining his life just when he thinks that it's over. That's the loudest theme right now."

"Well, I can't wait to read it," she said. "We'll all be saying we knew you when."

A blast of frigid air took his breath away when he pushed through the door.

He climbed the stairs to the tiny apartment above the post office and dropped the bag of laundry at the foot of the bed. Barely chewing large bites of the sandwich, urgency sizzled beneath his skin, and he itched to type his outline up and send it off. There had to be holes in his plot that he was too close to see, and the sooner he closed them up, the sooner he could finish the first draft. But a draft wasn't a book. A draft wouldn't please the dean. He wouldn't be able to coast along on his own good fortune and his father's name forever.

"No," he said, his mouth full of bitter rye bread. "Stop."

He couldn't let self-doubt and worry slide into the wake of his rapid writing slipstream. He had to stay in the zone. Rising to his feet, pacing the apartment, he pressed his forehead against the window's cool glass, shutting his eyes against the setting sun. He wouldn't give in to this. He had to keep moving.

Grabbing his notes and his phone, he locked the door, and raced down the stairs, pausing at the edge of the park.

To his right was the bar, where he could sit and type out his notes on his phone, send them to Mohl, and wait out his thoughts. To his left was the library, a place of diversion with worlds to explore and…Sandy. He should be setting aside the story for now, using his time to clean up other messes, figuring out what to say to Madison, to start, but he wasn't sure what he wanted. He was even less sure about what he needed in the long term. For now, he needed to stop putting his energy into his fears. Why couldn't he kick off his shoes just this once, celebrate the little achievements before they faded?

Turning right, he speed walked to the library, and pushed open the door breathless. Sandy jumped in her chair, tucking hair behind her ear. She painted on a smile.

The awkwardness of the moment hit Stuart like a brick wall. He had no plan, no clue what to say.

"Come to the bar with me."

"What?" She stood and turned her back on him, slipping into the library. He followed. She straightened magazines on the coffee table.

"I finished my outline. I'm really proud of it. I have to type it up, but I really wanted to celebrate. Come with me."

Her face blazing red, she turned from him again. "I can't, Stuart."

"Oh. You're busy. I'm sorry." He shook his head, searching for words. "I just barged in here."

"It's not that." Her ponytail swung when she faced him, determination and set in her jaw. "You don't live here. This may just be a vacation thing for you, being here and writing this book, and that's great, but I have to live here when you're gone."

"I didn't mean to—"

She put her hands in the back pockets of her jeans, her eyes wandering to some distant spot on the carpet beside him. "I'm not going to apologize for protecting my heart."

"I don't want you to." He stepped back into the doorway, inching his way out. "I'm the one who should be sorry. And I am."

A thick fog of silence rolled between them, cold and sobering.

"Hey." He put up his hands, inching backwards. "I don't want you to think I'm that guy, that this was some game to me."

"No, I don't think that. Not at all. I'm responsible for my own feelings here. I'm just…I have to get some work done, if you don't mind."

The creaking floor tolled out the distance between them as he stepped out onto the porch and pulled the door closed behind him. He paused there, the chicken salad and rye sitting sour in his stomach. Sandy was kind, but she was wrong. It had been a game to him, but not one he'd played with any intention. It would be cruel to go back, to explain it to her now, to tell her she was right, and he'd been an ass for projecting his wants onto her. He had been cruel all along, seeking comfort with her, giving into the sick machine in his brain that craved her soft validation, but it was time to put an end to the torture. He had to stop looking at the short term and find something on the horizon to aim for. It was time to sit down, to face the blank piece of paper, and craft a future that he wanted.

CHAPTER TWENTY-FOUR

Fluorescent paper rainbowed across the bar at Helen's Tavern. Typing on his phone had never been Stuart's strong suit, so huddling over the glow of his screen, pounding out a detailed outline without major typos gave him a strange satisfaction while making him yearn for a laptop that was probably under a pile of Edward's clothes by now.

Every time he pushed Sandy out of his mind, telling himself he'd apologized sufficiently, she popped back up again. Maybe the matter was closed for her, but his sins ran deeper than she knew, and he wouldn't be able to rest until he found absolution. He wasn't any better than Madison for his affair of the heart, and he owed it to her to sort this out even if she hadn't paid him the courtesy.

Self-flagellation wouldn't get the outline typed, though, so he shoved it aside, putting some final polish on his last chapter notes, and shooting it off in an email to Mohl, tapping his foot on the barstool to let off some nervous energy. Mohl was a friend, but he was also a talented writer, and there was no reason to expect less than a harsh critique. That's what he needed, to find the major flaws before they took over his whole life. For once.

He cracked his knuckles and chugged his lager, letting the empty glass land on the bar with a thud. Bracing himself, he sent Mohl a text letting him know the outline was in his email, and he leaned back, arms folded. Mohl sent a thumbs-up and said he'd get right on it.

It was like the first gas stop of a long road trip, finally setting off after weeks of planning and packing. But this time he had no home to return to.

The bartender snagged his glass and his attention.

"Another?" She cocked the glass at the taps.

"Please."

Some ten years his junior, she'd been behind the bar every time he visited, scampering between the office and the customers, but he'd only spoken to Helen.

"Your book's coming along then." She set the lager off to the side as he stacked his kaleidoscope of notes.

"You heard?"

"Of course. The whole town knows. Good luck with it."

By the time he set his notes aside and turned back to tell her the gist of his story, she was gone. There was no one to tell.

Fingers aching to dial Madison, he stopped himself before making the mistake of rushing into a phone call unprepared. She only cared about his stuff and how fast he could clear it out. An argument was unavoidable and always had been with her. If she wasn't tearing down his enthusiasm with bleak observations, she was rerouting him to unmet obligations and peppering her phrases with *shoulds* and *would haves.* But she was all he had. For years she'd been the first one he called. Nothing felt real until he told her. Never mind the fact that she always chewed up and spit out anything in his life that was irrelevant to her.

Never again.

He swore it would be the last time as soon as he pressed the call button. She would knock him down, and he would get back up, but she wouldn't bruise him this time. He'd been lonely for so long with her, even without having a name for the ache, that he wouldn't allow it to persist a day more. He knew what she was to him now, what he'd been to her. And not one bit of the adhesive from those old labels would be allowed to stick once he'd scrubbed himself clean of her.

He tapped his foot while the phone rang.

"Hello?" She was someplace noisy.

"I did it. I'm finished."

The old man across the bar scowled at him and ducked back behind his newspaper. Stuart vowed that before he left Ramsbolt, he'd find a way to study that guy's every move.

"What does that mean, you're finished?"

"It means what it means," he whispered into the phone. "I wrote the outline."

A man's voice punctured the background. It had to be Edward's. Stuart cringed and backed away from the phone. He didn't want Madison; he just objected to someone else taking his place while the seat was still warm. It was a violation of an unspoken code, an audacity from a man who made every excuse not to be in a room with him. The guy couldn't look him in the eye. A little ache in his chest sought to remind him that he could have done the same with Sandy if given the chance, but *could have* was miles away from the fact that he hadn't. Madison, however, had, and she admitted it.

Another brush of laughter came through the phone. It wasn't the typical kitchen sound.

"Where are you?" he asked.

"At work." It was a lie. He could hear her moving around, the scene behind her growing more distant and quieter. She closed a door and the sound dropped out. "Are you coming back? We have to divide up this stuff."

She didn't even hint at congratulations. At least she wasn't insulting. "Not yet. I can't head back just yet. I'm going to finish out the month here, try to get as much of a first draft down as I can, and I still have some unfinished business."

There wasn't much left to do in Ramsbolt, except to thank Warren for his hospitality and deliver the books back to Sandy and explain himself. He still hadn't told her about Madison, and she deserved to know the truth. She'd done him a favor by brushing him off and pushing him away, and she didn't deserve to be his diversion. Rather, she deserved to be thanked and to hear the truth. He had to come clean.

In Philly, however, there was enough unfinished business to keep him busy for a year. He didn't belong there, though. He needed to be in Ramsbolt with his book, taking care of his own wants and needs for once. With some coffee, he could easily head back home with an entire draft in his pocket.

"Madison, I have to tell you something, though."

She huffed through the phone. "Yeah, well, you have obligations here, too. I want to work this out."

A tall guy in a knit cap dragged a stool up to the bar and sat a few seats away. The bartender gushed over him. Stuart plugged one ear. There's no way he heard Madison right.

"You what?"

"I just...I made a mistake."

Silence swelled the ground between them. There was nothing but the chiseled edge of cold stone, a divide neither could cross if they wanted to. What had been was gone, and nothing would follow. She had to know that. For too long he'd let her control his emotions, steering their relationship without regard to his feelings. She'd pushed him aside to make room for Edward and now she wanted what? To keep both of them?

"No," he said. "You may have changed your mind, but you didn't make a mistake. You were right. This is over."

"You have obligations to me." Her voice was pleading.

"Oh, I do have obligations there, but not the way you think. I have textbooks there, coursework notes. My laptop. I need my stuff, Madison."

All of that stuff could be replaced. If he never saw his old sneakers again or all those old paperbacks, he wouldn't really miss them. His real obligation was to the guy he'd be on the other side of all this. He owed it to himself to draw an emotional curtain over the whole chapter of his life. He deserved a great new start.

"I need to find an apartment, too. When I get back, I'll stay with Mohl or something."

Her tide turned to anger. "You have to set a date, Stuart. You can't just show up here whenever you want."

"It's still my home. For now."

"Not really. You aren't *living* here. Your stuff is here. There's a difference. You can't breeze in here and start packing without talking to me first."

"What do you mean I'm not living there? I am for now. Is Edward afraid I'll take your television? I guess he's already walking around and taking stock of what I'll leave behind, huh? Has he staked a claim on any of my records? And before you get ahead of yourself, don't even think you can manipulate me into being your toy on the side. At least treat Edward with the respect you didn't show me."

"Don't do this." She rolled her words at him like an exasperated mother. "It's selfish."

"Oh, well, now that you mention it, I guess it was kind of selfish of me to plan this whole trip to Maine just so you could shack up with your Easy Bake boyfriend. Oh, wait. No. It was you who planned this whole thing to get me out of the way."

"Now you're just being mean."

"Am I? I'm the one being mean?" Maybe he was. "I don't have a lot of experience fighting with you, Madison. You're the one who always picks the fights. So, this is what being mean feels like?" He leaned back in his bar stool. The bartender flirted with the guy next to him. Further down the bar, the old man scowled around his newspaper. Stuart didn't care about any of them.

"I think I like the feeling of being mean. If I recall correctly, you found this place, put a nonrefundable deposit on it, and made it sound like a vacation. Then, as soon as we got here, you went running back home to Edward, leaving me a note in the car to end a relationship you hadn't been in for a very long time. Then you change your mind. It feels a lot like a professional hit to me, and if I were a betting man, I would say you planned the whole thing. It was all your idea."

The sputter of a laugh came through the phone. "Not how it happened but whatever. Now it's my idea for you to come back to Philly and clean up the mess, since you obviously won't think of it on your own."

He wanted it over. He wanted to fast forward the whole thing, past the anger and finding a new place and moving his stuff and get straight to the distant day on the horizon when he saw her on the street and didn't even recognize her. Rushing home now would be giving in again. It would mean putting his fate in her hands one more time. How many times had he been close to a story and she crushed it out of him with a snide remark or a snorted laugh? How many times had he been energized by an idea and she smashed it flat? He'd put so much weight on what she thought and so much belief in her ability to know what was good for him that he forgot to see it in himself. He forgot that she wasn't in charge.

He wanted to say he'd be home tomorrow, but instead he said, "No."

"What do you mean, no?"

"No. I'm not rushing back there. Period. I want to stay here to finish this draft. I need to see the door close on whatever this is between us. I want us to have a peaceful conclusion, and that won't happen today. I'll be back to get my stuff. I'll give you a ring when I'm on my way so you can make sure the door is unlocked. But it won't be today, and it'll be on my terms."

He ended the call before she finished her syllable and returned the angry glare of the man in the corner.

Helen was on him like white on rice, wiping the bar beneath his drink. "I couldn't help overhearing that."

"I don't guess anyone could."

"Good for you," she said. "Figuring it out like that. Sounds like a lot of things have unraveled for you in a good way lately."

"I won't miss that relationship." He downed the remainder of his beer. "Who am I kidding? I will for a while. Just the usual closing of a chapter. Once I stop feeling sorry for myself, I'll be fine."

"Of course, you will." She opened a cooler door and counted bottle caps. "I like to crochet. I make a lot of mistakes. Sometimes I have to pull it all out and start over. It's important to keep trying until you get it right. The yarn is worth a lot when it's a comfy scarf."

He tilted his empty glass at her. "As a writer, I applaud that."

Stuart's phone buzzed and a notification lit up his screen. It was Mohl. The first paragraph was fluff about work and the girl he'd been flirting with from the coffee shop.

But this book! THIS is the book you should have been writing all along. I made a few notes in the middle, just small stuff. This is great. Send me the draft asap! Can't wait!

Helen put another beer in front of him, and he slid a five from his wallet across the bar.

"Keep the change."

CHAPTER TWENTY-FIVE

Stuart locked himself in the apartment for nine sunsets and ten sunrises. He cranked out three chapters each day, except for the day that he wrote four. Breaks were spent at the bakery, staring out the window at the pet shop across the street, eating one of everything Marissa baked and gorging himself on chicken salad on everything bagels. People strolled by with bags of groceries, and for a fleeting few days, he felt like a part of it. From his chair behind the pane of glass, he observed the town much like a visitor at a zoo, but the town was hardly a spectacle to behold. It was more like a mirror with each passing day. He saw himself in the town, in the coming and going, the routine of life, and the calm of a morning walk.

On his last evening in the little apartment, he sat at the tiny table with the hardcover sketchbook he'd bought at Warren's shop to crank out the last chapter of his book. He rarely drank when he wrote, but he treated himself to a six-pack of beer for the occasion.

As sunlight narrowed itself into a golden wedge on the tan carpet, Stuart paused, his pen above the paper, to take in the details. He wouldn't miss the hard mattress on which he'd spent some sleepless nights, but he had a soft spot for the corner kitchenette where he made sandwiches and drank tea straight from the jug. Of all the places he could have stranded himself to write a book, this one turned out pretty great.

Arthur counted out the wad of cash. Six hundred bucks, just like the guy said. He stood back and watched as the old blue Gremlin got loaded onto the flatbed trailer, creaking and groaning on its rusty suspension.

"Can't blame it for complaining." Arthur put the envelope in his back pocket. "I don't like to move much myself anymore."

The guy nodded and gave him a polite smile, the kind that said he had no use for old men. If only guys his age knew what they'd become and how much they'd lose to get there.

He was about to turn back to the house when Noah's Jeep rounded the corner. Arthur rested his bones against the garage door while he did the math. If it was March, it was The Mother's birthday. He returned Noah's wave and kicked mulch from the driveway back to the neglected flower bed where it belonged.

At twenty-five, Noah was tall. Taller than Arthur had been at that age. He lived in some noisy town a few hours away with his girlfriend and a loud, fast life. They always connected when Noah came back to town, but the kid liked his email and his computer things, and Arthur wasn't going to become a robot at the age of eighty-five. He preferred mailing letters despite the low response rate, but the kid had to make his own way, and nobody had time for paper and pens anymore. Arthur wrote anyway. The short walk to the mailbox was good for him.

"I got your letter." Noah stomped over the last mounds of melting snow that

separated the driveways. "Gosh, it seems like every time I come here, the place gets smaller."

"I'm shrinking, boy. I'm a thousand years old. My bones are decomposing faster than my fat."

Noah's eyes were glued on the Gremlin. "I loved that car. We worked on that when I was a kid."

"You changed the starter yourself. You were in middle school."

"Where's it going? What happened to the Nova?"

Pushing his loaf of a frame away from the garage door took more effort than Arthur wanted to admit. He steadied himself on Noah's arm without asking and pressed the code that opened the door. It rumbled and rattled, the world's worst theatre curtain opening to display Arthur's garage of discontent.

"Where is everything?" Noah stepped inside and spun. "The tools."

"You said you didn't want them. I asked last time you were here. You said you didn't want it."

Running his hand through his hair, Noah inspected the workbench. "You're getting rid of everything. You're saying goodbye to things. I'm not ready for this."

"It's been going on for a while. I wrote you letters."

"I read them. I know. But you've only got two cars left."

"One, I'm keeping. I ain't selling the Citroën. No matter what. I don't need all this stuff anymore."

"If it's money, we'll figure it out. I got a raise. I can—"

Arthur grabbed his arm and turned him around. "Listen. Listen to me. It's not money. I got plenty. Come inside."

Noah followed him down the hall. Arthur kept pausing, looking over his shoulder like a cat guiding its owner to an empty bowl. "The town don't want all that mess out there anymore. I don't want it either, to be honest. When I'm gone, there won't be anybody to clean all this up."

"There's me. And mom."

"You're mom's almost sixty years old. She doesn't need to be cleaning up after some senile old man next door. She raised her kid." They were never that close, anyway.

"So…what? You're just selling everything."

Arthur paused outside a guest room door. Not many people had visited them over the years. Aveline's sister had stayed for a month back in the early 2000s when her French chateau was being restored. But mostly the bed gave the illusion of company that some days was a comfort and on others a reminder of the isolation. It was wasted space.

"I'm glad you stopped by." He flung open the door and patted Noah's back until he shuffled inside. "Nobody else would want this stuff, son. Take what you want, and I'll throw the rest away. I asked around. Some of it has some value. The trophies and maybe that suit. That ain't all the trophies. Most are in some room in Europe."

Aveline would have his head for plopping that cardboard box on the comforter. Dust bunnies clung to the corners, and some old grease stain saturated one side. Metal flames and crystal bowls stacked in the box.

Noah touched the edge of the box, leaning over it. "You're just giving away your trophies?"

"I'm letting them live on."

"There's a helmet in there."

"I know." Arthur's hip told him to sit, so he wiggled himself onto the chair by the window.

"I've never seen this stuff before. You never talk about it."

"It was in the closet there. And under the bed. Took me a damn day to get them out." Arthur pointed a twig of a finger at a white dress box with a cellophane lid. "That's the suit I was wearing. Ave put it in a wedding dress box. Stupid thing to save, but there it is."

Noah asked to open the box with a lingering plea in his eyes. Arthur nodded.

The smell of the char had faded years ago, but the singe was there on the sleeves and shoulders. He could still feel the crinkle of fabric against his hips when he walked, how tall he felt when he wore it. It had never been a second skin. The comfort some drivers felt had never been his to enjoy. It was a work suit, the last he ever wore.

"It's yours now. I don't care what you do with it. Take it down to the curb for all I care." He listed to the side, pushing the closet door open. It scraped against the high-pile carpet that never wore down like the rest of the house. "More stuff in there. That fluffy coat. That stays until I'm gone."

"Aveline's?" Noah lifted a sleeve, held it like a kitten in one hand and stroked it with the other.

"It's a memory. There's a newspaper in the pocket. Don't mess it up."

Noah bent to squint at it. "It's in German."

"It's from the day she decided I was worth her time."

The stoic set of the boy's jaw gave away the grief. Arthur remembered well his grandfather's last years in that Baltimore row house. It was hard to take seriously the flashes of remorse, the endless stream of things not done, repairs not made. Propped in his chair, gripping glasses of unsweetened tea with a strong hand, his claims flung like curses that his days were ending, and Arthur better decide soon what would go and what he'd keep.

"I've been around the block. I know half the time you don't believe me and the other half you wish you didn't. I'm eighty-five years old. My clock is ticking pretty fast." Arthur *wiggled his foot in his shoe, testing his joints before pushing to his feet.* *"All this garbage is one of two things: crap I want out of here and crap that stays until I'm gone. I'm giving you the chance to pick before I start filling the cans each week."*

His shoe caught on the carpet, and he tumbled forward, arm flailing for the door. Noah caught him before he fell.

Stuart's cell phone rang. Arm extended, reaching across the table to silence it, he accepted it instead. His mother didn't call that often, and he didn't call her enough.

"Happy birthday, early," he said.

"I got your flowers." Her voice was flat.

"What's up?" Gritting his teeth, he cringed. Deep in the zone of his last chapter, the last thing he wanted was an emotional sidebar rehashing his failed relationship with his father.

"Stu has been…Your father is very upset."

"I really don't want to talk about this right now."

Her voice shot up. "Well, you should have taken care of it a long time ago. A lot of things should have been said a very, *very* long time ago."

Stuart stood, scraping his chair against the worn linoleum, and paced the sagging floor of the kitchenette. "What was I supposed to say? He holds me to impossible standards, he withholds affection, demands I fawn on him in order to get his approval. It took me three decades to realize that I don't have to seek permission for living my own life."

She sighed deep. "Maybe sometimes you were hard on your father, and maybe things could have been said differently, but I mean us. Your father and me. We should have told you some things a long time ago."

"Like what?" The sound dropped out of the room, and his mouth went dry. His heart knew.

"Honey, your father was gone a lot."

"Stop. Don't start with excuses."

"It's the truth. He had someone else, too. But after you were born, everything changed."

"You've had almost four decades to tell me this. And you choose to do it while I'm in Maine trying to write a book. I have to drive home tomorrow." He stopped at the chair, lightheaded and sight white, like sun glaring off a field of snow. Everything seemed to dissolve—the kitchen, the rough wood of the chair back where he knew the paint was chipped and cracked, but his fingers couldn't feel it. The notebook, his pen, the world of Ramsbolt outside the window ceased to be.

"He's upset. I know it doesn't seem like it. He always defaults to anger. That's what he thinks strong means. But when he thinks you're not looking, the sadness is there. Every parent thinks they'll fail, Stuart. It's even harder when your brain is like his, when you see meaning in everything, and you're just like him. The whole world is a heightened experience for people like you. He was afraid that he couldn't raise you because you weren't his son. All he sees is the mistakes he's made. And he knows that he's made them."

"Stop." The word broke into four syllables, caught in his throat. "How many other lies?"

"We never lied." She pleaded. Whether it was forgiveness or to be believed, Stuart didn't care.

"You didn't tell me the truth either. What kid doesn't believe his parents are his parents? That's the default. Shit." The chair wobbled when he fell into it. Running his free hand through his hair, so many questions formed in the ether. His father gave up when he wanted to play catch. He never stayed for his T-ball games. They paid someone else to teach him to swim. He learned to shave by watching television. His mother was the one who taught him to drive. The day they dropped him off at college and his father...his mother's husband...asked him one last time if he was sure being a writer was what he wanted to do with his life.

"I gotta go. I can't listen to this."

"Stuart. Honey, believe me..."

"Oh, I believe you. I believe you cheated on my father, and he resented me for it. If I were his real son, my entire life might be different. I wouldn't need so much validation from people who never give it to me. I never would have bent for Madison until I broke."

"Are you and Madison..."

"Is that what you're taking away from this? That Madison and I are done? Jesus."

She gulped back air, and he was not going to hold her hand through this.

"I can't believe you did this. Why are you telling me like this?"

Her voice sounded small, scared. "There was never a good or a right time."

"So, you picked the worst one. I have work to do. I have to save my career. Maybe fit an existential crisis into my schedule this week. Happy birthday, Mom. Let me know when you get back from Cabo."

He ended the call and slammed the phone down on the table. Expletives escaped him, staccato reflections of the cannonade within. Sucking down the last half of his beer, he opened a new one and flipped through the pages of his scrawled-on sketchbook.

No wonder his father never wanted him to carry the name, that no matter how hard Stuart worked, he couldn't live up to family demands. No wonder the man wouldn't lend him support when he needed it the most. Tough love was just an illusion, a story the son of a bitch told himself to get out of stating the truth. That man put so many words together, so elegantly he was a classic before his time was due, and he couldn't bother to tell his own son the truth.

"It must take a lot of practice to lie so very well."

He swallowed a bitter sip and inspected the label. He hadn't recalled beer tasting so bad. The sudden urge to throw everything out the window gripped him. On knees that were surprisingly strong, he stood and leaned on the windowsill. The street below was empty. Stores were closing up for the evening. His last night in Ramsbolt would be uneventful. There was no way he was walking to the tavern now, not to celebrate a book he hadn't finished, but he gave himself a pass and considered his first draft done. It only needed a sentence or two anyway.

Slamming the cover closed, he packed it in the cardboard box along with the crunchy old notebooks that belonged to a man he never really knew.

Throwing on a sweatshirt, he locked the door and pounded down the stairs. Winter was coming early to Ramsbolt, and Stuart wouldn't be there to see it through, but as flurries swirled in the flickering yellow streetlight and landed in his eyelashes, he couldn't help but wonder what that town looked like covered in white. With all of its features stripped away and smothered in ice, would he even recognize it at all?

The park in the turning circle had two benches, and neither of them were in any condition for sitting, but he took his chances and sat on the one that faced the sailor statue. It peered at the horizon, one hand raised over his eyes, filtering out a sun that wasn't shining.

For Those Who Never Saw The Sea.

No statue or plaque had ever angered Stuart more. Hands balled into fists in the pockets of his sweatshirt, he clenched his jaw through the fury and the cold.

"What a dumb statue. Middle of nowhere with no water. Doesn't make a damn bit of sense."

Ice mixed in with the snow, pelting the statue and the sidewalk, taking over the ringing in his ears. A door closed down Main Street, and two women laughed, holding hands as they crossed the road, pausing for a kiss before slipping into the tea house. A group of men stepped out of the church, stomping their boots on the steps, testing their footing and groaning about the weather. Stuart shouldn't be able to hear it from this distance, but something about the brick buildings and the stillness of the night brought everything in closer. The entire town was like one organism, all of the people and parts working together like gears in a watch. Why couldn't he have that? Why couldn't he be a gear in some town, doing his job and being a part of things instead of constantly being on the outer edge, clinging on for dear life?

It would pass, the anger and the fear. The confusion over who he was and what his life would look like once he got home and cleared his stuff out of the home he shared with Madison. Someday all of this would look better, funny perhaps, a story he'd tell in pubs to people who thought they were having a bad few weeks. *Oh yeah*, he'd say. *Get a load of this shit.*

The man who raised him hadn't given him talent. If loves and fears were inherited, we'd all be the same. Everything he had and everything he was had been of his own doing and his own creation.

Kicking his feet out onto the brick walkway, snowflakes falling on his sneakers, he told himself that the truth didn't change anything. It was just a different hue of light, the same sun passing through panes of a stained glass window. Yesterday it was green. Today it's yellow. Tomorrow would be a different day.

* * *

Stuart loaded the Subaru with his laundry and box full of wrinkled old notebooks. Many of the pages were impossible to read, barely worth the room they took up in the car, but there was a time and a place for bidding farewell to old crutches, and this wasn't it. He'd know it when he saw it.

He made one last trip down the apartment stairs, locking the door as he went, and trudged through the frigid morning. Notebook in one hand, bottle of wine in the other, he slid two doors down to Marissa's and waved her up from the back of the shop. He held out the bottle of red.

"I know you won't accept any money for doing my laundry. I wanted to say thanks." He plopped the bottle on the counter. "I drove into Colby last night and got this for you. I hope it's good. I mean, I haven't had it."

She spun it around and looked at the label, smearing white powdered sugar on it that she wiped off with a cloth. "It's from Argentina. My parents were from Argentina."

"Nice coincidence. I know it's not much, I just wanted to say thanks. I named a character after you. A nice one. I promise."

She smiled and swatted him with the towel. "You're silly. I'm flattered. So, you're done?"

"Not quite. I have a first draft, and it's really solid. I'll do a few rounds of edits, but I feel good about this one."

She placed her hands on her hips, a genuine look of satisfaction widening her grin, and motioned to the display. "Can I send you home with anything? It's twenty-dollar-box day. Fill a box for twenty bucks."

He pulled his wallet from his pocket. "I'll take a whole box. On second thought, make it two. One won't make it back to Philadelphia."

Leaving the pastries in the car, he dodged boys on their bikes and pushed open the door to the newsstand. The bell rang out as it shut behind him.

Warren sat on a stool behind the counter, and the two older men held their daily court by the newspapers. They stepped aside to make room for him, eyeing him up with the same old suspicion. Warren must have noticed it, because he issued a rebuke in the form of a stern look.

"I brought you something." Stuart passed him the key and a bottle of whiskey. "I'm more of a scotch guy myself, but Helen said you're a whiskey guy, and she suggested this."

"Hey!" Warren beamed at the label. "This is my favorite. Thank you, man. So? You're done? Whole town's been waiting for an update. You're the most excitement we've had around here in a long time."

Sarcasm frizzled off the town hecklers, and Stuart straightened his shoulders. "I would hate to disappoint you. It could take years for anything to come of it, if anything happens at all. I cleaned the apartment for you. Thanks for letting me stay. And sorry about the cabin."

"Nothing to worry about." Warren set the bottle by the register. "Insurance will cover it. Should be done in the spring. You'll have to come back for a week on the house once it's done. We'd love to have you."

The two older men exchanged a furtive glance that Stuart caught anyway. With nothing to prove to the town's cheap seats, he could have easily let it go, but he was still riding in the slipstream of his win against Madison's will, his father's will, the dean's will, and what felt like the entire universe.

"Everything all right there?"

The taller, wider man hiked up his dark gray pants by the suspenders. "News around here is you ain't all right."

Warren rolled his eyes. "The two of you are something else. You read those damn papers cover to cover and never learn a damn thing. Stuart didn't do anything wrong."

"Says you." The shorter man seemed pleased with himself, grinning like a detective who'd finally cracked a case. "I didn't read anything about some guy coming into town, pretending to be something he's not. You FBI? CIA? What are you? Who are you after?"

It was Stuart's turn to roll his eyes, exchanging an amused glance with Warren.

Warren jabbed a thumb in their direction. "This town doesn't need a newspaper. It's got these two to make it up as they go along."

Stuart laughed. "Every town does." He stuck out his hand and shook Warren's. "I have one more stop to make before I head out of town. Just wanted to say thanks and hope to see you again."

He locked eyes with the shorter man for a brief moment before slipping out the door, slowing his step to enjoy the bell as the door closed behind him.

The street was dead but for small birds that hopped in and out of potholes and sifted through pebbles at the curb. A small flock took off as he approached his car and climbed in. He secured the remaining bottle of wine on the passenger seat, started the engine, and steered toward the library.

CHAPTER TWENTY-SIX

The library wouldn't open for another hour, but Sandy was in. The light was on, and her shadow passed by the windows, pulling her cart of books. Stuart's heart raced, his guilt getting the better of him. Was he stepping out of bounds by saying goodbye? He hadn't imagined the connection, however brief, but she regretted it enough to let him know. Weighing her regret against his, he cut the engine, grabbed the books and wine, and gave it a shot.

It was only a thank you gift, a simple bottle of wine to show appreciation for the hospitality and for lending an ear. Giving wine to a woman he liked still felt like a betrayal, though he owed nothing to Madison. Sandy deserved to hear the truth, a point driven home to him by his mother. Some lies were even more painful for their omission, and Sandy deserved better than that.

He paused at the book drop box, but the slot was too narrow for a bottle of wine and even if it were, given his luck, the bottle would smash and destroy all her books. Hardly the sentiment he wanted to express. No matter what would pass between them, at least he'd know the book drop was never really an option.

His sweaty hand slipped on the doorknob. It was locked.

Tapping at the door with his knuckles, part of him hoped she'd be in some back corner, too far to hear, saving him from the red-faced sputtering about how she helped him over a hurdle and how it was totally normal for some guy from out of town to thank a librarian with a bottle of wine and a lot of adolescent blushing. He tapped again and held a deep breath to calm his stomach, counting to ten. If he reached fifteen, he would drop the book in the box and head for Philly, keeping the wine for himself.

The door cracked open, and Sandy's expression went from stern objection to a slightly warmer welcome. She held the door open and waved him in.

"Books don't fit in the slot," she said.

"No. Neither does this wine." He held up the bottle twisted tight in a brown paper bag.

She nodded. "I haven't seen you for days. I thought my books were gone forever until I saw your car was still downtown."

He held out the books, owl up. "I was in hiding. Writing."

She ran her hand over the cover. "The poor book has been through a lot."

"So have I." He placed the bottle on her desk. It sat next to her reading tablet and her box of golf pencils. "I know it's silly, but I wanted to say thank you, and I'm sorry, and…a lot of things."

The way she stepped closer, open, the scent of her shampoo so close and getting stronger, his hand ached to grasp hers, and the need for closeness and comfort he'd deprived himself of for so long rolled and stirred within him. The air between them warmed, his knees weakened. His instinct said to step back and closer at the same time, a jumbled confusion of mixed messages between the need and the want, but a voice in his head belted out *unfinished business* in an unbroken tempo, a metered chorus.

He shoved his hands in his back pockets and tilted his head to the floor.

"That's nice of you," she said. "You're leaving?"

"Yeah. Just stopped by on my way out."

"I'll miss seeing you around town. Your book?"

"Finished. Well, the first draft is done." He could sense her nodding, though he only saw her sneakers, winter gray and sky blue with a broken stitch.

She shifted her weight. "I hope something comes of it. I look forward to reading it. Is it still about that race car driver?"

"Arthur. Yeah. I'll mail you two copies, one for you and one for the mantle in there."

She peeled away and stepped behind the desk. No library had ever been quieter. It seemed like every floorboard and book groaned under the weight of his silent need, and the walls constricted, threatening to snap his want into pieces. It wasn't a physical urgency, though he did ache for her nearness. It was an emotional poverty, a fear of insufficiency that he tried to brush off as the fodder of a breakup. But as she scanned the book back into circulation, the grace of her hands and the confidence of her movements denied him the hope that she'd be a ghost in his rearview mirror.

"Were the books any help?" She held it up before putting it on a cart with a slew of colorful children's books ripe for reshelving.

He opened his mouth to say that the library had been helpful. He wanted to say that it wasn't the book as much as the librarian, that she was a piece in his ill-fitting puzzle. That all along he'd been picking the wrong books off of shelves, judging them by a genre he didn't know existed. That he thought he knew what a muse was until he stood in front of one. He wanted to say that he appreciated every bit of inspiration, even the tiny seeds, but instead, he said the last thing that came to mind.

"The car book helped. Wildlife, not so much."

"Can't win them all, I guess. I was surprised when you grabbed it. So, you're leaving today?"

"Yeah. Now."

"It's a long drive, I bet. Not a day trip kind of distance?"

He locked eyes with her. "No. I'm…I'm afraid not. I'll do it in one day, though. I have a lot to think about. I have something to apologize for, too."

She took in air that hitched in her throat, her expression changing so rapidly he wasn't sure where it would land. She picked at a sticker peeling off a book cover and nudged the cart. Its wheels squeaked.

"Sandy, I have a girlfriend. Or…" He shrugged. "Had. We broke up. But it was after you and I met, and I feel like I may have led you on a little."

"You didn't." Her eyes were fixed on a Sue Grafton book. "If I felt anything it was my choice. Nothing happened."

"I wanted it to."

She blushed and folded her arms. "Yeah, me too. In another world, right?"

"In another universe, you and I were grand."

How could she be so graceful?

"I probably won't see you again," she said. "I…have a great drive back. You can stay in touch, if you want. The library is on social media, if you want to look it up someday."

"I'm not on social media. I try to avoid places my students hang out."

She grimaced. "It's a minefield in there. You're not missing anything."

"Except you."

She glanced away. "I can't believe you're a college professor. You seem so normal."

The laugh escaped him. "I hear that a lot. It really helps with my imposter syndrome. A professor went out on leave, and I took over the class for the rest of the year. Next thing I knew I was a college professor." He left out the part about his father's name, how the whole world expected him to be the next great magician, weaver of words into brilliant tapestries. Did it matter that it wasn't true, that he wasn't really his father's son? Would the pressure pop like a balloon if he no longer had to live up to his name?

"Nothing that cool happens around here. No one ever just accidentally becomes a college professor."

He shrugged. "I'm minimizing. It was a lot of work."

"I bet."

"And I have to write a book to save my job."

"Perk of being a librarian. I don't even have to read them. What comes next?"

He wanted to beg her to stay, to let him stay, to break the cycle of pleasing other people and going out of his way at his own expense to put someone else first. He wanted to put her first, but it wasn't meant to be. He was meant to be in Philadelphia. He was meant to write this book, and he was meant to keep going, to cross this divide into a whole new phase of his life. The fact that he didn't want it as much as he had a month ago, before he came to Ramsbolt, before he surrendered the longest relationship of his life, before he met Sandy, was totally irrelevant. He had to go back.

"I should go," he said. "Long drive."

"Of course." Her smile fell. That wasn't the way he wanted to remember her.

Turning from her, he paused with his hand on the door. "Thanks again, for everything."

On his way back to the car, his shaky breaths made little puffs in the chill. Ramsbolt would be covered by more snow than he'd ever seen in his life. He pictured it blanketed in white, smoke curling up from chimneys, moose roaming the streets, and that lanky mailman clawing his way through blizzards. The people of this tiny town were made of tougher stuff than he was.

The jaunt across town wasn't long enough to warm the Subaru. The steering wheel was still freezing. He rubbed his hands together while the engine settled to a purr and secured the box of pastries in the passenger seat. It had been a long time since he listened to music, so he found a playlist that looked worth streaming, something that would distract him just enough to forget how many miles stood between home and Ramsbolt. By the time he reached the intersection at Helen's Tavern where the light was red for only him, he turned it off. Silence was better than songs about heartbreak.

Just as the light turned green, a little blue Jeep blew through the light, nearly hitting Stuart's front corner panel. He slammed on his brakes and threw out an arm to save the pastries. He might miss a lot of things about that little town, but he wouldn't miss Bern.

CHAPTER TWENTY-SEVEN

At sixteen, Stuart was the only guy in the newsroom who still had hair on his head. He was also the only guy who didn't have a desk, but as an intern, he hadn't been promised one. Instead, he sat where he could, at tables in the breakroom, at an empty desk when someone ran off to investigate a house fire or went down to City Hall to investigate whatever new tangle the mayor got himself into. Bitterness seemed to find him no matter what dark corner he tucked into. It was no secret that news was losing money, sinking like a heavy stone in the rising tide of media waters, and having the son of a famous author sitting in their newsroom while benefits were being cut and coworkers were being laid off wasn't sitting well with the establishment. There was a life lesson in here somewhere, something his father wanted him to learn about working with people who don't want you around and carrying the weight of a reputation he hadn't earned. But far from learning it, Stuart was becoming an expert at avoiding them all. Hunched over some paper at a table by the fridge, he was out of sight for the woman who managed the classified ads and the man who edited the auto section. They plopped down around the corner from him and flattened out their brown paper lunch bags to use as placemats.

"Why would anyone buy a newspaper subscription when they can make up their own news on the internet? Nobody cares about facts anymore, Tiffany."

"There has to be something we can do to hang on to all this. It's really hitting my department hard. We used to get thirty calls a day just for used car ads. Nothing. It's crickets."

"I'm kinda glad my old man's not around to see it. He worked for Tastykake his whole life. Said only a lazy man would try to make a living by writing down words, and why wasn't that life good enough for me."

"Joke's on all of us. They're gonna fill this place with interns who'll work for free. Watch."

The pain in their voices took the air out of the room. Stuart heard plenty of lamentations over the death of the written word at the Saturday evening groan-fests his father called *Salons*. A bunch of writers would gather in the study, choking back scotch, whining about how underappreciated they were. It hit home to hear it in the real world from people he aspired to be. He wanted to point out that working for free wasn't sustainable, but their pain was worth a lot more than his discomfort.

"Stuart?" The local news editor clung to the doorway, hanging into the room. "You got a minute to talk about this gas station story?"

Gathering his papers, he danced the long way around empty tables, keeping his distance from the narrowed gaze of Tiffany and the auto editor, whose name Stuart could never recall. He made himself smaller than usual, papers clutched to his chest in his folded arms, head down as he stuck to the right side of the hall. He fell into the seat in his editor's office, watching the man wedge himself between his desk and a bookcase to settle in his place.

"Stuart?" He took off his glasses, templed his fingers. "First, what do you have going on next weekend. Do you want to cover the Broad Street Run?"

There was a football game that night. He had a green light to go, hit McDonald's with the guys, then go to the game. With any luck, Alicia would be there without that clingy best friend of hers. It was one of those big games that was important to people who weren't him. The memory of it would be fleeting, but the byline would last forever.

"I can do it," he said.

"Good. Now for this article you wrote." He pulled it from a desk drawer. He'd printed it out and scribbled on in blue pencil.

Stuart leaned forward to accept it. Big chunks of it, strings of paragraphs, were covered in x's and circled.

His chest constricted, and the world spun a little. The letters on the paper went blurry. Was any of it worth keeping?

"What did I do wrong?"

"Facts." The editor laced his fingers behind his head and leaned back in his chair. "There aren't any."

"I went to town meetings. I researched this issue a million ways. I called other towns in the county with the same zoning issues. I interviewed three people on the town council about it. And then I called a real estate lawyer to find out what the big deal is about putting a gas station down there. And then I wrote an article about it. What other facts are there?"

The editor gathered a bunch of pens from his desk, dropped them in a drawer, and closed it. It was one of those old metal desks that looked like it hadn't moved since the first world war. The thing could withstand nuclear fallout.

"Yes, it was clear that you did those things. And you wrote about them very well. Extraordinarily well, I should say. But you didn't write an article. You wrote a story."

"What do you mean? I talked to people who live next to the site. It took them years to get the old house torn down on that corner. It was full of rats. They couldn't even let their kids play outside."

"You mentioned that, too. But you didn't write the facts."

He scooted in his chair, dragging it beneath the desk with his weight like coaxing a horse to go, and it creaked like a sinking ship. "Journalism doesn't care about feelings. Sure, sometimes you're talking about the impact of something on the community you have to include the view of both sides. Editorial guidelines might sometimes demand that you take a stand. But you wrote a short story that includes quotes. Your voice was all over that piece. The assignment was for a straight news story."

Stuart let out the breath he'd been holding in. "I did do that, didn't I?"

"You sure did. You gave me your impression of everything you researched. You even gave me your impression of Councilwoman Flynn's outfit. It wasn't necessary."

"It illustrated how she doesn't identify with the neighborhood. It wasn't an insult."

"That might be true, and it's an insightful observation, but it doesn't belong in a straight news story. I gave your notes to Al, he's writing it up for tomorrow's paper. You'll get credit for research."

Stuart stacked the papers on his lap. The story he'd been writing about the orchestra capital campaign would have to wait. As if there wasn't enough tension in the newsroom, Al was one of the most intimidating men he'd ever met. It wasn't his size or stature, it was the reverence he commanded. Everyone from senators to the mayor sought his favor. His reporting had taken down half of the city council over the last few years, and he'd been shining a light on systemic inequality for longer than Stuart had been alive. The man lived on principle, he wrote with a sword, and for as much as Stuart wanted to learn from Al, he quaked at the idea of looking him in the eye. Having his subpar work pushed off onto a man of that stature made it even harder to lift his head in the newsroom.

"Is Al mad?"

The editor brushed a hand at the air. "No. It'll take him four minutes."

"Great." The weight of what Stuart didn't know pressed down on him. "So how do I get better at this?"

"Read Al's story. See what he did with it. And stop writing short stories instead of the news."

"I guess I mixed in too much human interest."

"Look, if this were a game of darts, it would have been a bullseye. But this is a game of horseshoes." He pushed away from the desk, gathered some papers and files into a stack, and shoved them into a tote bag that he draped from his shoulder. "Tell you what. For extra credit, I'll read it again if you fix it. The story won't run, but you'll learn a lot. Sit down and write out the facts."

He followed the editor out of the room in a thick wake of ink and newsprint smell. A roar of laughter thundered down the hall from an office on the left and a woman with a slice of cake on a flimsy plate smiled at them as she snuck by. The editor paused at the end of a row of cubicles and peeled back to face him.

"Stuart? Just remember that objectivity is important, okay? And it's also impossible."

He clutched the papers to his chest. "What do you mean?"

"You'll never be unbiased," he said without emotion. "Partiality is a good thing. It means you still have a moral compass. Denying it doesn't make it go away, either. You have to acknowledge your bias, check it, and rely on your editors and peers to help you overcome it. That's why I'm giving you another shot to write that article. I want to see how you can handle objectivity. It's a great learning experience for you."

"I don't have anything against objectivity. It's just that I see the emotion in this situation, and I think it's important that readers understand it. Isn't emotion part of the context?"

"It is. Let the words of the neighbors express it, though. Show opposing views. Get quotes from people, but don't steer them. The job of journalism is to arm the people with the facts they need to form an opinion, if that's what they want to do. Everything else is storytelling."

"But—"

"It's clear you want to defend that neighborhood. You were so fierce, if I didn't know better, I'd think you grew up there. You have what it takes. Just reel in your views. If you can't, there's always creative writing. God knows your father would love it if you followed in his footsteps."

CHAPTER TWENTY-EIGHT

It was trash day. The can outside Stuart's place in Philly was piled with Chinese take-out containers. By the looks of it, Edward was a moo goo gai pan guy. Stuart parallel parked in front of their place and sat for a minute. It looked the same. A few of the summer plants had faded, but the windows still needed washing, the shutters were still attached. He thought it would look older, like he felt. But time seemed to stand still here.

He checked his email one last time, a displacement activity to calm his nerves. He had a few emails from work and some spam. There was a new email from that agent Markus referred him to. She'd requested his manuscript, maybe as a courtesy. He expected a rejection, but her response was far from it.

Stuart, I loved the work. I have a few notes, but I'll spare you for now. Ordinarily, I would request a call and see if we're compatible before making an offer of representation, but in your position, you know the drill. I'd be happy to work with you if it's a good fit. When can we chat? ~Jessica

He sent her a reply, thanking her for her time, suggesting a call early

Tuesday morning. Drumming the steering wheel, he let his cheeks ache with the grin. It had been a long road. Years of rejection, most of it his own making lifted. The constant knowledge that he wasn't good enough, reinforced by the writing on his father's wall, on Madison's wall, finally fell by the wayside. There were many more miles to go, but this stretch felt like heading home.

"Get through this thing with Madison first. Then you can celebrate."

He checked his hair in the rearview mirror and climbed from the car.

A box full of smaller boxes and a roll of trash bags in his arms, he knocked on the door and gave Madison a chance to answer. It was still his door to unlock, his key still fit, but catching her, or them, off guard wouldn't do his psyche any favors. He didn't want to set himself up for an argument, but if history played out, this would be a hard enough day without seeing something he couldn't unsee.

Inside, footsteps groaned the floors. The door flung open, and Madison stood there in oversized sweatpants and a yellow tank top. Brown hair down around her shoulders. There was a time she'd relax when she saw him at the door. In the early days, back when she lived in that Fishtown row house, she never barked at him to take off his snow-packed boots or shake off his hat before coming in. This time, this last time, rigid as a closed door, she held it open just enough for the heat to smack into him.

"I turned the furnace on. I can finally sit around without a winter coat on." She opened the door and flung her head back, permitting him inside. He pushed back the resentment. "It's about time. You've been back for two weeks. Mohl's sofa must be comfy."

"I guess Edward's enjoying the mattress I paid for." Stuart pushed past her. The place still smelled like home in the surprising way home does. Despite a candle and the wraith of her dinner with Edward the night before, that underlying undeniable smell of home was still there, shocking in its sameness. Not that he'd given it any thought, but he expected it to be different somehow. Less him, more like the past, more like whatever her world without him would smell like.

He shallowed his breath, though he knew he was starving his lungs before the standoff.

A pair of large well-worn black shoes sat on the mat by the door, the toes spattered with the shine of oil and dribbles of butter. A zip-up sweatshirt in a shade of blue he'd never wear hung from a hook by the kitchen entrance. A magazine on the coffee table offered ten new ways to get flat abs fast and a fifteen second secret to bench more weight.

"Edward's a workout guy, huh?" Stuart dropped the box on the table, flattening the curl of the magazine's cover. He yanked out the smaller boxes and wasted no time pulling vinyl off the shelf. She never cared for records. Too much trouble to turn them over, she'd said.

"He reads it. I wouldn't say it's a religion."

Box full, he unfurled a black trash bag and breezed past her, to the narrow closet where they kept their winter clothes. He shoved his black pea coat in the bottom of the bag and piled hats and gloves and scarves on top. He wasn't there to keep things pretty. He was there to shovel as much shit as he could into his car and get out.

She leaned in the kitchen doorway. "Where are you staying?"

"Mohl's."

"I mean, long term. Are you staying in the city?"

"I'm staying at Mohl's." That's all she needed to know.

"That'll be a frat party." With a huff she spun into the kitchen and ran water in the sink, filling a glass. No offer for him. He wouldn't have accepted anyway.

He slid a big plastic tub from the floor of the closet and threw off the lid.

"That's your container. Those are my socks, though," she said. "You can dump them."

The place would look like a bomb went off if Edward wasn't a stickler for tidiness. He dumped her socks on the closet floor and stuffed the plastic crate with his gloves.

"You know, Mohl is a really smart guy. Two white academic men in a room is not automatically a frat party."

She rolled her eyes, the sharp edge of her laugh setting him on edge.

"You know, I get really tired of you talking down to me all the time," he said. "As if cooking a piece of meat and making some pasta is the epitome of human endeavor and anything else is beneath you."

He breezed past her, into the hall. He'd leave her the coffee table, though he paid for it. She could keep the dishes he hated, but he needed a few of the towels. Mohl's always smelled like mildew. He tugged his favorites from beneath the stack in the hall closet, but one was missing.

"Where's the other gray towel?"

She didn't answer.

Into the bathroom, he found it on the hook on the back of the door, still damp. It went into a trash bag all its own in a wet ball. Washing Edward out of his life would be gratifying later.

The medicine cabinet held little he valued. He'd taken his razor with him to Maine. He found his spare blades, his shampoo and soap and tossed them into a box. Madison trailed him the whole time, sipping a glass of water.

"How soon are you taking all those books? I want the shelf space."

Suddenly he was overcome with the urge to collect one book a day.

He couldn't let her see him sweat. She didn't deserve the satisfaction of knowing his breath hitched a bit, that his heart bucked in his chest when he faced their bedroom door. It was open, but barely. Sun came through the street-facing window and lit up the corner of her white dresser. They'd grabbed it from Ikea one night when it was snowing. He did a donut in the parking lot, and they brought home a tray of cinnamon rolls. She hated putting together furniture, so he did it on his own. He knew exactly where he'd left things, his clothes taking up half the closet, some on hangers, the rest in drawers. Were they strewn on the floor to make room for someone else? How long would it be before the memory faded?

He strode into the room without a wobbling knee. His books were still on the shelves. His clothes were still in the closet, though they'd been pushed aside to make room for a few new tops that Madison had purchased, some still decorated with tags.

"All of that needs to go." She swept her arm toward the shelves.

"Why do you hate books so much?" he asked, though he really didn't care to know why.

"What's happening with that thing you wrote?" The list in her voice nudged him into tormented waters.

"Why, Madison? Why? It's already not good enough for you. There's already something wrong with it. Aren't you done controlling my emotions? Here." He slapped hangered shirts between his hands and yanked down. They came away in a sandwich of colors, hangers clanging, some falling to the floor. He turned and heaved his clothes on the bed then pointed at the vacancy they'd made. "Look! Space! I made all kinds of room for you to bring in someone else you can tear down for a while. Call Edward. Go ahead. Tell him to rush over here with his clothes and his magazines so you have something else to judge. He's like…"

Stuart searched the ceiling, his breath quick, eyes frantic. The dopamine hit was cathartic.

"A blank slate. He's your personal tabula rasa, and you can turn him into any groveling fool you want. Why are you hovering over me? Did I bring the wrong trash bags? Are they the wrong color? Maybe I'm packing in the wrong order. I walked down the wrong side of the hallway. For years, I have entered every conversation with you giving you the benefit of the doubt. But every time I fail to prepare myself you come in swinging. And when I do prepare, you just keep digging until you find that one thing I didn't expect. So there. Let Edward fill the damn closet with things you're bound to hate."

Jaw set, eyes narrowed, Madison carried her satisfaction with a ramrod spine. Leaning in the doorway with her arms folded, there was no doubt she'd formed an opinion about his word choice and tone of voice. But having said his piece, he didn't care anymore. All the resentment he'd carried around, the words he'd packed down deep in his lungs had been set free. He was glad he stopped when he did, else all his anger at his mother and the boiling flames of rage he felt for the man who pretended to be his father would come spilling out, too.

Madison cocked an eyebrow. "Is there any chance this will all be gone today, or are you gonna drag this out?"

He cinched his clothes in the trash bag and slung it over his shoulder. Passing her in the doorway, he paused, inches from her. Their shoulders touched for the first time with freed contempt.

"Oh, I really don't think there's anything left to drag out. Do you?"

The bag landed in the living room next to his box of records, on top of the bag with his winter clothes. It rolled off and crinkled to the floor. Back in the bedroom with an empty carton, he swept novels into tight, neat layers. Madison hovered.

"You hate me. I get it. What about your book?"

"Entirely without your fault-finding condemnation," he said, "I finished writing a book. I got an agent. My endeavors are no longer yours to consider. Just like you wanted."

"When will you know something?"

"Whenever the universe feels like telling me."

She drifted closer, peering down into the box as he loaded paperbacks. "You sure don't seem very excited about it."

The box full, he closed the flaps. Over and under. He'd started sweating at some point, and he wiped it from his brow with the sleeve of his flannel shirt.

"Why should I be excited right now, Madison? Why should I be anything? This isn't exciting. I'm closing a chapter of my life that I should have closed a long time ago. This?" He pulled an empty box closer and dropped a stack of books in. "This is checking something off a to-do list. This is scrubbing up a mess. It's the next chapter I'm excited about. I don't owe you anything."

There was a whole new him on the horizon, someone he'd only begun to know. There'd been glimpses of him up in Maine, sitting at the bar and writing in the bakery. He was lost in Philadelphia. Somehow without the sound of the city and the constant flurry of obligations and expectations pecking at him, he'd been twenty pounds lighter and taking in better air. Since he'd been back, hiding in the university library to finish revisions on his book, talking to the agent, and having lunch with colleagues, he'd counted down the days until his sabbatical ended like he was facing a prison sentence. The closer he got, the more he feared the cell he'd made for himself.

But the end of this tunnel was plenty bright. The writer's block had been cracked open. He had dozens of new story ideas stirring in his head. Every time he sat down to write on a bench in a park or at a noisy cafe, he felt like he was back at the beginning, back at the core of what he loved at the start. The power of a story was its ability to transform him, not just taking him to a distant land or another planet but making sense of human struggle and carving sharp edges off universal truths. Stacking them all like stones in a wall, he could build a fortress where all of the layers of want and need could peel back without judgment.

Dropping a stack of books in the box, taking in the drug of paper and decades-old ink, he couldn't wait for his visions to take that form.

Arthur, as characters went, was imminently more flawed than he was. If Stuart could craft redemption out of thin air for that imaginary man, then he could find it for himself out in the real world, too. He just had to keep moving forward.

The shelves empty, he carried three boxes of books to the living room where he left them with the growing stack. It was finally happening. Neat and orderly, he was reclaiming his world from the pile of rubble that had swelled around it. He bit his lower lip and held back the smile. It was only for him.

Pushing past Madison, he wove through his stuff into the kitchen. The counters, as always, were spotless. Hours old coffee had gone bitter in the pot, but it was still on and warm.

She was hot on his heels. "So, what's your plan? You can't live with Mohl forever."

"It's none of your business what I plan to do." He hummed the tune that had been stuck in his head since he heard it at that cidery in Fishtown, Kurant, where he wrote out a few scenes for another book and some hipster girl tried to buy him a drink.

"Have you thought about what you're going to do? You seriously need to take control of things. What if Mohl gets married?"

"He's not even dating anyone." Except that girl from the coffee shop, but neither of them were taking it seriously.

"Someday he might. Are you going to meet someone new and take them to Mohl's place? That'll impress her."

Three rows of coffee cups deep, he found his favorites and pulled them onto the counter one at a time. There was the one *Star Trek* mug with the *Enterprise* on it, the small glass one with Garfield the cat, and one with Ziggy and his dog from the old cartoon strip. His father had given it to him for Christmas one year. It had been full of Hershey's Kisses. On second thought, he opened the trash can and chucked it in.

"Hey." She dove in after it, but he pried it from her hand and chucked it again. "I liked that mug."

"That mug was my mug, and I want it gone. If you like it that much, find one on eBay." He rolled his two mugs in paper towels.

"Your dad gave that to you."

Nostrils flaring, he bit his tongue. He wasn't arming her with the truth about the man who posed as his father.

"Whatever." She threw her hands in the air and backed up to the doorway. "Look, I'm just saying that a book isn't the solution to all your problems."

The rubber band that held his sanity together snapped, and he couldn't have held back his laugh if he tried. "Oh, I know that." He gathered the wrapped mugs in his hands. "I am really glad that you're taking on so much of the emotional burden for me. I appreciate it. It frees me up a lot to focus on other things. Like getting out of here as soon as possible."

She took the mugs from his hands and put them on the counter.

She grabbed an empty one from the cabinet, filled it with coffee, and pushed it at him. God only knew how old that stuff was.

"Here," she said. "I'm not your enemy."

She always knew when he needed coffee. That might have been the extent of her positive impact on his life. He took a sip and wrapped his hands around a mug covered in Smurfs.

"I know you're not the enemy." He shrugged. "No, I don't know that. There are three kinds of people in the world: friends, enemies, and strangers. You're definitely not my friend. I'm keeping a really good eye on that group lately, and it's been clear for a long time that you're not a friend."

Something resembling resignation rolled across her like a rapid tide. When it washed back, it left her looking honest and almost raw.

"I don't even like who I've become most days." She sank against the counter, arms folded, her eyes fixed on something in the tiny back plot of weeds they'd called a yard. "I walk around with a million things and none of them really matter here, it's just…I know we aren't what we used to be."

"Haven't been for a long time."

"I hear myself talking, and I think…God. What have I become? It's not just you. I'm mixed up, too."

He raised his eyebrows and set down the cup. He almost gave into the instinct and offered her sympathy. He almost said that he'd blamed himself for a long time, that it wasn't until he was alone in Maine that he realized how wrong they were for each other. He'd blamed himself for way too long, analyzed his every move with more precision than she ever had looking for faults to correct before she found them. He arbitrated himself to inertia. Avoiding the conflicts gave him a greater reward than moving through his own life.

"It can't be good to think the way you do all the time." He sipped the coffee and struggled to swallow it. "I'm not saying that to pick a fight. Don't say anything back."

The flinch in her jaw said what her eyes didn't.

"We used to be close, you and me," he said. "Yeah, I want to start my life over. There's good stuff for me out there. Better stuff. Same for you. But if you ever need anything, I'm around. Sometimes it's good to have people in your life who've known you a long time. I mean, it's been twelve years."

She kicked at the broken edge of a floor tile.

"This coffee is absolute crap." He poured it in the sink and rinsed the cup. "Can I ask you something? Has nothing to do with us."

She gasped and sighed. "Sure. Why not?"

"Do you think I'm objective enough to be a newspaper reporter?"

Snapping to attention she curled a lip and flared her nostrils. "Why on God's green earth would you want to go from being a college professor and novelist to being a newspaper reporter?"

He shrugged. "Just something I'm kicking around. I can make real change in the world that way. Tell people's stories."

"There's no money in it. The work never ends, newspapers are closing everywhere. Money is drying up."

"Everything has challenges. But journalism is really important. Not just breaking news that affects the world, I mean communities and small towns. They need a way to stay connected."

"But they're all drying up. How many have closed here in the last decade? Philadelphia is crawling with journalists out of work. Why would you want to be one of them?"

He waved a hand. "All of that aside. I just wonder if I could be objective."

"Those mugs are gonna break wrapped in paper towels." She flung open a drawer and dug out three old dish cloths, wrapped the mugs and shoved them in his hands. "I'd say you being a journalist is a dumb idea for about a hundred reasons, but not for the reasons you think."

"It's always negative with you."

CHAPTER TWENTY-NINE

Winter lingered into spring, and the semester started with the heat on full blast. Stuart tugged at the collar of his sweater, scratchy against his neck. He checked the time on his phone where he left it on his desk, so he didn't run over. Three classes in and he was on autopilot already.

His class was almost twice the size it would be at the end of the semester, once students cut back on their workload and skipped class to spend time in the sun. For now, he had to talk louder to reach the back rows. Just a few more bullet points, and he could wrap this up, issue some homework, and get some coffee.

"Master of two worlds." He scanned the tops of students' heads. Whether they were taking notes or passing notes didn't matter much to him anymore. "Joseph Campbell's monomyth. Anyone with me here? What is it?"

A guy with short dark hair in the third row raised his hand. It was one of those noncommittal third-row waves from a student who wanted to be seen by the professor instead of his fellow classmates. Stuart gave him a nod.

"It's, um." The student cleared his throat. "The main character learns to live in his old world with his new knowledge. He isn't who he used to be."

"Yes. That's right. In this part of your story, the character has transformed his view of the world. All of his old reactions are gone. His old fears are gone, along with his old motivations and needs. They've all been replaced by a new version of himself."

Stuart paced before the whiteboard. His new sneakers squeaked on the linoleum.

A woman in the front raised her hand. "I have a question."

"Cassie? Go ahead."

"I tend to drag down this part of the story by spending too much time having the character reflect on what they've learned and how far they've come. How do I fix that?"

"Transform it into action." He wrote on the board as he spoke the words *show, don't tell.* Sit back and ask yourself what situation your character could be in that would illustrate that change the most."

He wrote *Newton's First Law* on the board.

"Every object sits idle until it's hit with force. Then it reacts with equal and opposite force. Hit your main character with something big. How will they react as a changed character in a way that shows a reader how they've overcome their obstacles?"

Her hand shot up again. "What if the character is on the cusp. If they've already undergone that transformation, they just don't know it yet?"

A woman a few seats to the left laughed and shot up a hand.

He pointed at her. "Yes. Go ahead."

"I want to write chick lit." A wave of giggles erupted.

"Don't knock it," Stuart said, his chin lifted. "There's a lot of heart in chick lit. What were you about to say?"

"This happens a lot in the real world. Your best friend is stuck. She has all kinds of power she doesn't know about yet. She keeps asking you for advice, and you're just sitting there waiting for her to figure out that she already knows what to do. She already has all her power."

Stuart turned to the board. He wrote *Ultimate Joy* and underlined it three times. His marker hit the tray, and he lost his gravity. The walls extended beyond him, the ceiling lifted. There was a weightlessness to the moment, to seeing the words come out of him. He caught his breath and faced the class.

"Ultimate joy. Right? Isn't that what we all want? To find our ultimate bliss and hold on to it? Your character, come hell or high water, is heading in that direction. The whole journey up to this moment is about figuring out what the ache really is, and the main character is rarely right. That's where the drama comes from."

He hopped up on his desk, feet dangling. "They think if they go out there and find this one thing, they'll be happy. That's their *want*. But their *need* is even greater, and most of the time they have no idea what they really need."

"Like finding something you lost." The guy in the third row chimed in. "There's a breathless moment when you find it, but it doesn't last all day."

"Right. The journey's done. You found it. Now is the moment

when your character sees that joy for what it is and has to go back to his or her old world to share it."

The girl to the left of him jumped, her hand shot in the air. "Professor."

"Go ahead."

"What happens when the character doesn't want to go back?"

The guy to the right smiled and tapped his eraser on his notebook. "I think they call that a happy ending."

A few of the students laughed, but Stuart shook his head. "It's funny, but they're not at the ending yet."

The alarm went off on his phone. Chairs scraped against the floor as his class got up to leave. He didn't have the heart to give them an assignment. He'd only have to grade it later.

"See you next week." He yelled over the murmur of a departing crowd. "Find examples of this in modern literature. Or something."

He hopped from the desk and gathered his things. Mohl pushed against the tide and flopped down in a vacated front row seat. His wavy dark hair had grown longer since the coffee shop girl started running her fingers through it regularly.

"I came to steal you," he said.

Stuart shoved books in his messenger bag. "Coffee?"

"Nah. Class. I want you to sit in on my next one."

Nose wrinkled, mouth curled in a sneer, Stuart shook his head. "I paid my dues. What do I want to sit in on an art class for?"

"Visionary art. This is a good one. I think it might speak to you. Anyway, I know you don't have anything better to do right now."

Bag on his shoulder, Stuart motioned to the door. "Fine. But this better be good."

Mohl leapt to his feet, and they walked down the corridor crowded with students. Stuart hit the door with his hip, and they spilled out into the spring sunshine. Daffodils dangled from bright green stems in pots along the walkway. The last clumps of snow huddled in the shady spots between buildings.

"I'm really jealous of you art people sometimes." Stuart shuffled the weight of his bag on his shoulder. "You never carry anything."

"You say that, but you've never put every slide in a deck upside down and had to change it in the middle of class. So, what's up with that publisher? They like the revisions you sent?"

"Yeah. She loved it. I was surprised at how little she wanted me to edit. Usually, they have their finger on the market, and they want to make drastic plot changes to help the book sell better, but in this case, I guess I got lucky."

"That's cool. What about the synopsis?"

"She loves my ideas for the next one, too."

The art building had its own smell. Paint, mineral spirits, and earthy clays hit him as soon as he walked in the door. It was a creative process he envied, molding something from nothing, melding it with your hands until it softened and stiffened and became the thing your vision craved. He wanted to pause and admire the colorful works that lined the walls, and Mohl must have felt the pull of his attention.

"Come on. Running late." Mohl pushed through the double doors and launched down the aisle toward the front of the classroom. Stuart fell into a seat in the back row, next to a guy who was barely awake.

"Isolated artists searching for belonging." Mohl planted his feet, arms outstretched, as if ready for his crucifixion. "Who am I? Where am I? These are questions asked by every artist, visionary or applying himself to any great art movement. There's a reason that Realism Art was a prerequisite for this class. In order to understand what makes an artist a visionary, you must understand the realism it acts against. Visionary isn't just a transcendence of the realistic sensory world we know. And it isn't always a view of the divine, spiritualism or invisible ideals in the clouds. Some of the most compelling art of this century comes from visionary artists who are bringing into being a world they wish was real. What they all have in common is a drive to create that often comes from…" He held his hands up to the sky. "Somewhere else. Some voice within them. For them, in many cases, there's a longing and a yearning in the art for something other than this physical realm. Today, we're going to look at a few of those artists. If someone could wake up the back row, let's get started."

He slapped a row of lights, and the room went dark. The hum of the slide projector escalated to whir, and, with a *ca-chunk*, the first slide appeared. A ship on a storm-tossed sea beneath a sky of impossible purple was tossed on the waves. You could almost hear the groaning of wood, the slap of sails and masts in the howling wind.

Stuart's body went limp, one cell at a time lightening, loosening, his shoulders falling. He'd seen that work. He knew it well.

"Degory Howland." Mohl was shadowed from where Stuart sat, but he caught the wink, nonetheless. "Degory painted at the end of the nineteenth century in northern Maine. He was the son of a railroad man. The family was shaken when his mother died giving birth to his sister, and Degory, haunted by the sounds of her death, battled the ghosts in the walls as he isolated himself in their family home, alone, painting the sea for the rest of his life."

The slide changed. An old photograph of a house in ruins, sliding off its foundation, and the roof caving in. Stuart didn't recognize it, but there was no way it survived. Stuart's breath hitched, and he fought the ringing in his ears, hanging onto every word.

"After Degory's death, the town raided the home of his art. He'd painted on wood, on paper, on folders. He'd painted on an old stove door. The walls and floors were covered. How the art was retrieved is lost to history. Some say it was a coordinated effort done in a day, and others say it was more like a series of thefts, people sneaking in and taking what they wanted. But oral histories from the town all agree that it was an act of seeking forgiveness. Degory was isolated because people didn't understand him. Saving his art was the only way they could make amends."

The slide changed again. The painting wasn't identical to the one that hung on the cabin wall, but it was pretty close. His chest caved with an ache, a longing to be back in that place, to hold that painting, to appreciate it. He hadn't claimed every moment he could in Ramsbolt. He hadn't breathed in deep enough, taken enough of it in, let it soak in and become part of him.

"Much of his art ended up in an antique store in town, run by a woman named Eliza. Degory's brother told her that the artist's fixation with boats was tied to their father's regrets. He'd been a successful railroad man, but all he ever wanted was to see the sea."

The slide changed. *Ca-chunk.* Mohl highlighted parts of a ship. "If you look closely at some of his work, you can see hints of train features woven throughout. If you did this week's reading, you'll remember this painting from chapter thirteen of *Visionary Art at The Turn of the Century.*"

The student next to Stuart was asleep, his head hung over his desk, hair shielding his eyes. Without care for his nap, Stuart took his books and found the yellow textbook. Frantic, his mouth dry, he flipped the pages while the guy next to him snored.

There it was. The painting from the cabin, or one much like it. A ship tossed on a dark sea, but the foreground was markedly calm. As if the storm raged only for that ship.

Stuart slammed the book shut. "I don't need to be here. I have to go."

The student startled awake, rubbing sleep from his eyes, glaring at Stuart for having taken his books.

Stuart's phone buzzed in his pocket, some reminder perhaps or a spam text message. He listed to the side to fish it out as the student next to him reclaimed his expensive books.

It was a text from his mother.

Your father's had a heart attack. At the hospital now. On 11th St.

CHAPTER THIRTY

Stuart rushed through campus, around students and parks, down city blocks with his messenger bag fully of heavy books slamming into his hip. His throat burned, and he couldn't catch his breath, but he couldn't stop either. He told himself that it was all fine, it was probably spicy food or some kind of pulled muscle from shelving books too high without a ladder. There had to be a reason other than catastrophic failure of the machine that made his father run.

He flung himself into an admission desk and pleaded with the nurse who responded with the business end of her humanity. She waved at a hand down the hall.

"Red line. Follow it. There's a desk."

"Is there a water fountain somewhere?" He raked the back of his hand across his forehead, wiping away the sweat from his run. The deep thirst might be an emotional diversion, but it demanded it be quenched.

"Vending machine. It's down there, on the right."

The overhead sign said Cardiac Emergency. He rushed down the hall, following the line, dodging scowling people slowed by their own anguish. The hall opened to a wide vestibule. Midcentury modern waiting room furniture sat in rows. People clustered in little lumps, noses in magazines and trade paperbacks, in their own diagnosis purgatory. The chairs made him think of Sandy. No sign of his mom, but a vending machine full of blue water bottles got his attention, and he patted himself down for his wallet, but he only had a fifty, and that wouldn't work.

Back to the red line, he followed it past patient rooms and offices, janitorial closets, and a unisex bathroom. The dark hall dumped him into a bright waiting area, a desk straight ahead was void of attendants.

"Stuart." His mother grabbed his arm out of nowhere. She was wearing one of those housecoat sweaters that she'd never leave the house in even to check the mail. It had some kind of red sauce on the front, and its pockets bulged with tissues. Her eyes were red and puffy, but she was in full makeup and her hair was, of course, perfect. "Come. Sit."

Stuart dropped his bag in a chair and sat in the one next to it. The waiting room smelled like Listerine and industrial cleaners. A woman sat knitting something off in one corner. Other than that, they had the place to themselves.

He shifted to face her. "Mom. What happened?"

"He was making breakfast. We had one of those pizzas from Felicia's last night, and he was going to reheat it. Pizza for breakfast. So stupid. I was on the phone with Gillian. She called because her granddaughter is selling Girl Scout cookies. All of the sudden he fell. He didn't say anything when I called out to him, so I rushed down the kitchen and found him clutching his chest." She dabbed at her nose.

"How long ago?"

"A few hours. He's in surgery."

"Why didn't you call me sooner? Breakfast? It's one thirty." Stuart couldn't keep the urgency out of his voice, but a part of him knew it wasn't his to feel. The man was his mother's husband, and this was her wound to carry. It had nothing to do with him, no matter how deep the stab in his chest buried itself.

His mom wiped at the red stain on her sweater. "There wasn't anything you could do here. You had a class to teach. He wouldn't want to interrupt your work. Look at me, covered in pizza sauce." She turned her eyes from the stain and put the tissue away, down in a pocket with the rest.

"So? What's happening?" Stuart flexed his hands, palms up.

"I said. He's in surgery. He'll be out soon. We just have to wait."

"What surgery? What are they doing?"

She shrank three sizes. "I don't know. I can't understand what they're saying to me, because all I hear is that my husband is dying, and my son hates him and probably me for lying to him his whole life, and as soon as I call you to come over here it's going to be even more complicated, and I just want him to come through that damn door over there so we can go home. Okay? Can you help me here? Can we do all the other stuff later?"

He grabbed her hands. "Okay. Listen. I got this. I don't hate him.

Or you. I'll figure it out."

Leaving his bag with his mom, he went to the desk and leaned over it, peering down the hall behind it and tapping his fingers on the cool counter. He could hear the woman in the lab coat before he could see her. Clicking a pen as she walked, she gave him the kind of smile that said she was used to answering questions from people.

"Hi. Can I ask you about my dad?"

The question sounded foreign coming from his dry throat. There was an asterisk attached to the word dad. He hadn't come to terms with it enough to understand it yet. He hadn't even visited his parents since he returned from Maine. He'd had lunch with his mother, but he never told his father, the man, about his trip or Madison or his book. There'd been time, plenty of it, to figure out the future.

"Stuart Dolan, right?"

He gripped the edge of the counter. He really could use that water. "Right."

"He's out of surgery and being monitored. They'll have him in a room in a few minutes, and then you can go see him." She pointed behind Stuart, to where his mother sat staring at her hands. "That your mom? Let's loop her in."

Stuart nodded, and the doctor slipped from behind the counter, weaving through the waiting area.

"Mom, this is Dr.…" He looked to the woman in the lab coat for a name.

She stuck her hand out. "Hansen. Dr. Hansen. I performed your husband's angioplasty and stent insertion. It took about fifty minutes, and it was uneventful. We opened his blocked artery and caught it before it did more damage. No bypass was needed. He's in recovery, and we'll get him into a room for overnight observation, then you can go in to see him. You'll be given some information about medications he should take and some dietary suggestions."

His mother blinked up at the doctor, the abject look of scorn on her face was well known to Stuart. She always looked like that when she was confused or tired.

"Mom. Don't worry about remembering any of this. I got it."

Her face softened, slackened, and she turned to the window. It looked across to third-floor apartments above a pretzel shop.

"Do you validate parking?" his mom asked.

Stuart rolled his eyes, offering the doctor an apologetic sigh, but she patted his arm and put him at ease.

"There's a lot going on. Everyone deals with it differently. I can't make promises, but I'm pretty sure that everything will be okay. Nurse Dean will be out in a minute, and she'll take you back to see your dad."

It took half an hour for the nurse to come. His mother spent it focused on immediate normalcy, fretting over her sweater and the pizza still lying on the kitchen floor. By the time the nurse came, he'd found change for water in the recesses of his mother's purse. She'd dictated a list of things to do that filled two pages of his college-ruled notebook. Call their handyman, Darby, to power wash the back patio. Check to make sure that shutter on the second floor is okay because she swore she heard it rattle in the last thunderstorm.

Nurse Dean had a brown bob haircut and square rimmed glasses, and she reminded him of Velma from Scooby-Doo cartoons with a comforting air of competency. He followed behind her, his mother clinging to his arm, and they paused outside his father's room. The nurse gave him a few warnings about needles and monitors and how he might look, she stressed the importance of not upsetting the man, then she opened the door and left them to it.

"I can't go in there. Not yet." His mother parked herself on a chair in the hallway, clinging to the purse in her lap. "You go first."

There was no arguing with her, and the door was wide open. If his father could yell, he'd be screaming about growing up in a barn and demanding his modesty. With no time to brace himself, he stepped into the stillness of his father's unwellness and closed the door behind him.

It was bright. Sunny. Light came in through the open curtains. All the wires and monitors were as Nurse Dean described them, dangling and beeping like a robot octopus sucking the life and color from the man who raised him.

"How you doing?"

The man's gray eyebrows did the work of conveying his disdain for the situation. "Damn catheter. Hungry. They gave me applesauce back there. Probably cost me six grand."

Stuart nodded. "I'll get you something more substantial. There's a bunch of new dietary requirements."

"Do I look like I give a shit?" There was a defiant twinkle in the man's eye.

"You'll be just fine." He stopped before calling the man Dad. He wasn't ready for that.

"We have to come to terms, you and me. Now. Before your mother sees any more of the slop in the middle. I know she told you. She shouldn't have. Because it didn't matter one bit."

Digging his nails into his palms, the fists he made quelled none of his fury. "This isn't fair. You have a heart attack, and the nurse is out there telling me I can't upset you, so I can't even speak my mind. You can't just demand that this all go away. You lied to me my entire life. And, you know, when I look back… It's almost like you wish you never had to."

Stuart clenched his jaw. He'd said too much already.

"I don't think you understand what I'm saying." He plucked at a cable attached to his arm, unwinding it from his hospital gown. "You and I are different people. We have things in common, but we have different minds. You would have been you no matter what, and I was never going to be anyone but who I am. If you were my son by immaculate conception, I would have raised you the same way because I raised you the way my father raised me."

He folded his arms and stepped into the ray of sun that warmed the air. "You're telling me you didn't resent my mother one bit, and you never blamed me for it."

It was a statement, not a question, but Stuart Senior answered anyway. "I'm not going to get into the past of my relationship with your mother except to say that there was nothing to resent. We worked it out a long time ago, before you were born. And now it's past time to work this out with you, before I die."

Stuart rolled his eyes. "You're not dying."

"We're all dying every day."

A monitor beeped, and a nurse came in. She looked at machines and nodded and smiled. Stuart barely moved, letting his father control the air. The door clicked closed behind the nurse, filling him with resolve.

"You're saying I'm supposed to just forget about it. Just pretend it never happened."

"No, I'm telling you that it happened, and you'll have to incorporate this new information into your life in a way that helps you be happy. If you were processing this information productively, you wouldn't have withheld the news about your book deal."

"You've never been proud of me. Not once. You take every achievement and roll it into something negative. I'm never good enough."

"It's because I raised you. I know you can do better. I don't mean achieving things or publishing books. I only ever pushed you to do things you said would make you happy. That's what all dads want. More for our kids than we had. If I'd have been happy, your mother might not..." His father pushed up in bed. The heart monitor beeped, and the line jumped, settling when his father did. "I just want you to be happy. And then tell me that you're happy."

Stuart flung open the door. He waved his reluctant mother in and pointed at the chair by his dad's bed. She fell into it, at his father's side, clinging to his needled hand.

A million unsaid things passed between his parents, touching each other's hands, tracing veins and lacing fingers. Stuart sometimes forgot that they had a world before he showed up, and suddenly he felt like an intruder in it.

"I don't want to talk about this…thing anymore. Maybe I'll have questions someday, but I don't right now." Stuart ran a hand down his face. "Dad's right. I can't change any of this. All I can do is live with it. It doesn't change who I am or who you are or what we are to each other. And maybe the timing is wrong, but I'm quitting my job, and I'm moving to Maine."

His father blinked up at him. He'd been a statue of a man teaching Stuart to play T-ball. He'd been an immovable mountain when helped with math homework. He'd been a force of nature when Stuart was in college, and an incomparable work of art when he became a professor. Every student, every colleague, everyone he met on life's path judged him by his father's measurements, and yet again the man was right. It would be frustrating if it weren't exactly what he believed in his heart to be true. Ultimate joy lay in a town where no one cared one bit who his father was. The only criteria in Ramsbolt was that he do right by his own standards.

"Are you sure?" His mother reached out for him, and he squeezed her hand.

"I've never been surer of anything in my life."

* * *

Stuart's office was closer to the hospital than Mohl's apartment. He stopped in the cafeteria for a chicken sandwich and some fries, sat at his desk overlooking a bike rack and a row of mature elms, and wrote his resignation letter. He texted Mohl that he'd be late, and that he had news, but his dad was okay. Then he shot a note to his editor, begging to include one last scene. He received a fast reply.

Can't wait to see what you have, she said.

Noah approached the graveyard like a man touring a museum. Something about age and the lightness of his bones made his visits different somehow these days. It was hard staring down at the ground, knowing he'd be in that dirt one day, next to Shelly. He would ask her what it's like, if it's cold, if she can feel the damp. But he couldn't talk like that with Tyler there. Their son had always been sensitive, thoughtful. He'd only think Noah was crass, though it was just his way of coping with the thought that Shelly couldn't feel the sun or the snow because she'd disappeared. Because the universe just opened a pod bay door and yanked her out, and no matter how old he got, death would never make sense to him.

He preferred to come alone, to make the walk from the car to see her, to stay as long as he liked, then he'd walk a few rows back toward the hedges to see Arthur. But today Tyler and his stepson both came—the boy to see his mother and the son to see his gran.

Jared plopped in the soft grass about where Shelly's knees would be. He ran a toy car back and forth on the grass, making ruts where the wheels ran.

Tyler reached for him. "Not there. Stand back. You have to show respect here."

Noah groaned his discontent. "Leave him be. He's a kid. People used to picnic in graveyards. They were pretty parks back in the day."

Tyler stood. "I feel like I'm always getting it wrong. I don't know the first thing about being a dad."

"Neither did his real dad. But he left, and she picked you. Just keep doing what

you think is right."

Noah left Shelly to her company, and he passed between stones until he found Arthur's. Moss had covered it, thick and green in places, gray and worn in others. He abused his knees to collect a rock and placed it on top of the stone.

"I never knew Arthur," Tyler said from Shelly's plot. "It's kinda nice they're close together."

"Shelly never knew him either. And I never knew Aveline. I have her coat somewhere, though. I should give it to you."

Tyler stood beside him. He didn't look over, but he could feel his son there.

"It's funny," Noah said. "He was like a dad to me. All those years, I never knew he was teaching me to be a man. I thought I was playing with the old guy next door. He taught me everything I knew about cars. Told me I could be an engineer. Said I could do anything I wanted, and I believed him. He taught me how to have an argument, how to apologize, how to keep a promise. He taught me how to pay for dinner and woo a girl, when to keep my mouth shut."

Noah turned to Tyler. His son's face was reddened by the last of the daylight. Summer would be ending soon, and the boy would be going off to school. Tyler would be saddled with homework and T-ball and kids' social events. He could see the worry etching the young man's eyes.

"Son, fathers come from a lot of places. What's important is that you have people in your life who can help you through the doors, not just when they open but when they close, too. It's not just taping up skinned knees and finishing up the homework. You have to teach him how to live in this world. Teach him how to know what happy is when he finds it. The rest is icing on the cake.".

CHAPTER THIRTY-ONE

The sun had mostly set by the time Stuart pulled up to the cabin. The tombstones were fading into the grass, and the sky darkened. Only a faint hint of blue remained on the horizon. It seemed fitting that the black lab sprawled at the top of the porch steps. He lifted his head and yawned before returning to his nap, a most indifferent welcome committee.

Stuart made a mental note to buy a water bowl.

His hands shook as he pulled his suitcase from the back of his Subaru, antsy to get inside, to see if the new place looked like the old one.

He pulled his laptop off the passenger seat, stretched his lower back, and leapt onto the porch, dodging the dog and pulling the suitcase behind him.

The trim around the front door was shiny and unmarred. The ceiling was free of cobwebs, the porch swept, no coffee stains. The two old rocking chairs had survived the rain of terror last fall, and

Warren had left them right where Stuart remembered them with the same little table between them. The view was the same looking out across the graveyard, like seeing an old friend who never seemed to age no matter the distance between them. For hours behind the wheel on narrowing roads, leaving behind the highway knots of the dense east coast, he'd puttered in silence, allowing himself to feel the dread of a savings account that would have to last, the unease of leaving behind a world that placed faith in him in favor of a sea where he'd have to earn it. He had no idea how to start a newspaper for a town that may not want one. How would he crack that hard shell exterior? Would they talk to him, let him tell their stories? If anything could be comforting and terrifying at the same time, this was it. It did smell, for all the world, like heaven, though.

Stuart slid the old flowerpot to the side and found the key where Warren said it would be.

The dog stood and stretched, circling to the door, nose pressed in the jam and his tail wagging.

The key fit into the lock without resistance, and Stuart followed the dog inside. Everything smelled new, like wood and stone, paint and adhesives. The tiffany-style light above the kitchen table was on, shining down on a basket wrapped in cellophane. He dropped his laptop bag next to it and made a beeline for the bathroom.

The water pressure was better than he remembered.

The fireplace had been restored, and the kitchen was the same but newer. There was a fridge and dishwasher but no scratched glasses or chipped ancient plates. The cabin was bare but for the bed and table he'd ordered and had delivered weeks before. There was a lifetime to collect the perfect things.

The Degory Howland painting was tacked to the right of the door. Stuart traced the frame with his finger. It was just like as remembered. That big wooden ship in a storm-tossed sea.

Warren left a note by the gift basket.

Welcome back. The bank's never done a settlement like that before. You drove a hard bargain, but I'm glad to find a buyer for the place, and I'm extra glad it was you. Welcome to your first house! The town missed you, and we'll really enjoy having a newspaper here. I kept my promise. No one knows. Our next town meeting is on the third at six thirty at the library. Once you're settled, come on by for a visit. Can't wait to sell your papers at the newsstand. ~W

His stomach clenched at the mention of the library. Sandy had been on his mind for a long time. She'd never left his mind, really. He'd looked up the library and started drafts of emails to her dozens of times, but he hadn't once been able to write any sentiment that either concealed or revealed how he felt. There was a very good chance she'd have forgotten him by now, that everything he imagined between them wasn't real, just a figment of his willful imagination. If that was the case, fate would hand him what it may. But of all the people he knew here, she would understand his need to let go of his past.

He peeled back the overlap of the cellophane and peered inside the basket. There were little sheep cookies from Marissa, some coupons from the hardware store, fresh fruit from the market, a note from some woman named Adelle. The town manager.

His car was still full of his clothes and his things. It took a few trips to get the bulk of it inside and settling in wouldn't take very long. With any luck, he'd find a sofa and some furniture at Penny's Loft, and he'd be cozy and finishing revisions on his book in just a few days. His editor said he was crazy, buying a house and moving with such tight deadlines, but he was nothing if not driven.

He found a bowl and filled it with water, placing it on the kitchen floor. The dog lapped it up.

Stuart pulled a sweatshirt out of a trash bag and snugged it down over his hips. Outside, the dog at his side, he rounded the cabin, collecting large rocks that he gathered into a pile in the back clearing. Nudging the rocks into a circle, he cleared its center of leaves and twigs.

He would leave the old energy there, burn it to the ground, turn it to ash. The old rush to get through door after door, to jump through the hoops and check the right boxes would be gone, up in smoke. He would warm himself with its fire one last time, breath in the peace of letting it all go. And then he'd breathe in new air, let this place become part of him.

His mother was right. He was a lot like his father, the way he saw meaning in everything, the way he felt things deeper than most people. He took the last box from his car and nudged the door shut with his hip. He didn't need a gratifying slam, and he didn't need to listen for an echo. It didn't matter if the sound of it never came back to him.

He carried the box to the center of the circle and turned his back on it. Later, it would burn.

CHAPTER THIRTY-TWO

The thin blue band on the horizon faded to black as Stuart crossed town, stepping into lakes of yellow streetlights that flickered to life in his passage. The last time he trod that path he was out of breath, out of shape. A lot had changed for him since he last faced the Ramsbolt Library and the woman inside.

If the website was right, Sandy would be locking up in about ten minutes. Standing in the golden puddle across the street, he watched her shadow pass from window to window. Winter had been closing in back then, when he was there before. He'd rushed in, not knowing what to say. She was grace personified, as always, and they'd parted on good terms. Since then, the town had been blanketed by heavy snows, washed clean by the melt and thaw. And he had worn himself smooth, chiseling down his harder features. He wasn't the same. She might not be either.

He loosened the collar of his sweatshirt, tugging the hem down over his hips as he climbed the steps and tested the doorknob. The door gave way.

He crossed the threshold into a thick wall of different air. Old books and new ink tucked in an old house. He'd bathed in it a thousand times in dreams that left him longing for the feel of it.

The lobby was empty.

Sandy's tablet sat on the desk, its screen dark. Somewhere in the back, the squeaky wheels of a library cart gave her away. It was worth risking the wrath of the librarian to make some noise, to make himself known. He stepped into the doorway like cracking open a time capsule, breathing deep the air from a place he'd feared was lost. It had only been a few months, and yet a lifetime, and to his surprise, nothing had changed. The colors were just as vibrant as he'd remembered.

"Sandy?"

She emerged from behind a shelf, clutching a book with a green Jeep on the cover. She tugged ear buds from her ears and let them fall to her shoulders. Book pressed to her chest, shock registered on her face and faded to confusion.

"Maybe you don't remember me," he said. It seemed to take ages for recognition to dawn. "I'm sorry I startled you."

"Remember you?" She abandoned her cart and crossed the room, dodging chairs without looking. "How could I forget you?"

She fell into his arms before he was ready, and he returned her hug, warmed by citrus and cinnamon, comforted by the smell of home after a long and arduous journey. Maybe she held on as long as he did, but by the time they parted his heart pounded, no longer his own.

"Your book. I saw the publication announcement." She wrapped the cord of her earbuds around her phone and tucked it into her back pocket. "I put in a preorder for the library. The whole town is excited. What brings you back?"

He wanted to say that it was her, it was the feeling he had when he was with her, that it wasn't easy to go on living out there when a whole town existed where he could belong, and the rules were easy to follow. He'd been given a taste of it, of fitting in and being part of something bigger than himself and going back to the city where he was so very lost—a son who didn't belong to his father, a professor who didn't fit in a classroom—made him want Ramsbolt that much more. It was Marissa's cookies and paper cups of coffee, kids on bikes and grumpy old men planting their feet in the newsstand. Maybe it wouldn't work out, and he wouldn't fit in. Maybe they had no need for a newspaper, but if he crashed and burned at least he'd know he tried to find a world of his own instead of wedging himself into one that someone else made for him.

It was too much of a mouthful. All of that was meant for the burn pile.

"I bought a house. Here."

Eyes wide, she gripped the cart's handle and shook her head. "What are you saying?"

"I moved here. I bought that cabin from Warren. I never thought I'd want to live in a cemetery, but…" He lifted a shoulder. "I never thought I'd leave Philly either."

She crossed the room in slow motion and fell into one of the orange faux-leather chairs. He tried to read her expression, but her hair obscured her face. He sat on the coffee table in front of her, pleading with the universe that she still had room for him, that she hadn't found someone else or developed an aversion to writers in his absence.

Her fingers were laced, and there was no room for his, but he touched her forearm, the fuzzy lilac sweater was the softest thing he'd ever felt.

"I can't believe you moved here." Her eyes turned up at the corners when she looked at him and smiled.

"The way I felt when I was here is how I want to feel all the time. I kept trying to wedge myself into a life that wasn't meant for me. Like, I was living someone else's truth. Sure, everybody feels like that sometimes, but I did something about it. I bought that cabin."

She swallowed hard and blinked. "When? How?"

"I called Warren. I offered him money for it, and he accepted. I need a job, though, so I'm going to start a newspaper here. It's time to live the life I want, not the one I stumbled into."

She fanned her face and rubbed her eyes. "I'm sorry I'm so…ugh. I'm in shock."

"You and me both." He stood, the old floor creaking beneath his feet as he moved to the blocked-up fireplace. "I have a lot to do, and I could really use a friend to show me around. I don't know the first thing about surviving a Maine winter, about engine heaters for my car, or how to use a snow blower. I don't know the best stores. I need pots and pans and a kitchen full of dishes. I need a surge protector for my laptop."

He turned to face her. "Will you help me out?"

She crossed the room and grabbed his arm, an excited skip in her step. "Of course. This will be so much fun."

"I hope this isn't too forward or New Agey for you, but I want to celebrate. I have a box of notebooks full of things I don't want to hold onto anymore, and I want to burn them. It's nothing toxic, just lots of old writing, false starts by the guy I used to be. I want to let them go. I can't think of any better way to christen my new place and this whole new life than by saying goodbye to the old one and making room for new things. Better things. I have everything I need. Wine, a fire pit, fuel. There's even a dog. I think I have a dog now. I just need some good company. People company. Do you want to drink wine around a fire pit and burn the past with me?"

"I don't know." The mischief in her smile was unmistakable. "You're asking a librarian to help you burn books? Seems a little bold to me."

"No books. Just..." He rubbed an eyebrow with his ring finger. "Old notes, written by a version of me who wasn't ready to talk to the world yet."

"But don't you want to save those things? You might regret it one day if you don't. What if you're so eager to move on that you don't realize how much you'll want to revisit?"

He shrugged. "Let's just say that I've learned a lot about who I am lately. And nothing in my future is contingent on holding on to the past."

He helped her shelve the last of the books, and he turned off the light before she locked the door. They walked side by side back to his cabin. She poured the wine while he started the fire, twisting up papers to use as kindling.

The dog lowered himself on his haunches, settling by the fire, content.

Sandy tangled her arm in his, and he pulled her close, his arm around her shoulder. In silence they warmed by the glow of the flames, as sparks shot up and wisps of ashen pages danced toward the stars.

ABOUT THE AUTHOR

A Maryland native and Pennsylvanian at heart, Jennifer M. Lane holds a bachelor's degree in philosophy from Barton College and a master's in liberal arts with a focus on museum studies from the University of Delaware, where she wrote her thesis on the material culture of roadside memorials. She resides with her partner Matt and a tuxedo cat named Penny.

Receive free prequel stories, news about upcoming releases and more by signing up for the author newsletter at jennifermlanewrites.com

OTHER WORKS BY THE AUTHOR INCLUDE

Of Metal and Earth
Stick Figures from Rockport
and the
The Collected Stories of Ramsbolt Books:
Blood and Sand
Penny's Loft
Hope for Us Yet
A Good Day for Pie
The Warmth of Fires